Murder at an Irish Session

Books by Carlene O'Connor

Irish Village Mysteries

MURDER IN AN IRISH VILLAGE
MURDER AT AN IRISH WEDDING
MURDER IN AN IRISH CHURCHYARD
MURDER IN AN IRISH PUB
MURDER IN AN IRISH COTTAGE
MURDER AT AN IRISH CHRISTMAS
MURDER IN AN IRISH BOOKSHOP
MURDER ON AN IRISH FARM
MURDER AT AN IRISH BAKERY
MURDER AT AN IRISH CHIPPER
MURDER IN AN IRISH GARDEN
MURDER AT AN IRISH SESSION
CHRISTMAS COCOA MURDER
(with Maddie Day and Alex Erickson)
CHRISTMAS SCARF MURDER
(with Maddie Day and Peggy Ehrhart)

A Home to Ireland Mystery

MURDER IN GALWAY
MURDER IN CONNEMARA
HALLOWEEN CUPCAKE MURDER
(with Liz Ireland and Carol J. Perry)
IRISH MILKSHAKE MURDER
(with Peggy Ehrhart and Liz Ireland)
IRISH SODA BREAD MURDER
(with Peggy Ehrhart and Liz Ireland)

A County Kerry Mystery

NO STRANGERS HERE
SOME OF US ARE LOOKING
YOU HAVE GONE TOO FAR
COME THROUGH YOUR DOOR

Stand-Alone Novels

THE PUB ACROSS THE POND

Published by Kensington Publishing Corp.

Murder at an Irish Session

Carlene O'Connor

KENSINGTON PUBLISHING CORP.
kensingtonbooks.com

KENSINGTON BOOKS are published by

Kensington Publishing Corp.
900 Third Ave.
New York, NY 10022

All Kensington titles, imprints, and distributed lines are available at special quantity discounts for bulk purchases for sales promotion, premiums, fund-raising, educational, or institutional use. Special book excerpts or customized printings can also be created to fit specific needs. For details, write or phone the office of the Kensington Special Sales Manager: Attn. Special Sales Department, Kensington Publishing Corp., 900 Third Ave., New York, NY 10022. Phone: 1-800-221-2647.

Library of Congress Control Number: On file

ISBN-13: 978-1-4967-4446-3
First Kensington Hardcover Edition: March 2026

ISBN-13: 978-1-4967-4452-4 (e-book)

10 9 8 7 6 5 4 3 2 1

Printed in the United States of America

The authorized representative in the EU for product safety and compliance
is eucomply OU, Parnu mnt 139b-14, Apt 123
Tallinn, Berlin 11317, hello@eucompliancepartner.com

This book is dedicated to all the fine Irish trad musicians out there.

Acknowledgments

Although all mistakes are my own, thank you to Jim McVeigh for his wealth of information on Irish traditional music. He's a fabulous musician, as is his son, Pierce McVeigh. If you're ever in the Wisconsin area in the States and they're playing somewhere, definitely get there!

Thank you to the usual suspects: my agent, Evan Marshall, my editor, John Scognamiglio, my publicist, Larissa Winterbottom, and all the other fabulous staff at Kensington Publishing.

Thank you to Caroline Lennon who always does a fabulous job as our audiobook narrator.

Chapter 1

Liam Noone, Ireland's "King of Matchmaking," stood in the back of Fitzgerald's Pub, tapping his feet and bopping his head to a lively trad session. It seemed the entire town of Kilbane had turned out for this music and matchmaking festival, and with five days to go until the official opening, anticipation was high and the atmosphere was downright electric. He wasn't surprised at the turnout—traditional Irish music sessions were always good craic. This evening, musicians of all ages and sexes were grouped together in the corner of the pub, forming as much of a circle with their chairs as they could manage in the cramped space. The instruments this evening included fiddles, guitars, a squeezebox, a bodhrán drummer, and several pipers. Trad music was a somewhat loose structure housed within a timeless tradition and that was part of its magic. The vibe of the session on any given night depended on who showed up with what instrument.

And as if top-notch feel-good music wasn't enough, throwing the prospect of love into the mix amplified this celebration to a whole new level. Liam never imagined he would have taken on this challenge a second time—to find matches for single Irish trad musicians—but after last year's stint in Doolin, where he matched six single musicians in a town known for its trad sessions, a local reporter featured him in an article, and it seemed word had spread. So, one year later, when a woman named Siobhán O'Sullivan contacted him and requested the same service in Kilbane, County Cork, Liam Noone jumped at the opportunity.

His job was full of surprises and he wouldn't have had it any other way. Irish traditional music sessions were played in a variety of places: pubs, festivals, out in the fresh air, gathered around a peat fire (when it was still legal to set peat on fire), or even around the dinner table. As long as there were skilled musicians who had the instruments and knew how to play jigs, reels, and waltzes, a trad session could be formed. Tonight, the session leader was Jim McVeigh, a seasoned local musician from what Liam had been told, and he was currently tuning his guitar and taking suggestions around the circle as to what to play next.

A robust and smiling man, Jim was somewhere in his sixties with whitish-gray hair and a matching beard and mustache. He was full of life and full of tunes. Jim nodded to the publican who ferried over pints for himself and his fellow musicians.

Liam's business was based on observing folks, figuring out who they were and what made them tick. His job was to dig beneath the surface, dive past who they claimed to be and discover who they really were instead. People rarely understood themselves, which is where Liam came in. This was a talented group, and Liam was thrilled to be tasked with finding matches for the single ones among them. Of course, that wasn't the only reason Liam wanted to be involved, but if he proceeded as usual, no one would ever be the wiser.

But time was of the essence: he had one week to interview potential love matches. Musicians were best suited for each other; not only were most of their free hours taken up playing their tunes, they spoke a language unto themselves. Musical notes replaced words, head nods and foot taps became exclamations, and eye contact between musicians was often intense and always engaging. If there was one chink in the armor, it was that Liam always felt a bit jealous to be on the outside of their circle. It was hard to imagine a stronger bond than one forged by the love of music. Trad sessions popped up even without audiences, impromptu gatherings spurred on by passion. There was no doubt about it, these people loved what they did, and the fact that they had an audience was simply a bonus. He could imagine that non-musicians who married into this lot might feel like a third wheel to their first love: music.

"If you're just joining us, welcome," Jim McVeigh called to the crowd. "I hope you enjoyed that set of polkas, and now we're moving on to our jigs: 'One Hundred Pipers,' 'The Rakes of Kildare,' and 'Cock o' the North.' "

As the first tune in this set rang out, their instruments blended seamlessly with one another, producing an optimistic and jaunty melody with just a touch of longing. The kind of song that conjured up images of lush green fields, family gatherings, and Irish pride. And although Liam couldn't tell a jig from a reel, he was thoroughly swept up in the melody that had nearly everyone bobbing their heads and tapping their feet.

The publican, a man with broad shoulders and puffy cheeks, sported a large grin as his head moved to the music. No doubt he was thrilled with the crowd that these seasoned musicians had drawn.

Across the room, Liam's two assistants, Grace Collins and Ron Gallagher, had their heads bent over a clipboard, hashing out the schedule for this weekend. All work and no play. Just the way Liam liked his employees. Grace had insisted on lugging that whale of a harp all the way here, and

Ron, with his fancy suit and determined expression, seemed poised to take over Liam's matchmaking throne.

That was never going to happen.

Liam clutched his Lucky Book and wondered what people would think if they only knew the secrets that were written within its pages. He never let anyone read it, and many assumed that was because he was too stingy. Why should he share tips he'd spent a lifetime accumulating?

But its secrets were the real reason he never let the book out of his sight. Lately, however, he'd been a bit forgetful. Leaving the book in full sight of Ron, putting it down somewhere and then having to search for it—and rifling through it in pure view of Nosy Nellies. What was happening to him? *Stress.* Forty-something was too young for his carelessness to be age-related. He vowed to be more careful.

He was the third professional matchmaker in his family, after his grandfather and his father, but despite their teachings, it hadn't taken him long to learn that the heart wanted what the heart wanted, and when it came to other people and their personal desires, secrets always surfaced. Capitalizing on that had turned into a lucrative side hustle. It was positively addicting and he couldn't stop now even if he wanted to. Sometimes he shuddered to think what his father and grandfather would say if they had lived long enough to see him in action. As far as he knew they had both taken the straight and narrow road, which was the reason they always fell short of the lifestyle they should have been living. Love was wonderful and romantic, but it didn't pay the bills.

"Blackmail" was such an ugly word. Liam preferred to think of it as engaging in "privacy protection" for a fee. After all, he didn't force people to divulge their deepest, darkest secrets, now did he?

Additionally, if one was willing to sweeten the pot for their preferred match, it proved they were committed, and wasn't that a good quality in a future partner? But some folks hadn't paid their latest installment, and this week he was going to have to rectify that. The ones who still owed would soon receive a message loud and clear that it was time to pay. Whether they interpreted it as a gentle reminder or a threat was their problem. Thank goodness he had his little rendezvous with a certain someone to take his mind off of business. She was probably waiting for him in the hotel at this very moment. What a delicious turn of events.

"I can't find my bow," a perturbed musician could be heard saying as Liam weaved his way toward the exit. "Has anyone seen my fecking bow?"

Liam's phone buzzed, alerting him to a text message, just as he reached the door. He glanced at it.

We need to talk

It was from an unknown number. *We need to talk* . . . that was something a lover said, wasn't it? It had better not be someone who owed him trying to wriggle out of the agreement. He shook his head, stuffed the phone back in his pocket and turned his mind back to the woman he would soon be holding in his arms. Given that himself, the six musicians he'd invited (all ones he'd previously matched), and Ron and Grace were staying at the Kilbane Inn, he'd booked himself and his paramour a room in Charlesville. The less people gossiping about his love life, the better. Everyone seemed perplexed as to why the King of Matchmakers was a single man. If they had his access to available beautiful women, desperate for love, they would do the same.

He stepped onto the footpath only to be greeted by a gust of wind so strong it slammed the door behind him. He pulled his jacket tight and prayed the weather would improve for this weekend's activities. His mind returned to the annoying text. Better to nip it in the bud. He dashed off a quick reply.

Who is this?

It wasn't the first time someone thought they could turn the tables on him. But he had something they did not—*nothing to lose*. He was the one holding incriminating evidence. Voice recordings, photos, letters, confessions. It was mutual destruction with them taking the brunt of it. And if someone did decide they would rather punish him no matter the consequences, he could always lie. Besides, he'd made sure to cover his tracks, and the only hard proof that he was a blackmailer was in his Lucky Book (and if anyone wanted it, they were going to have to pry it out of his cold, dead hands). The more he tried to dismiss the mysterious text message, the more he perseverated on it. Tonight was all about *ceol agus craic*. Music and fun. A whole lot of fun to be exact. But now he was totally distracted. Troubled thoughts were no aphrodisiac. Maybe he was taking the message too seriously. He needed to show this "unknown caller" that he wasn't taking the bait. He paused on the footpath outside the pub, and quickly sent another reply:

Talk is cheap

He added a smiley emoji so the person would know he wasn't bothered in the least. Immediately, his phone buzzed.

Cheap is the woman waiting for you in Charlesville

The kind of talk we need to have is going to be expensive

Very expensive.

He froze. Who in the world was he dealing with, and how did someone know about her? He was nothing if not discreet. And who talked like that? That reply was not only confident, it was downright ominous. What did they know? Had someone been rifling through his Lucky Book when he slept? That wasn't possible, was it? Enough of this. He would take the bull by the horns. He dialed the number and waited for it to ring. Someone picked up, then immediately disconnected the call. His phone buzzed again.

Meet me at the abbey in 15 minutes

Come alone
Bring two books: Your Lucky Book and a matchbook

A matchbook! What nerve. Just as he was contemplating what to do, another text buzzed in. This time he knew the number, it was this evening's date, and it included a sexy photo. Now *this* was the kind of text he'd been waiting for. His thumbs hovered over the tiny keyboard on his phone. *Wait.* Should he be worried that someone knew where he and this angel were meeting? Should he try and find another hotel? *Ding.* It was her again, a photo of her blouse . . . on the hotel room floor. And just like that he deleted the ominous texts and blocked the mystery caller. Let them wait at some local abbey in the cold and the dark. He had a much more exciting date to keep.

Chapter 2

Twins. Siobhán and Macdara were having twins. Four months in, and it still didn't feel real. Whereas herself and Macdara were over the moon about the babies, the challenges that lay ahead of them were daunting. She needed this festival to distract her from the terror that rose within her whenever she thought about taking care of two wee ones. She was still trying to get her head wrapped around *one*. She tried to remind herself that she'd practically raised her four siblings (five if you counted her older brother, James), although none of them were babies when her parents died. When the doctor handed herself and Macdara the sonogram, and pointed out the two little passengers inside her womb, Siobhán insisted there had to be some mistake.

"Having two isn't that much harder than having one," Macdara told her later, when they were back at home and Siobhán was sobbing into a vanilla milkshake. "People with dogs say that all the time."

Her head popped up. "I know you did not just compare our unborn children to *dogs*."

Macdara grimaced. "Fur babies are babies too." With that

he scooped up Trigger, their Jack Russell terrier. "Mammy didn't mean that," he cooed, as Trigger licked his face.

"I am not Trigger's mammy. If that dog could pitch me out and take over the household, he'd do it in a heartbeat."

Trigger yipped and gave her a look, proving her point. But one glance into his big brown eyes and she softened. "C'mere to me." She held her hands out for the dog. Macdara handed him to her, and she massaged his little head before a planting a kiss on it. "I didn't mean it. Of course you're our baby too."

"This morning, I saw him sniffing his own poo," her sister Gráinne piped up. She was sprawled on the living room sofa, flipping through television channels, manicured toes painted bright blue and propped up on the armrest, her long black hair hanging in messy waves around her pretty face.

James, the eldest O'Sullivan, was tending to the fire, but when Gráinne delivered her little zinger he threw his head back and roared with laughter. Siobhán was starting to regret luring the pair of them away from Lahinch for a week by talking up the matchmaking festival. The two of them had moved to the seaside town a few years ago after a family holiday. They seemed happy-out. James was doing construction, and Gráinne was running an oceanfront inn. And now, apparently, they were both dating, but neither had yet to cough up too many details. Siobhán was thrilled for them but there wasn't a day gone by that Siobhán didn't wish the six of them were still under the same roof. Even now with their youngest sister Ann away at University of Limerick, Siobhán felt anxious, like a part of her own body was missing. But Ann was thriving too, so much so that her visits home had become less and less. Siobhán knew this was what she wanted for all of them—to have full and happy lives—but did they have to have them so far away? Technically, Ann wasn't far from home at all, but far enough that they hardly ever saw her. Hopefully, the babies would lure everyone home—Siobhán would need the help, and who could resist newborn twins?

Five more months to go. It might as well be five years. The only sane thing to do was ignore the future completely and live in the now. It was bad enough that her mother-in-law, Nancy Flannery, had planted herself at their house and was nitpicking on everything Siobhán put in her mouth, whereas Macdara was fussing over her as if she was a porcelain cup teetering on the edge of a table. But the final straw came when the youngest O'Sullivan, Ciarán, floated the idea of moving to Australia, in search of love.

"Australia! Is this just because you want to see a kangaroo?" Siobhán asked.

"*And* find love," Ciarán said, thrusting up his index finger. "But if I *can't* find love, at least I'll see a kangaroo."

"We can go on holiday there sometime, you can see your kangaroo, and then we'll come back and you can find love right here in Kilbane."

He shook his head. "Kilbane is a love wasteland."

"What about Sara O'Grady? She's lovely."

"Sara O'Grady? A redhead?" He shook his head. "I'd rather chew me own arm off. And I need it to play the fiddle."

"You do realize you're speaking to someone who is in the redhead family?"

"You always say yours is auburn. But . . . yes, I realized."

"I don't just say it's auburn, it *is* auburn."

"Don't get your knickers in a twist. You're the one who just called yourself a redhead. But you're right—practically everyone else thinks of you as one."

"And you don't like redheads?" Maybe Australia wasn't so far after all.

"It's not that I don't *like* them, I just don't want to date my sister."

"Right." From somewhere behind her, Macdara was having trouble controlling his laughter.

"And you know," Ciarán added, "there's the whole temper thing."

Siobhán was forced to squash her gut reaction because she would only be proving his point. "What about . . ." She tried to think of another girl in Kilbane that would be nice for Ciarán but drew a blank. *Love wasteland.* "You just need to go into Cork city more often—or Limerick."

"Only another trad musician would understand me. And they're never my age. They're all grannies!"

"I'm sure they're not *all* grannies."

"Fine. I'll date someone in their *thirties.* Is that what you want?"

Ciarán was in his early twenties, and even so, he seemed much younger than his chronological age. But he was right about one thing. The dating pool in Kilbane was not only small, it was somewhat swampy. Falling in love in a town where everyone knew everyone else's business, specifically, everyone's embarrassing moments, and that was not for the faint of heart. Siobhán had been lucky in love, and she wanted the same for her siblings. Of all of them, Ciarán seemed the most clueless about finding a match. She hadn't even known love was on his mind until his pronouncement that he intended to fly Down Under. She couldn't imagine him so far away—it would absolutely break her heart. It was bad enough Gráinne and James were in Lahinch, but at least they were still in Ireland. And that's when brilliance struck.

She had just read an interview about this matchmaker, Liam Noone, who had successfully paired six young musicians. A year had passed and the reporter was checking to see how many of his matches were still together. Interestingly, all of the ones who were musically inclined were still going strong. Granted, none of them had gotten married yet, but Siobhán thought that was wise. Rushing into marriage was never a good idea. Could they afford to throw a festival here in Kilbane? Would Liam Noone even be willing to come? Siobhán immediately began researching what it would take, and when he finally agreed (for a price), it was as if heaven itself had opened the gates of love.

And focusing on this festival was loads better than listening to her mother-in-law's well-intended but very old-fashioned superstitions. Nancy had lists of things for Siobhán to do and lists of things not to do. Siobhán was all for the to do: adopting healthy eating habits, taking her prenatal vitamins, and making her husband rub her feet nightly, but the latter advice was driving Siobhán mental. *Do not walk into a graveyard. Do not walk past a graveyard. Do not look in the mirror. Do not lift your hands up over your head. . . .* When Siobhán had had enough, she'd asked Macdara to intervene. He'd agreed, but at the last minute, he panicked. "Maybe a compromise?"

Siobhán's hands instinctively went to her hips, as if she was already practicing her mammy pose. "Such as?"

"At least agree to this one." Macdara threw a desperate look to his mam before turning back to Siobhán. "Do not bring a mirror into a graveyard and raise your hands up over your head while looking into it?" Neither his mam nor Siobhán talked to him the rest of the day.

Siobhán glanced at the clock. It was nearly noon. Volunteers would be in the town square by now, setting up for the festival. Macdara was starting his shift soon and James and Gráinne had been busy all morning keeping things in order at the house. With all she had going on, Siobhán appreciated the backup. "Better get my legs under me. I'm meeting Eoin and Ciarán in the square." Eoin, the most artistic among them, had agreed to make a cardboard cupid that they could plant in the square, just past King John's Castle where participants would enter for this evening's opening trad session. He'd asked Siobhán to come take a look at it.

Before she reached the door, Macdara handed her a green smoothie. "Mam made this for you."

Siobhán gritted her teeth. It resembled a swamp in a cup. "How thoughtful." She missed her daily cappuccinos. Nancy had been up before the sun and was out doing her messages. No doubt picking up more rabbit food for the pregnant woman. "Thank her for me."

"If only she could see your face." Macdara grinned. "Your expression says it all."

Cupid's arrow was never meant to kill, but apparently, the giant cut-out that Eoin O'Sullivan created hadn't received the memo. With furled brows and menacing eyes, the winged infant looked less like a matchmaker and more like a hired assassin. "What do you think?" Eoin asked. "Honestly."

Many moments in life require complete honesty. This was not one of them. Siobhán hesitated as she tried to think of a polite way to tell her brother that if she had to look at his creation much longer it was going to give her—not to mention her unborn babies—horrible nightmares. The town square was starting to transform: A makeshift stage had been erected in the center of the square, covered by a large white tent. String lights were being hung around the circumference of the tent, food trucks were rolling in, vendors were setting up stands, and Eoin was testing whether or not his cupid display could withstand the wind. This week Mother Nature had been blowing her way through Kilbane, hurling advertisements, stray bits of rubbish, tree branches, and unsuspecting hats across town. Unfortunately, the weekend forecast called for more of the same.

It was one of the reasons that most of the music and

matchmaking events this coming weekend would take place inside local pubs, shops, and restaurants. This would allow attendees to hop from one location to another where they could mingle and listen to trad sessions. The twist was that whereas most traditional Irish music sessions consisted of musicians of all ages and relationship statuses, these would all consist of singles looking for love. But the kickoff event with matchmaker Liam Noone would take place here in the town square, where his previously matched musicians would play. Everything needed to be perfect. Or at the least . . . not hideous.

Siobhán forced herself to look directly at the cupid, but she could feel his menacing eyes boring into her as she tried to work out how to soften the blow. *Start with something positive.* "The bow and arrow are on point," she said, "and I love how he's pulling his chubby little arms back as if he's eager to let that arrow fly."

Eoin grinned. "Right? And we'll set up a giant heart across from it just waiting to be pierced."

Siobhán nodded enthusiastically. It was time for the truth bomb. "I should add that he does look a bit—" She hesitated. Artists were sensitive, and her brother was no exception.

Eoin ran a hand over his closely cropped chestnut hair. "A bit what?"

"Constipated," Ciarán, the youngest O'Sullivan, piped up from a few meters away, where he was arranging chairs in a circle underneath the tent. "Hopefully he hasn't been eating at The Six."

"Are you joking me?" Outrage was stamped on Eoin's face. He gave Siobhán a look, as if demanding she take his side.

"I'm afraid I must concur," Siobhán said, "although of course he hasn't been eating at The Six." The Six was Eoin's new farm-to-table restaurant, located on Siobhán and Macdara's farmhouse property, and despite Ciarán's cheeky comments, it was top-notch. The restaurant was booked up for months.

"He's not constipated, he's *concentrating*," Eoin said. "Matchmaking isn't easy, you know." He glanced at Ciarán, the only musician among them. "Especially when you're exclusively matchmaking *musicians*."

Ciarán grinned and pumped a victory fist. "Deadly."

Siobhán turned back to the cupid and mulled over her feedback. "Maybe he could look a little more excited about making a match," she suggested. "As if he's bestowing love on them rather than . . . *inflicting* it." She pointed out the menacing eyes and cruel mouth. "You could widen his expression and curl his lips up instead of down. You know"—she tilted her head—"more fairytale and less serial killer."

"Serial killer?" Eoin released the cardboard cupid who immediately did a face plant. He gave Siobhán the side-eye. "Being pregnant with twins has changed you."

"Changed me, how?" Siobhán placed her hand on her belly. She wasn't that big yet. Was she?

"You've lost your filter."

"I didn't realize I ever had one." She sighed and patted Eoin on the shoulder. "Just try your hand at making Cupid again, and maybe think of Aretta while doing it." Aretta, a fellow member of An Garda Síochána, was Eoin's love. Now that they'd finally went public with it, the pair seemed closer than ever. It felt good to see people in love. What was this life without it? This festival was exactly what the town needed.

Chapter 3

Siobhán O'Sullivan?" a male voice yelled out. She turned to see a thin young man in a baggy suit approaching. His gait seemed off, and he was tilting slightly to one side, most likely due to the double bass he was lugging in one hand, and bulging notebook in the other.

"Yes?"

He grinned, barely slowing down before coming to an abrupt stop in front of her. It was as if he'd skated across the square. "I was told to look for the redhead in charge, and here you are."

"Told ya," Ciarán piped in from underneath the tent. "You can say 'auburn' all you like, but you'll always be labeled a redhead."

He was going to be seeing a kangaroo much sooner than expected if he kept that snarky behavior up. Then again, it was quite possible he'd learned it from her. When the twins were born, she would have to constantly monitor her own behavior. Just thinking about it was exhausting. But just as she tried to turn her attention back to the stranger, Ciarán was at her side. He was staring at the double bass. "Why do you have that?"

The man tilted his head in curiosity. "I'm hoping to join a trad session or two."

"With a double bass?"

The man laughed. "Do you think I'd be carrying it around otherwise?"

"You might hear a double bass in a recording of Irish music but never in a session. Like *never*."

The man shrugged it off. "With the variety of sessions this weekend, I'm sure I can find someone who will have me."

"But we're already squished in the pubs. I'm telling ya, there's no room for that yoke."

The bass man was starting to tire of the lecture—it showed in his face. "If there's no room, I won't play."

"There won't be any room, I'm telling ya. Tiny pubs and stand-up basses don't mix."

"Ciarán," Siobhán said. "May I speak with you for a moment?"

No doubt also dreading a lecture, Ciarán shook his head and darted away. "Sorry about that," she said to the stranger. "I'm sure any of the sessions would love to have you and your bass."

"Honestly, he's probably right. Grace encouraged me to participate. I figured if she could bring a harp, I could bring a double bass."

"If it makes you feel any better, Ciarán will probably whinge about the harp as well, like. Now. What can I do for you?"

He set down his instrument and wiped his palm on his trousers before sticking it out. "Ron Gallagher at your service. I'm Liam Noone's assistant." He was in his early thirties at most, but he was styled like a much older man. Not just the ill-fitting suit, but his dark hair was slicked back, and he even sported a mustache. He leaned in, and she couldn't help but notice that his breath smelled extra minty. "I'm his protégé."

"Lucky you." As they shook hands, he stared at her as if he was waiting for her to say more. "It must be wonderful to help people find love for a living," she said. "I'm a big fan of love."

Ron grinned and nodded enthusiastically. "I wouldn't trade my job for the world. And Liam is thrilled to be working with musicians again."

"That's wonderful. When I read that article about his previous success, I just had to reach out."

Ron nodded and grinned. "Liam has a deep appreciation for trad music. He is also a perfectionist, and I mean that in the nicest way possible." The smile that followed this hearty proclamation seemed forced, like an actor reciting lines he didn't believe in. "He really takes the time to get to know everyone's personalities." A look flickered across his face, as if he found his own response irritating, but just as quickly it was gone and the happy demeanor was back.

"I can tell you all about the personalities of trad musicians," Ciarán said, ambling over with his chest puffed out. "Starting with the best of the lot—fiddle players." His thumb jerked back toward himself.

"This is my youngest brother, Ciarán O'Sullivan," Siobhán said. "And if you hadn't guessed already, he's a fiddle player."

"And the inspiration for this entire festival," Ciarán added throwing his arms wide open. "You're welcome."

"Oh?" Smiling, Ron turned to Ciarán.

Ciarán nodded. "I called Kilbane a love wasteland and threatened to leave town for a kangaroo."

Ron threw a befuddled glance Siobhán's way. Siobhán spread her arms out, palms to the heavens. "That explains that," she said. Sometimes, less was more.

"Worked like a lucky charm," Ciarán added.

"I see." Ron's gaze began to flick around the square like an escaped prisoner trying to locate all possible exit points.

"Well. We're going to do our best to find your perfect match."

"He has his work cut out for him," Ciarán said. "I'm picky."

Ron took a biro from the pocket of his trousers, jotted down a note and nodded to Ciarán before turning back to Siobhán. "Liam Noone and the successful lovebirds he's matched, or should I say *songbirds*, have been in town all week mingling with the new participants."

"We've also gone through multiple interviews and filled out a trazillion questionnaires about ourselves and our ideal match," Ciarán said.

"He sounds very thorough," Siobhán said.

"Liam is nothing if not thorough." There it was again, a slight edge to Ron's tone. Were his true feelings for Liam darker than he was portraying?

Ciarán had been unwilling to share the answers from the questions let alone answers from the interviews and forms with her, and she had to respect that, but apart from "no redheads—I don't want to date my sister," she was dying to know who he envisioned as his ideal match. Hopefully, he'd put more thought into it than wanting her to be pretty.

"You have not met Liam yet, is that correct?" Ron asked.

"That is correct." Although the Matchmaking King had been in town all week, Siobhán had been busy with doctor appointments. But he must have started giving pointers to the participants, for Siobhán had noticed changes in Ciarán. He was spending a lot more time on his hair, he'd traded his T-shirts for button-downs, and he had even taken to wearing cologne. She'd yet to break it to him that the latter wasn't quite agreeing with her or the Dynamic Duo. Pregnancy was making her very sensitive to smells.

"Let me just give you a brief rundown of the characters you'll encounter in a typical trad session." Ciarán stuck his index finger out. "Fiddle players. Life of the session." He stopped as if waiting for agreement, then pointed to Ron's notebook. "Aren't you going to write this down?"

"There will be time for that later," Siobhán said, noting the stressed look on Ron's face. "Will Mr. Noone be joining us?"

"Call him Liam," Ron said. "He's a people person." His left eye began to twitch.

"Grand. Will Liam be joining us?"

"Absolutely. He's helping Grace with her harp."

"Harp?" Ciarán said. His mouth dropped open. "A double bass *and* a harp? What is this world coming to?"

"Ciarán!" Siobhán had no idea what had gotten into him. He was being ultra cheeky today. "Just like the double bass, I'm sure there have been harps in trad sessions."

"Maybe autoharps," Ciarán said. "But only if they grease some palms."

Ron looked amused. "Grace and her harp go wherever we go," Ron says. "She'll play at a few opportune moments during the matchmaking portions—but don't worry, she won't infiltrate the sacred trad circle." He opened his notebook and jotted something down. Siobhán couldn't help but look, and then she did her best not to laugh. *Fiddle players*, he'd written. *Full of themselves*.

The sound of wheels clacking distracted her, and she turned to see a harp on a dolly being pulled by a middle-aged woman with blond curls, her cheeks red with exertion. Behind her, chatting to someone through earphones and clutching an even larger notebook than Ron's, was none other than Liam Noone. He was a tall and handsome man in his late forties, a "silver fox," as they say, and his deep voice was melodic. The compliments stopped there—whoever was on the other end of his phone call seemed to be getting an earful from the matchmaker.

"Don't ever call me again. I did not guarantee you a happily ever after, I guaranteed you a *match*. It's up to you to strike it, and then it's up to you to blow on it. What? No! I meant—blow on the fire. It's a metaphorical fire. You know—as in keep the flames burning." He suddenly looked at Siobhán, shook his head, then pointed to his phone à la *Get a load of this guy. . . .* "Now. If you would like to employ me as a dating coach, my assistant Grace will be in touch with my prices. But I warn you, I don't come cheap." He hung up and flashed a full set of white teeth. "A redhead," he said looking her over. "That could present a challenge."

Chapter 4

"I'm already married," Siobhán said. "And pregnant with twins."

Liam narrowed his eyes and frowned. "I'm afraid that goes against my rules."

So far, Liam Noone was not living up to his stellar reputation. "I'm neither a musician nor a participant," Siobhán clarified. "I have simply arranged this festival for my younger brother."

Liam looked visibly relieved, then grinned. "Only messing." He stuck out his hand. "I've heard all about you from your brother, Ciarán."

Siobhán felt a little foolish and laughed to show she could take a joke. "I can see you've already taught Ciarán a few things."

Ciarán strolled up and grinned. "Fiddle players," he said. "We're the life of the session."

Liam leaned in to Siobhán and lowered her voice. "He needed a confidence boost. I'm glad to see it took."

"I believe it implanted into his brain," Siobhán whispered back.

Liam laughed, then scanned the town square as he snapped his fingers. "Grace. Where are you?"

The answer first came in way of a harp strum. "Here," she sang, strumming again. As directed by the Gardaí, Grace had set her harp up halfway between the bookshop and the passageway to King John's Castle. The location allowed enough room for her to play but also granted space for people to pass by without running into her. Moments after Liam had shouted her name, she hurried over. "Here I am."

"I can see that," Liam said. "Please don't wander off."

"I was just setting up me harp." She turned to Siobhán. "I've parked my van close as I can to the town square for harp-loading purposes. Do I need to move it?"

"Stop in at the garda station and they can give you a parking pass," Macdara said on his approach. He pointed across the square to the station before joining Siobhán.

"Thank you." She turned to Liam. "You bellowed?"

"Where is my Lucky Book?" Liam demanded.

"You're holding it," Grace said, pointing to the book in his hand.

Liam looked at it and nodded. "This is my Lucky Book," he pronounced. "It's rarely out of my hands, but right now I have to help set up for the kickoff event, and I cannot lock it up in my office. So you, as a garda, will have to do." He thrust the book at Siobhán and waited for her to take it.

"I'm actually a detective sergeant," Siobhán said. The promotion was so new, she still got a thrill saying it. She turned to Macdara. "And this is my husband, Detective Sergeant Flannery."

"You didn't take his last name?" Liam sounded offended.

"I did—we've hyphenated it: O'Sullivan-Flannery—but for work purposes I go by O'Sullivan." She didn't need to get into all her reasons with Liam, such as people seeing her simply as an extension of her husband or giving him credit for her rise in position. And although it was true that everyone in town already knew each other's business, she preferred to keep her work name O'Sullivan. Unlike Liam, seemingly, Macdara had no issues with it.

"Well, Detective O'Sullivan, you must guard my Lucky Book with your life." He thrust it forward once more, as if challenging her to a duel.

"Me?" She was not going to be his pack mule. If she had met Liam Noone in person, she might not have hired him. Not if he had presented this version of himself.

"Who else would I be talking to?" It was settled. *She definitely would not have hired him.* She had a sinking feeling she had made a terrible mistake. But due to the excitement in town, and all the work everyone had already put into this festival, she could hardly call it off now. *You made your bed, now lie in it.*

Everyone was staring at her, waiting to see if she would take the book. "I can mind it for a short while."

"Grand."

Liam gave one final thrust, and once the book was in Siobhán's hands, her arms sagged from the weight of it.

"She's not supposed to carry anything heavy," Macdara said. No doubt her tall, messy-haired, blue-eyed husband had taken a dislike to Liam too, and he was trying to refrain from coming to Siobhán's rescue. Even though he knew she could rescue herself, the instinct was still very much alive in him. She loved that about her husband, but equally loved that he wasn't making his wish to jump in obvious to anyone else but her. The twins were going to be so lucky to have him as a father.

"The doctor specified that I should not handle anything over two stones," Siobhán said. "I think I can manage a book."

Liam wagged his finger. "It's sacrilege to call it a 'book.'

When you are holding it, you are literally holding the future of love in your hands."

Siobhán and Madara exchanged a look. "Well, then," Siobhán said, "I shall hold it as if it's one of my children."

"I would appreciate it." Macdara chuckled as Liam took in the square, his head swiveling as if he was analyzing every detail. "I need to know where the opening act will perform—and I need it to have only six chairs." He began to head off.

Wait. Why had she agreed to hold the book? She was a detective sergeant now. He hadn't asked one of the men to hold it. He had singled her out. She needed to rectify this. "Mr. Noone"—Siobhán made sure her voice was loud and strong.

"Liam," he corrected her. He stopped and waited, his impatience on full display.

"*Liam*. If you'd like, I can lock your book in the garda station, but I won't be carrying it around with me all night."

With a sigh, Liam shook his head, strode over, and yanked the book out of her hands. He scanned the area. "Has anyone seen Grace?" Once more the response came in the way of a harp strum. "Grace, you cannot keep disappearing. Come here."

Siobhán's fist curled at her side. Macdara leaned in. "Deep breaths."

The petite blonde rushed over once again. "I'm here."

Liam held out the Lucky Book. "Well? Don't just stand there like a fish out of water. Take the book."

Her eyes widened, and her mouth dropped open. "But . . . you've *never* let me hold your Lucky Book."

"There's a first time for everything."

"You said it would be a cold day down below before you ever let one of us touch it."

"Are you refusing to mind it?"

"Of course not." Grace took the book and hugged it to her chest. "I'd be honored."

"No peeking, and guard it with your life," Liam said.

"Of course." She grinned and remained nearby as if waiting to see if the King would need her to assist with anything else.

"Excuse me." Ciarán was circling the chairs counting them. "Trad sessions are open to all musicians," he announced. "We can't limit it to six."

"Fiddle players," Liam muttered under his breath. "Fear not, lad, it's temporary. In the opening act, I will be introducing three couples—all musicians that I have matched up in my notable career. They will perform a few songs—jigs and reels, that sort of thing, as I introduce their love stories. I want our participants to feel the excitement, witness the miracles I have performed!"

Ciarán took this in. "I take it there is a fiddle player?"

"There is indeed, my man. His name is Niall O'Malley."

"Who did you match him with?" Ciarán asked eagerly. "Please don't tell me it's a piper." He clasped his hands as if in prayer.

Macdara tilted his head and studied Ciarán with a bemused expression. "What's wrong with a piper?"

"Quiet, breathy, and mysterious," Ciarán explained. "I'd be tying meself into knots wondering what she was really thinking."

"I believe Niall O'Malley was matched with Tara McCarthy, a flute player," Liam said. He pointed to the Lucky Book. "I would have to look that up." As if thinking he had instructed her to do so Grace cracked open the book. "No!" he shouted. "Do not, under any circumstances, open that book." Stricken, Grace slammed it shut. "If you open that again, it's quite possible you will bring a curse down upon yourself." *Curse?* This matchmaker was more of a character than Siobhán had realized. This had been a bad idea.

"What do you mean?" Grace asked, her lips quivering. "What curse?"

"Years ago, a psychic I crossed paths with put a curse on my Lucky Book. Damning anyone but me who dared to open it." Liam's tone was surprisingly cheerful, as if he relished the idea.

Grace's lips trembled. "Why didn't you warn me? I opened it just a crack. Does the curse still apply?"

"There was no need to warn you because I had already forbade you from opening the book."

Forbade you. If Siobhán had to listen to this domineering buffoon much longer she was going to need more than deep breaths to keep her from exploding.

"I suppose I could date a flutist," Ciarán said out of nowhere. "As long as she's not too breathy." He nodded as if it was decided. "That's where I draw the line."

"I don't want to be cursed," Grace said. "Is there any way of reversing it?"

"Did you happen to see anything when you opened it?" Liam asked. "Even a single word?"

"No." Grace shook her head. "Not even a single word. I swear."

"Then you're probably fine." Liam waved his hand.

"How will I know? What kind of curse is it?" Grace began to wring her hands. "It's not a musical curse, is it?"

"What would a musical curse look like?" Ron asked. "Would you open your mouth to speak and only notes would come out?"

Grace pursed her lips and shrugged. "I wouldn't know because it's not my curse." They both looked to Liam.

"Curses are curses," he said. "I don't remember the details. I'm sure you can take a mulligan. Just don't open it again."

But Grace was not convinced. "Why don't you let Ron mind it?"

Ron immediately brightened. "I would be happy to mind it. I'm really just an amateur musician, so a musical curse suits me just fine."

"No," Liam said. "You will never touch that book."

"Are you saying you trust Grace more than me?"

"Yes."

Ron glowered. "Grace has always been your favorite."

"Is this the curse?" Grace asked. "Is Ron going to whine nonstop?"

Liam sighed and looked at Siobhán. "Do you see what I have to put up with?"

"I'm sorry," Grace said. "I'll take good care of it." Book in hand, she hurried away.

"If you had just handed the book to me, I never would have opened it," Ron said. He rubbed his eyes.

"Are you *crying*?" Liam asked.

"No," Ron said. "The wind blew something in my eyes."

"Do you have any ideas of who you'll be matching me with?" Ciarán asked, sidling up to the group once more. "And is she pretty? I made sure to underline 'pretty.' "

"Worry not, lad, leave the matchmaking to me," Liam said. "It isn't just my job, it's my passion, my raison d'être, my life's purpose." He turned back to Siobhán. "And I expect full payment by tonight."

Chapter 5

Although the matchmaking portion of the festival was only for single trad musicians, all of whom had a red heart pinned to their tops, the entire town had been invited to show their support, enjoy the music sessions, and rally around Kilbane's small businesses. The local shops were all onboard, evidenced by posters in their windows broadcasting music and love. Even Chris Gordon, who was getting darker and darker with his comic shop window displays, had switched the decorations to hearts and violins. Several folks, Chris included, had expressed their dismay that only trad musicians could join in the love fest. Maybe they would have to make this a yearly thing and open it up to all singles. Blooms, the local flower shop, had roses and bouquets spilling out onto the footpath, Turn the Page bookshop was showcasing their favorite love stories, and every pub had their doors thrown open. The people of Kilbane had their dancing shoes on.

This week and weekend were going to be a win-win, especially now that Eoin's Cupid had been transformed into an appropriately sweet cherub. By the time everyone was gathered at the kickoff event, ready to meet the six previously matched musicians, the town was overflowing with love. Even the wind had given them a break.

Ron Gallagher stood in front of the circle of chairs, preparing to speak to the crowd gathered in the square. The food carts were all ready to go, and sugary and savory scents mingled in the brisk air. Ron unplugged a set of cords at the base of the makeshift stage, then plugged them back in and the string lights hanging above them came to life, casting the stage and surrounding area in a golden glow. Next, he waved his hands until everyone settled down to listen. "Welcome, good folks of Kilbane." A cheer rang out and Ron grinned. Standing just off-stage, Liam gestured for him to hurry it up. "A year ago, when I heard that matchmaker extraordinaire Liam Noone was going to match trad musicians only, I was a little surprised. But then I started thinking about the relationship between trad music and falling in love, and suddenly it all a made perfect sense. They are alike in many ways. Take trad music for a start. Originally an oral tradition, trad music is not formally written down. Rather, the tunes have been passed from generation to generation—not unlike the matchmaking tradition being passed down in families. Liam's father and his grandfather before him were matchmakers. Although, in this case Liam does not have any children, so perhaps when he's ready to retire he'll find a suitable replacement—such as a stellar assistant." Ron indicated himself with his thumb, grinned, and looked at Liam who returned the mirth with a scowl.

"I won't," he said.

Ron laughed a bit too loud. "He's only messing." Liam rolled his eyes and shook his head, but Ron ignored him and turned back to the audience. "Many trad musicians learned to play by ear—whereas matchmakers learned to play by the heart. Music elicits action and strong emotion: listening and dancing, laughter, crying—and a sense of belonging. That sounds a lot like love to me. So, without further ado we thought it would be inspirational to kick off this matchmaking and music festival with our now infamous previously matched trad musicians. Ladies and gentleman, let me introduce the very first musical pair matched by the great Liam Noone—on the fiddle, Niall O'Malley, and on the flute, Tara McCarthy."

The audience politely applauded as Niall O'Malley and Tara McCarthy emerged from a set of curtains leading to a backstage area. They held their instruments in one hand and clasped hands with the other. Niall lifted his fiddle overhead like a rockstar and flashed a wide grin. No doubt his confidence was buoyed by his good looks: tall with a head full of curly black hair, and a mile-wide grin. Tara, on the other hand, seemed a bit on edge. She gripped her flute against her chest as her eyes flicked over the crowd. She was taking them in as if her life depended on memorizing their faces, and the corners of her mouth were turned down. She flipped a section of her long brunette hair away from her freckled face. She was the quintessential "girl next door" apart from the fact that the girl next door looked terrified.

"Thank you, thank you, what a nice welcome," Liam boomed. "Niall and Tara have been together for one year, and I cannot wait to hear how it's been going." He threw them a look. "Will they be the first of my happily matched couples to get married?"

"Hear, hear," someone in the crowd shouted.

"Let's not get ahead of ourselves," Niall joked. "I thought this was supposed to be a *fun* weekend." Tara's face reddened. *Interesting*. Was this a point of contention between them? Couples shouldn't be pressured to get married, especially after only one year of dating, but then again, maybe matrimony was the ultimate payoff for a matchmaker.

"Niall knew what he wanted in a woman," Liam continued, "and some free advice to those participating this weekend—knowing what you want is half the battle. The other half is accepting what you get." Liam laid his head back and roared with laughter. He didn't seem to mind that he was the only one who found it funny. "Niall is confident, he's outgoing and active, and at first, I thought of matching him with someone else who was high-energy—but in the end, what is it they always say? Opposites attract." He turned to smile at Tara, who stared down at her flute and refused to make eye contact. "Our dear flute player is also confident, even if she presents as a bit shy."

"A bit?" Niall said. "Her flute talks more than she does."

Tara squinted, but then lifted her flute and began to play the opening sequence from *Jaws*. Once the audience caught on, laughter rippled through the square.

"See what I mean?" Liam said. "That's confidence and smarts all in one package. And when pairing someone with a fiddle player, who absolutely has to be the center of attention anywhere, it's best to match them with someone that doesn't require all that constant reassurance."

"Let's hear it for fiddle players," Niall said, jumping up and once more parading his fiddle as if it were a guitar he was about to smash.

An enthusiastic "Woohoo!" rang out from the crowd. *Ciarán*. It took the audience a moment; eventually they politely clapped.

"That's enough showboating," Liam said, pointing his finger at Niall. "You've had your turn." For a second Siobhán was taken aback by the bite in Liam's tone. But then, as if realizing he'd slipped, Liam grinned. It was odd, looking between the older man and the younger one as they held their smiles—almost as if they were having a blinking contest with their lips. "Tara's calming energy was the perfect balance to Niall's breakneck speed," Liam continued. "And my genius worked—for here they are, as happy as a pair of clams!" In Siobhán's opinion, neither clam looked happy. Niall and Tara took a bow and then moved to their seats.

"You'll get a chance to hear their love story—all of their love stories—told from their point of view later this weekend, so don't miss the event titled "How the Matchmaking King changed our lives." And don't forget to bring tissues—if it doesn't bring a tear to your eyes—you might want to check your pulse. Next on deck, I'd like to introduce Edward Kavanagh, our uillean piper, and Róisín Doyle, our bodhrán drummer."

Row-sheen. Siobhán had always loved that name. *Little Rose.* If a girl or two were onboard, it was a baby-name contender.

From behind the curtain a drumroll rang out, followed by the sound of the pipes announcing a triumphant entrance. Edward and Róisín stopped center stage to take in the cheering and applause. Edward was bald with full cheeks that were currently bright red, and although he wasn't necessarily a beast, the black-haired and smiling Róisín was definitely the beauty. Oddly enough, Tara McCarthy seemed to be staring at Róisín Doyle with daggers shooting out of her eyes, and Niall O'Malley was doing the same to Edward Kavanagh. Did anyone else see that? It didn't seem so, even Liam Noone was grinning cluelessly. "Thank you," Edward said, as he took a bow. "We're delighted to be here."

"Delighted," Róisín said, in a tone that conveyed otherwise. She licked her lips and made eye contact with a young woman standing off to the side. A woman that looked exactly like her. *Identical twins.*

Siobhán touched her stomach. She didn't know if she was having boys or girls (or one of each), identical or fraternal. Anticipating the surprise was half the fun. Macdara and his mam, Nancy, both extremely prepared folks, were dying to know so that they could start shopping. The jury was still out for Siobhán. She just wanted them to be healthy and happy, but she also wanted each of them to feel like individuals, not just half of a whole. Did these women feel like individuals? They were dressed differently, but otherwise it was nearly impossible to tell them apart.

Liam Noone hopped on the stage, and Róisín visibly relaxed as the attention turned to him. "These two may not seem compatible on first glance," Liam said. "But in any parade, the piper files in behind the drummer, does he not?"

Róisín drummed out a parade march sequence. "What can I say?" Edward said, his bald head gleaming under the string lights. "Behind every good woman there's a great man!"

"Hogwash," Niall said, covering it up with a cough. Liam gestured for Róisín and Edward to take their seats.

"Last but not least, I'd like to introduce Aisling Byrne, our squeeze-box player, and Saoirse O'Reilly, who is often on the bass, but this weekend she will be playing the acoustic guitar."

Saoirse O'Sullivan-Flannery. Ser-sha. Siobhán liked the sound of it. She would add it to her mental list of possible names. The women came out, and although they were not holding hands, they were beaming ear-to-ear and positioning their hands in the shape of a heart. When the audience applauded, they blew kisses. Aisling's dark wavy hair bounced as her head swiveled to take in the crowd. Saoirse, on the other hand, white-blond hair sticking out of her cap, pulled the brim down low as if she was a celebrity who didn't want to be recognized.

Siobhán couldn't help but think about another Aisling, one of her best friends, along with her other best friend from childhood through adulthood, Maria. Both of them were married with children of their own now, Aisling had a boy and girl, and was living in Dublin with the husband. Maria and her beau were currently in Galway, and her little girl was almost one year of age. It was startling how fast the time was going, how long it had been since they'd been able to get together. Siobhán missed Maria's booming laugh and big personality and Aisling's dry wit and big heart. Even with the distance, they'd managed to stay abreast of each other's lives with calls and texts. But they were due to meet in person. Luckily, they'd been over the moon to hear the news of the twins, and they were both going to try to make it to the baby shower that Gráinne was hosting in Lahinch. An entire weekend by the sea with her family and best friends, gathered to celebrate these two little lives. And Siobhán would get to see their children again, and hopefully get some well-needed advice on motherhood. She could not wait.

"We're delighted to be here," Saoirse was saying. "Liam Noone was the only matchmaker I could find who was open to serving the LGBTQ community. Long live the king!"

Aisling looked stricken, as if this was the last thing she expected Saoirse to say. Saoirse gave her a nod as if she'd forgotten her next line and needed a nudge. "Love is love," Aisling added. Then, as if trying to one-up Tara's *Jaws* rendition, she played a few bars of "That's Amore" on her squeeze-box. The audience perked up, applauding vigorously as the women took their seats with the others.

"Our esteemed lovebirds are going to play a polka for you now, this is 'Britches Full of Stitches.' " Liam gestured to the group and stepped back as the polka started up, a lively bit that uplifted the crowd. Trad music favored melody over harmony, making it easy for an audience member to feel a part of it, as if the song had just opened a door and ushered everyone in. It was fitting how the tunes embodied Ireland, melodies that brought life to Irish culture. When words failed, music filled the gaps. Trad music was as essential as water or breathing, and Siobhán could not imagine what they would be without it.

Ron and Grace stood off to the side, bobbing their heads and beaming at Liam with pride. Siobhán could see why

Ciarán loved this world—it was very special indeed. And they were lucky to have a musician in the family. Many a night had been spent listening to Ciarán play his tunes, and it never failed to brighten them. Siobhán hoped her twins were enjoying a bit of it too. Maybe they would grow up to be musicians like their Uncle Ciarán. It was nearly impossible to imagine Ciarán as an uncle. Little by little, Siobhán was finally letting go of the notion that he was still a child. When the polka ended, Liam swept in once more.

"What do you think, folks? A round of applause for our amazing lovebird musicians?" This time the crowd didn't hesitate to show their appreciation. "Normally, I've been told, each category—polkas, jigs, and reels—is played in a succession of three songs. But I know that everyone is eager for the festival to begin, so we just wanted to give you a little taste. Now, as you all know, trad sessions are open to all musicians who know the art, and this festival will be no exception—only most of our participants will be single musicians—if you aren't sure, you only need to look for the heart pinned on their chest. Those are the ones looking for love. We will be adding chairs to this circle, and the instructions for this opening night are simple—play, chat, drink, and mingle. Tomorrow, the festivities begin bright and early! Food, music, dancing, and social games. For our singles, please only mingle with those wearing the same red hearts. We're not here to pilfer anyone else's mate! While you all mingle, I will be setting up first dates for our lucky singles. We'll have several activities for our love-starved contestants, and on Sunday eve we will close the event with a scavenger hunt! Throughout all the activities, I will be pulling singles aside for interviews. That is your chance to give me your 'wish list,' although please keep your expectations realistic. And all the while, you are free to attend the various trad sessions happening in all the pubs of Kilbane. On Day Two, you'll have another two matches, followed by two interviews, and on the morning of Day Three you will find out who you have been permanently matched with, and you will spend the rest of the day with this person. Just keep in mind that it's possible none of your first few 'dates' will become your perfect match. Does everyone understand?" Cheers rang out from the crowd, and Liam beamed. "We'll be taking a quick break, but I am going to ask that our three couples hang out in the middle of the circle for a few minutes—we have some catching up to do. Everyone else? Love is in the air, folks, let the festivities begin!"

The single musicians began to filter into the crowd, some chatting right away, others waiting with their instruments for the chairs to be set up. The sound of the harp rang out, and although Siobhán didn't know the name of the tune, it was beautiful. "Harp," she heard Ciarán mutter, as he passed by her. Liam joined the matched musicians, shaking hands, and exclaiming over each couple. Siobhán joined Macdara and Aretta by the garda station and was thrilled when Macdara presented her with a hot chocolate. The atmosphere was one of excitement, and despite Liam's demeanor, Siobhán was feeling good for following through with this idea. After a half an hour or so of chatting, she headed into the garda station to use the restroom. It was a frequent need lately. The Dynamic Duo was wreaking havoc on her bladder. She was just exiting the station when she heard a strange crackling sound, followed by a burst, and then suddenly the square was plunged into blackness.

Voices rang out in alarm. Although lights inside businesses and on the periphery were still on, the entire square had gone dark. One could make out shadowy figures moving about, but people were bumping into one another. Siobhán wished she had a bullhorn. Luckily, she had the second best thing, a husband with a good set of lungs. "Everyone stay calm," Macdara called out. "We'll get the lights on as soon as possible."

From across the square, the harp continued to play, and Siobhán had to give Grace credit for trying to keep everyone calm. Unfortunately, it didn't last long.

"Help!" a female voice yelled. "Man down! Man down!" The harp was drowned out by panicked voices. Lights from smart phones blinked on and off like glowworms. The crowd began to follow the voice.

"Who said that?" Macdara called out.

"Here," a female voice replied. "Hurry! He's bleeding!"

"Where's our first-aid crew?" Macdara could be heard saying. "Everyone, please, turn off your phone lights *except* the person who called out for help." Luckily everyone complied, and the lights began shut off until there was only a sole beam cutting through the dark. Siobhán followed Macdara and the two-person first-aid crew. When they arrived at the light, Macdara and Siobhán took out their phones to increase the illumination.

The woman who had called for help turned out to be the young woman that Siobhán had pegged to be Róisín Doyle's twin. She was kneeling on the ground right next to the cutout cupid. In front of her a man was lying in a pool of blood. It was none other than the King of Matchmaking, Liam Noone. As they drew closer, Siobhán could see there was something sticking out of his chest. His eyes were vacant and staring. "I don't think first aid is going to help," the young woman whispered. "I can't find a pulse. He's not blinking."

"Please give us some room," Siobhán said. "We'll take it from here." The girl sniffled, then got to her feet and moved back. "What's your name, pet?"

She paused as if she didn't want to divulge that information. "Helen."

"Helen Doyle, is it? Is the drummer your sister? Róisín?"

Helen nodded and absentmindedly touched her hair. "We're twins."

"I could tell," Siobhán said, momentarily forgetting this was not a happy time. "How wonderful."

"Wonderful?" the girl said. "Is it?" The change in tone was abrupt. Siobhán's stomach turned as Helen stalked away. What was that all about? A little sibling rivalry perhaps. Siobhán wondered if she should apologize to her unborn twins and assure them that most twins she'd met were thrilled to be a twin, and that they couldn't take one distraught woman's word on it, after all she'd just found a dead body, but she'd save that speech for when they were old enough to understand her.

Macdara focused his light on Liam, and for what felt like eternity, Siobhán could not make sense of what she was seeing. Their victim was lying directly beside the cutout cupid, as if the cardboard had come to life and shot him. For the object sticking out of his heart was indeed an arrow. But unlike Cupid's, this one was very real. And yet, there was something odd about it. Siobhán steadied the light and inched closer. The arrow looked like . . . were those strings? Siobhán had recently learned that individual horse-tail hairs were used in the making of the strings.

"Is that what I think it is?" Macdara asked.

"Yes," Siobhán said. "If you're thinking it's a bespoke arrow made from the bow of a fiddle—"

"You're wrong." Siobhán and Macdara turned. Once again, Ciarán was in their midst.

"What do you mean, I'm wrong?"

"Look at the shape of it," Ciarán said. "That is the bow of a double bass." He shook his head. "I told you it doesn't belong in a trad session."

They watched him walk away. Macdara and Siobhán exchanged a glance. Macdara stared at the bespoke arrow. "Astute observation," he said. "But I'd venture to say it doesn't belong lodged in a man's heart either."

Chapter 6

"Is he dead?" Helen cried. Siobhán had joined her a few steps away from the body at the underpass of King John's Castle.

"Petal, I'm going to need to ask you a few questions," Siobhán said. "Let's move onto Sarsfield Street." There were too many big ears nearby.

"There's nothing you can do to save him?" Helen asked, as Siobhán guided her away. One didn't need to be a professional to know that Liam Noone had been beyond saving, but Helen was in shock, and from the sounds of it she was in the "bargaining" stage of grief. But there was one thing puzzling Siobhán. Shock was understandable. But did Helen know Liam well enough to be grieving?

Once they were past King John's Castle and had found a private spot on Sarsfield from which to talk, Siobhán stopped. "Were you close to Liam?"

Helen's eyes widened. "Why would you ask me that?"

"Don't try to read into my questions, pet, just do your best to answer them." Siobhán didn't want to supply the truth, that Helen's reaction was less like a stranger coming upon a man on the ground and more like a lover.

"I knew him, of course. He helped my sister find love. But no, we weren't close." She bit her lip and looked away.

"I need you to take me through your steps before the lights went out. Where did you go when the session was over?"

"I tried to talk to my sister, but they were all meeting with Liam." From the look on her face there was a story there.

"Okay. And then?"

"I didn't think the meeting would go long, so I hung around and waited. But as soon as they were finished, Edward and my sister walked off. I started to follow, but I could overhear them and it was obvious they were getting into it."

"Getting into it? Do you mean they were arguing?" The other interpretation didn't make sense in this context but one had to ask.

Helen nodded. "I love my sister, but lately she's not been too happy. Everything Edward does is sus to her."

"Sorry. What?"

"Sus. She's all paranoid, like."

Sus. Suspicious. Siobhán knew the lingo, but hadn't heard anyone actually use it before. Having twins would mean she'd stay a little more attuned to "what the kids were saying," but it would be quite some time to get to that stage. "Paranoid about . . . ?"

"She's worried Edward isn't in love with her." She crossed her arms. "She even thinks he's cheating on her."

"I see." Liam Noone probably wouldn't have been happy to hear about this, but it hardly seemed related to his death. Then again, at the beginning of an investigation, it was important to note everything equally and weed out what didn't belong at a later date. But it was interesting that Helen seemed to be siding with Edward over her own sister. "What do you think?"

Helen frowned. "What do I think about what?" Siobhán was starting to think that she was the one who was "sus."

"Do you think Edward is in love with your sister?"

Helen crossed her arms and sighed. "I *know* he's not in love with her." She chewed on her lip. "At least, not anymore."

Siobhán had not been expecting such an emphatic statement. "How is it that you know?"

She tilted up her chin. "I just know. Trust me."

"I am afraid that the nature of this job does not allow me to automatically trust you. I need to know how you 'know' he isn't in love with her."

"It's just not my story to tell. All I can say is that they are not in love." That was not a satisfactory answer either, but Siobhán was starting to realize that she was not going to get one. "Do we have to talk about this?" Helen asked. "It has nothing to do with what happened to that poor man."

Earlier she was calling him Liam, and she had just switched to 'that poor man.' Was it on purpose? Did she want to emphasize that he was nothing to her? Was it possible Helen had a crush on Liam? Were they seeing each other? He was much older than she was, maybe not May to December old, but at least May to September. Either way it wouldn't be the first age-gap-romance in history. "Again, I would prefer if you would simply answer the questions I ask rather than analyze them. I assure you, there's a method to my madness." Or a madness to her method, but Siobhán didn't need to bog the poor woman down in the details.

"I work at a coffeehouse back home. Edward started showing up every day—without telling my sister. At first, I didn't think anything of it—but then he brought me a rose—and then one day he said, 'I think I was matched with the wrong sister.' "

"Have you spoken to Róisín about this?"

"Yes, alright? And she was fine with it. More than fine."

"And yet they're still together?"

"They are here at this festival together." Helen was choosing her words very carefully.

"Is Róisín interested in someone else?"

Helen tilted her head. "Róisín is a really private person. She doesn't talk to me about those things." She paused. "However . . ."

"However?"

"Everyone thinks that Niall and Róisín would have made a better match. I mean based on looks alone—they would be stunning together." She paused. "I suppose Róisín is never satisfied. Whatever path she takes, she's always wondering if the other route would have been better."

"Are you basing this on something you think or something you know?"

"I already told you. We don't talk about those things."

The statement did not ring true. Didn't twins talk about everything? Emma and Eileen, identical twins who ran the Kilbane Inn, were so close they finished each other's sentences like an old married couple. And didn't some twins make up languages? Communicate in the womb? Of course, there had to be exceptions, twins who didn't speak to each other at all or twins who simply did not get on, but the silent exchange Róisín and Helen shared during the opening session had been telling, so Siobhán just wasn't buying it. She was going to have to take everything Helen said with a grain of salt. Or an entire mine. "Let's backtrack to your movements this evening. After you realized your sister and Edward were in the middle of something, where did you go next?"

"I was heading here," Helen said, indicating Sarsfield Street. "To get a taxi back to the hotel."

Taxi drivers had been lining the street toward the end of the evening this past week, no doubt thrilled with the extra work, mostly ferrying people from town to their inn or hotel rooms. "When you say hotel—you're staying at the Kilbane Inn?"

Helen shook her head. "I'm at a hotel in Charlesville."

"Which one, pet?"

"I don't mind telling you but—you're asking me a lot of questions. Am I, like, sus?"

"It's too early to tell if you're sus," Siobhán said. "But the more information we gather—from everyone, mind you—the better."

"I'm staying at the Hotel Charlesville," Helen said. "I wanted to stay near my sister, but the Kilbane Inn was full."

That made sense. Emma and Eileen had a limited number of rooms. "So you came out here to get a taxi . . ."

"I was nearly to the underpass when I stopped to listen to the harp. It was a haunting melody. That was my thought right before the lights went out. It startled me, as I'm sure it did everyone. I stumbled forward, and that's when I almost tripped over something—or as it turned out, *someone*." My foot hit something—I hope it wasn't his head—but if there's a mark on his head due to my shoe or something? Then let me say, I'm so sorry—I nearly lost my footing, and then I rammed my foot into something *again*. And I was so angry, because I thought, who would be so careless as to leave something on the ground for people to trip over? That's the only reason I kicked him again—I didn't think it was a person! And he made no noise, so I know I didn't contribute to his demise in any way. I mean the kick was pretty hard, so believe me, he would have cried out if he felt it. I swear I've never kicked a person in the head—*never.* That's when I turned on my phone light and shone it on the ground. The sight of him!" Helen shivered. "And then, I think I screamed."

She had most definitely screamed. Siobhán gave some thought as to where most people went during the break. The food vendors were on the other side of the square, and many people had gathered around them, but there were loads of people in town, and thus, they had spread out. In addition to the singles, trad musicians had come in from all over Ireland, to join in the week-long sessions. During the break, most people had congregated near the food tents, which meant it was possible that no one saw anything sinister take place on the other side of the square. How many seconds did it take to shoot an arrow? Could a novice pull it off—i.e., get lucky—or did one need to be a skilled archer? And why make an arrow out of the bow of a double bass? As Ciarán pointed out, it wasn't a very common instrument in trad sessions. And Ron Gallagher was the only one they'd seen so far lugging one around.

Was he so bold he wanted advertise that he was the killer—or was someone trying to set him up? *Maddening.* Either way, Siobhán was inclined to believe the weapon was some kind of a message. It would be much easier to use a regular arrow, and it wouldn't be difficult to procure one. Either way, she was going to have to speak to Ron Gallagher as soon as possible and check whether or not he still had his bow. Then again, this arrow would have taken some time to make and she had no way of knowing if the bow had even been in Ron's case. "Was there anyone else around you?"

"There were people on either side of me, but not too close."

He must have been struck with the arrow right after the lights went out. But how had someone managed to hit him in the dark? The bow struck him too close to the heart to be an accident. "Did you hear anything out of the ordinary?"

Helen shook her head. "Just people exclaiming when the lights went out, overlapping voices, and the harp."

Siobhán handed her a small notepad and biro. "Can you give me your digits in case I have any follow up questions?"

"Not a bother." Helen jotted down her number and handed it back.

"Thank you, pet."

"I don't know how you deal with murder," Helen said. "This is going to give me nightmares."

"I try and focus on what I can do," Siobhán said, "which is get justice for our victim."

"Better you than me," Helen said. She pulled out her phone. "Are we finished?"

"Yes, for now. Thank you for your time, and if you're alone at the hotel, maybe you should ask your sister to join you."

"Why do you say that?"

"It's been a traumatic evening, and it can be dangerous to be alone with one's thoughts."

"Good advice." Helen bit her lip and nodded. "I'll call her."

Siobhán headed back through the underpass. She had been dealing with death and murder for many years now, but she could still remember the first time she'd encountered a murder victim. How she'd come downstairs in their family bistro to find a dead man in the dining room with a pair of hot pink scissors protruding from his chest. The shock was like nothing she'd ever experienced before. Here she was all these years later, and it didn't get any easier, but the first time was always the most traumatic. Like love, the first time was the one that stuck with you.

The wind was starting to pick up, rattling the colorful bunting hanging above Sarsfield Street and whipping Siobhán's hair into her face. Bad weather was the last thing they needed. Guards had placed a sheet over Liam and surrounded him with evidence markers. Although it was still dark, the lights from phones and torches helped to navigate her way. Macdara was soon standing in front of her.

"I just talked to the young woman who found the body," Siobhán said. "Helen Doyle. She's Róisín's sister. Her *twin.*"

"Róisín?" Macdara asked.

"The bodhrán drummer," Siobhán said. "From the opening session."

"Did she see anything?"

"No. According to her she almost tripped over Liam when the lights went out. She thinks her shoe came into contact with his poor head—in fact she said she thinks she kicked him in the head, but she insisted he must have been already dead for she didn't hear him make a peep. We'll have to remember to mention that to Jeanie." Dr. Jeanie Brady was the state pathologist, and she had become a good friend over the years.

"We'll definitely mention it, but if I had to guess I would say it's the arrow sticking out of his heart that killed him."

"I would have to concur."

"Did she see or hear anything?"

"She said there were people milling around on either side of her but not close enough to see Liam Noone lying on the ground, and other than a chorus of voices and the harp, she didn't hear anything unusual."

"We need to figure out how the lights went out," Macdara said. "Join me?"

"Of course." Armed with proper torches, they made their way through the town square. All available guards were working the perimeter, cordoning it off, while others were trying to keep the crowd contained. Because they had already been prepared for a large gathering, guards from nearby stations were already on hand to help with security. They needed to keep people away from the murder scene, but on the other hand, they didn't want anyone sneaking off. Every single person who was in the square had to be interviewed while the events of the evening were fresh in their minds.

"The streetlights are still on," Siobhán pointed out. "As are the pubs, the shops, the garda station. It's only the string lights in the square that are out."

"Maybe the killer is an electrician," Macdara mused, as they approached the circle of chairs. Siobhán located the extension cord for the string lights. It ran the length of the stage and continued past the curtains. Once Siobhán stepped through them and into the small backstage area, she saw straight away that the cord to the lights was unplugged. "I'd say we can discard that electrician theory." She bent down, picked up the cords, and plugged them in. The overhead lights glittered on and the square was once again aglow.

Macdara stared at the cords. "Well done, Sherlock. I'd say you solved that one."

"Indeed," Siobhán said. "I took one look at it and thought it was *sus*." Macdara raised an eyebrow. "Suspicious—just a little lingo I picked up from Helen."

Macdara laughed as they made their way back through the curtains. He scanned the square. "Unfortunately, knowing how the lights were killed does not help us in the least. Anyone had access through the curtains, and the ability to unplug the cords."

The curtains wrapped around the back, thus hiding the staging area from view, but it was true, anyone could have slipped through them.

"Where did Liam meet with all his musicians after the session?" Macdara asked.

"Right here," Siobhán said. "Right where we're standing."

"It would have only taken a few steps to unplug the cords."

"Correct."

"I'd say that narrows our suspect list down."

It was looking like one of their lovebird musicians was a killer. "We'll have to find out what time this impromptu meeting ended. If there's an extensive amount of time between the end of the meeting and Liam's murder—anyone in the crowd could have murdered him."

"It's highly unlikely that a random stranger killed him," Macdara said.

"I agree. Let's hope somebody saw something." Then again, eyewitness accounts were often flawed, even when the witness was confident about their version of events. Memory was a fickle sense. "The murder weapon is very distinct," Siobhán said. "We're going to need to meet an archer. Learn a little something about bows and arrows."

Macdara nodded. "We also need to find out how long it would have taken to get in position and hit the target, and whether or not it took practice to make a shot like that."

"Great minds think alike." Siobhán touched her belly.

"I hate that they have to listen to all of this," Macdara said, glancing at her stomach.

Siobhán laughed. "I don't think they'll remember. And if they do—it means their memories are off the charts."

Macdara grinned. "Do you think they'll have a language all their own?"

"It's possible. Many twins do."

"If they do, I'm going to crack the code, learn every word," Macdara said, rubbing his hands together.

It was Siobhán's turn to laugh. "Me too." They could not have their children talking about them behind their backs, plotting . . .

Macdara straightened up—he was back in business mode. "Let's section the town square into zones and figure out which area had the best vantage point to the murder," he said. That way when we're conducting interviews, we can see if their actual view matches what they claim to have seen."

"Good idea." That is, if anyone saw anything at all. "Of course, we should also pull CCTV footage, but the square was so crowded I don't think we'll notice anything."

"You're probably right, but I'll assign a few guards to it anyway." Macdara was already sending a text.

"Have them start the footage from the moment Liam and his entourage arrived. I have a feeling that whatever happened this evening must have been brewing all week."

"It would have taken time to fashion a weapon out of the bow of a fiddle," Macdara said. "This was premeditated."

"If anyone had been walking around with a bow and arrow someone will remember it," Siobhán said. "I wonder if they stashed it somewhere so that, when the time was right, it wouldn't take long to grab it."

"We could try and locate the owner of every car parked on Sarsfield Street and see if they'd voluntarily let us search it," Macdara said. "But that's only if we could figure out the owner of each car and then locate said owner in a timely manner."

"Grace Collins parked her van close to the passageway, remember?"

Macdara nodded. "And since we gave her a pass to do so, I can't imagine she'd refuse to let us search it."

"I'm thinking the bow has to belong to the killer. Otherwise, wouldn't someone have noticed if the bow to their fiddle was missing?"

Ciarán, who was now standing nearby, piped in, "A musician was missing their bow Monday last—in Fitzgerald's."

Chapter 7

Siobhán didn't realize they'd been talking loud enough for him to catch any of their conversation. Then again, he was young and had excellent hearing. She turned to face her brother who was standing just on the other side of the crime scene tape. "Who?"

Ciarán shrugged. "Some little old dude. He was going around asking everyone if they'd seen it."

"Old dude like me?" Macdara asked. "Or old dude like a grandpa?" Ciarán tilted his head and studied Macdara, his expression conveying that to him there was little difference between Macdara and a grandpa. "Never mind." Macdara sighed.

"You didn't recognize him?" Siobhán asked.

Ciarán shook his head. "He must've been a visitor. He was short. And he played a mean fiddle. It shouldn't be too hard to figure out who he is."

Short and played a mean fiddle. With this many visiting musicians in town, it could be anyone. "Thank you." Siobhán took out her small pad of paper and biro. "I'll add Fitzgerald's to the list."

"Fair warning. He's a talker."

"We're detectives," Siobhán said. "The more they talk, the better for us."

"And the worse for them," Macdara quipped.

Ciarán shook his head like he couldn't fathom it. "I'm so lucky I'm a fiddle player."

Siobhán laughed. Ciarán was really coming into his own, and she loved that he had a passion for music. It pained her heart that this weekend wasn't going to turn out as they planned. But of course, they were still alive, and it wasn't helpful to feel sorry for anyone but Liam Noone. She may not have liked his personality, but he didn't deserve an arrow through the heart.

"I found something," Aretta said, approaching them with an evidence bag. She'd been canvassing the square. Most of the "evidence" would no doubt turn out to be random bits of trash or lost items, but you never knew when something would become a clue. Siobhán and Macdara gravitated toward her.

"What is that?" Siobhán asked, peering into the bag.

"The cap off a lipstick tube," Aretta said. "Unfortunately, there's no way to tell if it's the same neon-pink color Liam has on neck."

"His neck?" Siobhán and Macdara said in unison. They simultaneously whipped around and stared in the direction of the body.

"I have a photo." Aretta pulled out her phone and showed them the screen. Liam Noone did indeed have a partial imprint of bright pink lip prints on his neck.

"It would be one thing if it was the cheek," Macdara said. "But the neck suggests something far more intimate."

"Helen Doyle reacted to his death in such a way that I wondered if they had a close relationship. But it was too dark to notice if she was wearing lipstick." Siobhán mulled it over. "Do you think Jeanie will be able to get DNA from the lip prints?"

"I have confidence in her," Macdara said. "The lab, on the other hand—"

"Will move torturously slow," Siobhán finished. It was true: it didn't matter how much of a hurry they were in to solve a murder: when it came to test results it was never fast enough.

"Pink is a common color," Aretta said. "But I will say the shade on him is particularly bright."

"Nearly fluorescent," Siobhán said. A thought began to creep in.

"I know that look," Macdara said. "What is it?"

"What if the lipstick was a way to see the target in the dark?"

"Interesting thought," Macdara said. "Although wouldn't that line up better if he was struck in the neck rather than the heart?"

"It would. But it probably wouldn't have been hard to figure out the position of his heart once you located the neck."

"Are we thinking the killer is a woman?" Aretta asked.

"Either that, or the killer is not the kisser," Siobhán said.

"A man could have put on lipstick, then wiped it off," Macdara said.

Technically that was true, but it would have been a strange maneuver, and wouldn't Liam have seen it coming? "You think a man got close enough to kiss Liam on the neck?"

"We don't know anything for sure about Liam's sexual orientation," Macdara pointed out.

"I suppose anything is possible," Aretta said.

"It's true that we do not know Liam's sexual orientation," Siobhán said. "But if a man in the crowd this evening was wearing neon-pink lipstick, someone is sure to remember it." And although she didn't like the fact that a witness would remember it specifically because it was a man wearing it, the sooner they identified this person—no matter the sex—the better.

"Finding the owner of that shade of lipstick will be quite the challenge," Macdara said. "It's not like we can approach every single woman in Kilbane who was here this evening and demand they show us their tube."

"An interesting take on looking for Cinderella's shoe," Siobhán added.

"If you want to test it out and need a willing neck for beautiful women to kiss, mine is available," Ciarán said before sauntering away.

"Liam Noone seemed to have an effect on him," Siobhán said. "He's way too cheeky."

Macdara laughed. "Or the thought of love has buoyed him."

"He'd better find an anchor before he floats into space."

Aretta cleared her throat. They looked to her. "I think we should make a plea to the public to send in any photos they took during this event, starting from the moment these visitors arrived."

"That's a brilliant idea," Siobhán said. "We should make the announcement before everyone goes home."

"I can fetch the bullhorn from the station," Aretta said.

Macdara raised his. "I'll do it."

Siobhán gave him the side-eye. "You just like using the bullhorn."

"I don't dislike it." He grinned. A few minutes later, Macdara announced to the crowd that he would like any photos folks had taken this entire week to be sent to the garda station. He thanked them in advance and gave out the station's email address.

"Do you think the killer could be someone who is unhappy with their match?" Aretta wondered.

"Possibly," Siobhán said. "Although wouldn't it be much easier just to break up?"

Aretta nodded. "One would think."

"Maybe his Lucky Book—which he was very protective of—will have some answers," Siobhán said.

Macdara perked up. "Grace was given the Lucky Book, correct? After you stood up for yourself?" Macdara winked to show his approval.

"She was, indeed," Siobhán said. "She was asked to mind it, along with dragging along a harp, and driving the van."

"Should we see if we can find her?"

"Absolutely. Her harp is set up between the underpass of the castle and the bookshop, but since we told the public to stay out of the square, I've no idea where she might be." People had begun filtering onto Sarsfield Street, filling the footpaths, wandering into the pubs. "She worked closely with Liam, so I would guess she's either having a stiff drink or she's situated herself somewhere near the body." Siobhán navigated the area behind the crime scene tape, looking for a section that would have a direct view of Liam's body. Sure enough, when she found it, she also found Grace and Ron, huddled together, tears streaming down their faces. Guards had set up spotlights near the body, and now that the string lights were back on, it gave them clear visibility. Grace and Ron wore expressions of shock.

"I'm very sorry for your loss," Siobhán said. "I know both of you were close to Liam. But I'm afraid I'll need to ask you a few questions."

Grace looked past Siobhán, as Macdara and Aretta approached. Her tears stopped, and a look of concern crept over her face.

"Ron," Siobhán began, "may I ask where you left your double bass?"

"My double bass?" he looked at Grace as if to see if she could make sense of this. "It's behind the curtain of our little stage. Why?" Slowly, they turned to the sheet-covered body. "No," he said, pointing a trembling finger at it. "Tell me that's not—"

"I can neither confirm nor deny a thing. But I would like to see your double bass."

"Ron," Grace said. "What did you do?"

"How can you ask me that?" Ron said. "You know I'm opposed to violence in all forms." He gestured toward the stage. "If you follow me, we can have a look right now."

"You need to remain behind the crime scene tape," Macdara said. "But with your permission we'll look in the case right now." He pulled out a pair of gloves. Ron stared at them, dumfounded.

"Be my guest," he said.

"We need the pair of you to remain where you are," Macdara said. "Is that going to be a problem?"

Both shook their heads. Siobhán and Macdara hurried over to the backstage area. They pushed through the curtains and entered the makeshift backstage. The bass case was lying in the center of the small area. With gloved hands, Macdara knelt next to the case and opened it. The large instrument was in place, but the area designated for the bow was empty. They looked at each other. "This doesn't look good for him," Siobhán said.

Macdara took out his mobile phone and snapped a photo. "And why did he need to bring it this evening? He didn't play in the opening, and he could have easily left it in one of the pubs."

"But if he's the killer—how could he be so obvious? So brazen?"

Macdara sighed and stood up. "I don't know. But we cannot allow that kind of thinking to get in the way of the facts."

"He seemed genuinely surprised when we asked to look in his case."

"Let's see how surprised he looks when we tell him the

bow is gone." They headed back to where they'd left the pair. When they arrived, Ron was staring at them, a look of pleading in his eyes.

Macdara opened his phone and showed him the photo. Ron shook his head. "I'm being set up," he said. "It was in there. I swear it was in there."

"When was the last time you opened the case?" Siobhán asked.

"To be honest—it's been a while. I grabbed it at the last minute when I saw Grace's harp loaded in the van. I thought, why not? I haven't opened the case in months."

"Isn't that a bit unusual for a musician?" Macdara asked.

Ron shook his head. "I'm not a regular player. Honestly, I didn't even know if I'd get to play it this week. It was just a spur of the moment thing."

"Would you recognize your bow if you saw it?"

Ron shook his head. "No. I mean, as far as I know they all look alike."

"If it helps," Grace said, "if the murder weapon is made from the bow of a bass—that would have taken some skill."

"And?" Macdara said.

"And I've never known Ron to be that handy."

"I'm not," Ron said. "I don't even know how you would make an arrow out of a bow."

"We are going to have to take your bass as evidence for now," Macdara said.

"You can have it," Ron said. "I'll never play it again."

"We will also need to search your van," Macdara said, turning to Grace.

Grace frowned. "My van?"

"If you have any objections, we can get a warrant, but honestly it's to your benefit as much as ours."

Grace reached into her handbag, pulled out a set of keys and gave them to Siobhán. "Does it have something to do with the murder?"

"It's possible the killer hid the murder weapon nearby," Siobhán said. "And your van is parked directly behind the overpass, is it not?"

Grace nodded. "The station gave me a permit."

"Is there anything in there we should be aware of?" Siobhán asked.

Grace shook her head. "I haven't loaded my harp back in, so the back is empty apart from a rubber mat to protect my harp. I don't think there's much in the front—a map, chewing gum—I think there's a bottle of water."

"That's alright, we just need to know if there are any animals or weapons."

"Heavens, no."

Siobhán nodded. "This won't take a second." Aretta handed Siobhán a pair of gloves, and the two of them headed over to the van. Seconds later Siobhán had the back open. Apart from the rubber mat covering the floor it was empty. Siobhán closed it up and moved to the front. She checked the front and backseats, under the seats, and the cubby bin. No bow, no additional arrows, and it was relatively clean. She returned to Grace and Ron and handed back the keys. "Thank you." She glanced at Macdara. "All clear." She looked at Ron. "Are you parked nearby?"

He shook his head. "The three of us traveled in the van." Which meant that Liam did not have his own vehicle here. That was too bad, as sometimes people hid a lot of secrets in their vehicles.

"I know we shouldn't stare," Ron said, his eyes flicking to the sheet-covered body. "But it feels wrong to just leave him there."

"Once we get approval from the state pathologist, the coroner will be out to collect him," Siobhán said.

"Do you know who killed him?" Grace asked in a whisper.

"And why?" Ron added.

"I wish we worked that fast," Siobhán said. "But no, we've only just begun our inquiries."

"It has to be one of the musicians," Grace said. "Who else would make an arrow from the actual bow of a double bass?"

"Someone who has it out for me," Ron said.

"Like Liam?" Grace said.

Ron's mouth dropped open. "No," he said. "Liam didn't have it out for me. Did he?"

"He certainly didn't want you taking over as matchmaker."

Ron crossed his arms. "That was just because of his giant ego. It was nothing to do with me personally."

"Did anyone else know you were bringing your double bass this week?" Siobhán asked.

"No," Ron said.

"Yes," Grace said.

Ron's head whipped around and he glared at Grace. "Who?"

"All of us."

"What?" Ron sputtered. "When?"

"The night we all got together to plan for this week," Grace said. "It was Liam, you, me, and the six lovebird musicians."

"And how did everyone know?" Ron seemed incensed. Either he was truly caught off guard or he was an excellent actor.

Grace tilted her head and stared at Ron. "Because you announced to the group, 'Hey lads, do you think I can bring my double bass?' "

They turned to stare at Ron. "Oh," he said, "that."

Chapter 8

Ron started to hyperventilate. "I didn't do this. I swear I wouldn't hurt a fly. I *couldn't.*" He began to pace. "If only I hadn't brought that bass . . . do you think"—he swallowed hard—"do you think Liam would still be alive?"

"Why don't you try and put it out of your mind for now," Siobhán said. "We are not jumping to any conclusions."

"And we need to insist that you do not repeat these details to anyone—especially not about the murder weapon."

Grace nodded. "I understand. I won't say a word."

"Neither will I," Ron said. "Because the minute everyone hears, they're going to think I'm a killer."

Siobhán wasn't going to attempt to assure him otherwise, because she couldn't control what people thought, and it was probably a correct assumption. "I'd like each of you to take me through your movements when the session ended and everyone was on break."

"I was told to play a few songs after the session," Grace said. "I was at my harp."

Grace's phrasing was not accidental. *Told.* She was told to play, not *asked* to play. Liam had certainly been a dominating figure, or maybe Grace was the type who perceived all men in that role, or a combination of both. Siobhán just knew she would have never let Liam speak to her the way she'd heard him speak to Grace. "Your harp is located between the underpass and the bookshop," Siobhán said.

"That's correct."

"It was a beautiful song," Siobhán said.

"Thank you." She sniffled.

"What was it?"

" 'Inisheer,' " Grace said.

"It was Liam's favorite," Ron added. "It was even his ring tone on his mobile phone."

Phone. Was it on his person? Siobhán held up her finger. "Do you mind stepping away from the body?"

"We're behind the tape," Grace said.

"Why don't you step all the way out onto Sarsfield Street. I'll meet you in front of Fitzgerald's in a moment. They exchanged a glance that conveyed they were checking in with each other on whether or not they intended to argue with Siobhán.

"Of course, Detective," Ron said. The pair moved away slowly as if hoping Siobhán would change her mind and call them back.

Siobhán held up a finger and asked Macdara and Aretta to step back with her. "His mobile phone," she whispered when Grace and Ron were far enough away. "Was it near his body? Could it be in one of his pockets?"

Macdara shook his head. "I patted down his pockets. Wallet and keys are there but no phone."

"And it wasn't near his body," Aretta added.

Siobhán took out her notebook and began jotting down her thoughts while they were still fresh in her mind. "The killer must have taken it—most likely because he or she texted to Liam to meet him or her by the underpass."

"Which is why Liam reacted that way to Ron," Macdara

said. "Maybe he didn't want anyone to know about this meeting."

"And maybe the killer was able to line up his or her shot before the lights went out," Aretta said. "Perhaps that wasn't even part of the plan."

"In that situation, the killer would have been holding the weapon in plain sight," Macdara said. "That seems unlikely."

"You're right," Aretta said. "I didn't think it through."

"It's not out of the realm of possibility," Siobhán said.

Macdara raised an eyebrow. "What are you thinking?"

"The killer could have been hiding in the underpass. He or she would have been shrouded in darkness." They all turned to look at the underpass. It was entirely plausible that someone could have been positioned inside and no one noticed. Then again, he or she would have been taking a big chance. Someone could have entered the underpass in either direction at any time.

"Will you search the underpass?" Macdara asked Aretta. "Maybe we'll get lucky and our killer left some kind of a clue."

"Straightaway." Aretta headed off as Siobhán headed through the underpass and when she reached Sarsfield Street turned to the left, where she spotted Ron and Grace standing on the footpath in front of Fitzgerald's as requested. She joined them.

"Do you happen to have Liam's phone?" Siobhán asked, hoping her tone sounded casual. It was a shot in the dark, but sometimes those hit a target. *Like the arrow and Liam's heart.*

Ron tilted his head. "Why would I have Liam's phone?"

"It wasn't in his pocket?" Grace asked.

"To be honest, we haven't searched his pockets yet. We'll wait for the coroner."

Siobhán switched gears, hoping they wouldn't draw too many conclusions from the question. The killer must have taken it. Which could only mean they were worried that something on the phone would point to their guilt. Had this killer been communicating with Liam? They could still get Liam's phone records but of course that would take time. For now, the less information these suspects had, the better. She continued questioning Ron. "What were your movements when the session ended?"

"I saw Liam head in the direction of the castle's underpass, and so I started to follow him. But the minute he realized I was behind him—he did something strange." Ron paused, letting the moment build as everyone stared at him. "He said he was going to the jax."

Siobhán raised an eyebrow. "I would hardly call that strange." What she didn't add was now that she was four months pregnant with twins, she was constantly going to the jax.

"The strange bit is, I got the feeling he was lying." Ron stared out into the distance, as if the answer lay just within reach.

"And what made you think that he was lying?"

"Honestly, just a gut feeling. Maybe it was his expression—as if seeing me had just interrupted some grand plan. It was very obvious he was trying to get rid of me."

"I see." As a garda and now a detective, Siobhán often relied on gut feelings. It was possible Ron's gut was right, but it was equally possible he was throwing out a red herring. After all, would the everyday person find it odd that someone didn't want to be followed? Then again, Liam Noone was not your everyday person, and she'd seen for herself how snappy he could get. Ron would know better than she whether or not he wasn't himself.

"Besides," Ron continued, "the bookshop and the garda station already said we could use their bathrooms, but they were in the opposite direction."

Were Ron's hunches correct? Was Liam hurrying to meet

someone? Had his killer lured him to the exact spot where he was killed? He had been standing next to the cutout cupid. It would have been simple. Someone sent a text that said to meet them by it. "Was there anything else about his demeanor this week that seemed off?" She addressed the question to both Ron and Grace.

"He was up and down," Grace said. "One minute he seemed on top of the world, and the next he would be glowering. I don't know what it was, but I too had this feeling that something was going on with him."

A lovers' quarrel? Who but romantic partners could make someone feel euphoric one moment and enraged the next?

"Take it from me," Ron said. "There was definitely something going on that he wasn't sharing."

"I just told her that," Grace said. "Are you tuning me out?"

"I was his protégé," Ron said. "I knew Liam better than most everyone. And as his shadow, I'm in the best position to observe him."

"Better than everyone?" Grace cleared her throat in a not-so-subtle manner.

"That's not what I said." Ron glared at her. "If you were listening—I said I knew Liam better than *almost* everyone."

"I accept your apology." Grace nodded her approval.

"I didn't apologize." Ron shot an exasperated look Siobhán's way. "Moving on to other matters, I have absolutely no doubt that Liam would want this festival to continue. He would expect me to take up the reins and go forth."

"Ron!" Grace said. "How could you even think about such a thing in this moment?"

"I can think of such a thing because I am a professional. Besides, I truly think it's what he would have wanted." Ron's voice hitched as he wiped nonexistent tears from his face. "I'm trying to *honor* his memory."

"I want his murderer caught," Grace said. She was crying for real but made no move to wipe away her tears. "But I cannot imagine going through with a matchmaking festival when Liam has been *murdered*."

"Then you're forgetting how dedicated Liam was to his passion!" He turned to Siobhán. "I hope I don't sound callous," Ron said.

"Well, you do," Grace interjected.

Ron shook his head. "I know it's what he would have wanted."

"That doesn't mean he would have wanted you to take over," Grace said.

Macdara was approaching, which caused the pair of them to fall silent. "What have I missed?" he asked, stepping up next to Siobhán.

Grace pointed at Ron. "He wants to continue with the festival!"

"As a way of honoring Liam," Ron said. "It's what he would want."

Macdara held up his hand and glanced at Siobhán. "Normally, I would say no to a matchmaking festival continuing after this—everyone is traumatized, which is to be expected, a man has been murdered—but if you want his killer caught, continuing with the festival is a sure way to keep all of our suspects in town."

This caught Grace's attention. You could nearly see the wheels turning in her poor head as she thought about it.

"It would also help to keep everyone distracted," Siobhán added. Even if they didn't cancel the festival, people had traveled a long way to get here, especially the musicians, and they would hang around. As for the rest of the visitors, it was dangerous to have people hanging around, getting worked up about a killer, with nothing to do. Idle hands and all that. "Keeping people busy is vital to this investigation."

"It feels disrespectful," Grace said. "I don't know if I can be a part of it."

"We certainly won't act like none of this happened," Ron said. "I meant what I said. We can turn this weekend into a tribute to Liam. A memorial service of sorts."

"Liam was passionate about making matches," Grace said. "So, if during our tribute, Cupid's arrow happens to strike—" She stopped and slapped her hand over her mouth. When she dropped her hand, her mouth was still open in surprise. "I didn't mean it that way," she said.

"It's okay," Siobhán said. "We know what you meant."

"Thank you," Grace said.

"Liam would understand too," Ron said. "Remember, matchmaking was his life's purpose."

"I am going to ask both of you a broad question," Siobhán said. "Try not to think too hard about the answer." Ron and Grace stared at her in anticipation. "Did any of the musicians have any kind of problem with Liam? Did anything unusual happen since you arrived?"

The pair exchanged a look.

"Yes?" Siobhán hoped this would be the lead they needed.

"Tell her," Ron said.

"I'm sure it's nothing." Grace stared off into the distance.

Siobhán held up her hand. "Let us figure that out."

"Liam was rather secretive this week," Grace said. "Even more than usual."

"We've told her that already," Ron said. "If you don't spit it out, I will."

Grace sighed. "We saw him come and go from the Kilbane Inn at odd hours."

Macdara perked up. "How many times, and what were the hours?"

"He'd leave close to midnight and return early in the morning," Grace said.

"I'm sure trad sessions went on all night," Siobhán said. "Maybe he was at one of them?"

"He wasn't known to frequent trad sessions," Grace said. "He much preferred if the attention was on him."

That definitely rang true.

"That isn't unusual," Ron said. "He's a bit of a ladies' man."

"I see," Siobhán said. "Any idea who he might have been seeing?"

"No," Ron said.

Grace looked at her feet. "Grace?" Siobhán prodded.

"I would only be guessing."

"Go on, so."

"He wasn't the only one who came and went from the Kilbane Inn at strange hours." She was dragging it out. Siobhán waited. "Please. Don't mention my name."

"You have my word," Siobhán said.

"It was either Róisín or Edward. Or both."

"You're not sure?"

Grace shook her head. "It was dark. I could make out a figure, but only a glimpse. But they came in the same car and it has a bad muffler. Every night after Liam left, I would hear their car start up. By the time I peeked out the curtains I could only make out a figure getting into the driver's seat, and I would watch them leave."

"You said them," Siobhán pointed out. "Was it one person or two?"

"One," Grace said. "I just don't know which one."

"But you said they returned a few hours later, right?" Ron asked. "Whereas Liam stayed out all night."

"That's correct," Grace said.

"Thank you," Siobhán said. "I take it you did not mention this to Liam or Róisín or Edward?"

"Absolutely not," Grace said. "I don't stick my nose into other people's business."

Ron snorted.

"*Much*," she added.

"I understand. I'll ask that you both keep this to yourself as well. Grace, I have to ask that you return Liam's Lucky Book to me."

Grace stared at Siobhán for a moment, then her mouth dropped open. "Oh, dear," she said, her gaze flicking about. "Oh, no." Her breath became shallow and she began to wring her hands.

"What's wrong?" Macdara asked.

"Yes, Grace," Ron said, "why do you look like you just swallowed a lemon?"

"Because when all the chaos started, I forgot all about the book," Grace said. "I tucked it inside my harp cover."

"We have to get it," Ron said, the panic in his voice rising. "Let's go."

"The harp is inside the crime scene tape," Siobhán said. "And I will be taking the Lucky Book as evidence."

Ron frowned. "Evidence of what?"

"That's yet to be determined," Siobhán said. There was no doubt about it, Ron was gagging for the book.

"It has to still be in my harp cover."

"We'll search it for you," Macdara said. "And we can also cover the harp and wheel it back out to your van."

"Thank you."

"Feel free to walk on the other side of the crime scene tape, and join us at the harp," Siobhán said. "You can give us instructions on the proper way to put the cover on and transport it."

"Thank you," Grace said. "It's larger than most autoharps but not as big and bulky as the harp I usually use." A funny look came across her face but just as quickly it disappeared.

"Was there something else?"

Grace shook her head. "No, sorry. I was just thinking of Liam."

By the time Siobhán and Macdara were gloved up and arrived at the harp, Grace and Ron were standing on the other side of the crime scene tape, waiting anxiously. Siobhán half-expected Ron to scale the line of tape and grab the book. She opened the cover as wide as she could and Macdara shone his torch inside. It was empty.

Chapter 9

"The book isn't here," Siobhán announced. She shook out the harp cover to prove the point.

"No, no, no, no," Grace said. "It was in here." Grace pointed at the cover as if Siobhán hadn't understood the assignment. "I dropped it right in here, and zipped it up so that it was safe."

"Are you sure it's gone?" Ron said. "Look again."

"It's not in there," Siobhán said. Grace began to hyperventilate. "Deep breaths. Take deep breaths."

Grace began to suck in air. She clutched the top of her head with both hands. "I'm sorry, Liam. I failed you. You asked me to do one thing, and I failed you."

"Maybe you moved it," Ron said.

Grace shook her head. "I did not move it."

"Maybe you put it in your van for safekeeping?" Ron seemed on the verge of panic. Siobhán had already searched the van, but she kept her gob shut. It was obvious they were reaching for straws.

"It was safe by my side," Grace said.

"Until it wasn't," Ron said.

"Until that woman screamed. I ran to see what was the

matter. And then, when I realized what had happened—" She stopped. "You can't possibly blame me for momentarily leaving the Lucky Book."

"He should have given it to me," Ron said. "I wouldn't have set it down for a second!"

Grace began wiping her eyes, sniffling all the way. "I couldn't very well play the harp whilst holding the Lucky Book."

"Take it easy," Siobhán said to Ron, hoping he caught the warning in her tone. Hysteria never helped anyone.

"I'm sorry," Ron said. "I'm sorry. I just know how upset Liam would be." He stopped. "I'm not blaming you, Grace."

"Funny," Grace said. "Because it feels like you are."

"Why don't the pair of you take a break from each other," Siobhán said. Their arguing was going to give her a headache. "When you left it, was the harp cover zipped or unzipped?"

Grace stared at the cover as if she expected it to answer. "It was zipped. I'm sure of it."

"It was unzipped when I arrived," Siobhán said.

"Do you think you can get fingerprints off the zipper?" Ron asked.

"No," Siobhán said. "The surface is too small." Was it just Siobhán's imagination or did Ron look relieved? Of all people, he would be the one who wanted Liam's Lucky Book the most.

Macdara, who had been listening from a few meters away, approached. "Who would have taken this book? I don't see why the average person would have any interest in it." More often than not, Macdara seemed to read her mind. Slowly, everyone turned to look at Ron.

"Me?" Ron said. "You think I took it?" He shook his head. "Did you not see my genuinely freaked-out reaction when I learned Grace had lost it? I'm a matchmaker, not an actor!"

"I'm not implying that you took it, Ron," Grace said. "But you cannot pretend you didn't covet it. Nearly as obsessed with it as Liam, I'd say."

Ron narrowed his eyes. "And yet—if I stole the book—do you think I'm only *pretending* to be devastated that it's gone?"

Grace shrugged. "Isn't that exactly how you would play it, if you did take it?"

"Seriously? And here I was feeling guilty for accusing you."

"And what exactly were you accusing me of?"

"I understand everyone is on edge, but let's just take a deep breath," Macdara said. He glanced at Siobhán. Ever since learning they were having twins, they'd both been doing breath work. Not necessarily for the delivery, but just to quell the panic whenever they thought of taking care of two babies.

"I tried that already, "Siobhán said. "It didn't take."

"I attempted to give the book back to Liam before I began to play." Grace stopped, tilted her head, and frowned. "I think you're right, Ron—something wasn't right with him—he didn't even react when I tried to give him back the book." She glanced at Siobhán. "Liam was very, very strict about that book. He's never let me hold it before today. Something was definitely wrong. I should have been more alarmed. Why wasn't I more alarmed?" She began to pace. "They say people give things away when they're thinking of ending their own lives. Do you think Liam—?"

"What?" Ron said. "Shot himself with an arrow?"

Grace stopped pacing. "You're right. You're right. No one could shoot themselves with a bow and arrow." She shook her head. "But he wasn't himself. I should have been more alarmed."

"Your reaction is normal," Siobhán said. "People often try to blame themselves when something like this happens. But the only one to blame is the killer."

Ron put his arm around Grace. "I'm sorry," he said. "We need to stick together."

Grace chewed her lip but didn't move away from his embrace.

"We should spread the word to the pubs that the trad sessions can continue this evening," Macdara said. "But we should assign all available guards to Sarsfield Street, just to ease minds and show we have some control over this."

"Do you think one of the matched couples murdered him?" Grace asked, her voice hitching.

"At this point, all possibilities are on the table," Siobhán said.

"There was one person who decided to play Ron's double bass last Monday evening," Grace said.

Ron whirled around. "What?"

Grace chewed her lip. "Niall O'Malley thought he'd have a laugh—I saw him playing the bass that evening."

"It wasn't mine," Ron said.

"How do you know?" Siobhán asked.

"Because I was busy that evening running around for Liam. My bass was still in Grace's van." He seemed to perk up. "Do you know what this means? It means there *was* another double bass floating around."

"Any of the musicians around could have laid their hands on a double bass," Grace said.

"Of course," Ron said. "They're around musicians and music shops all the time!"

"And people have been preparing for this festival in advance."

"Premeditated," Ron said.

"Thank you," Macdara interjected. "We'll take it from here."

"Sorry," Ron said. "We listen to a lot of true-crime podcasts."

"If we need a podcast listener, we'll let you know," Siobhán said.

"Do you want us to question the suspects?" Ron asked. "We can be subtle."

"Let's make a deal right here and now," Macdara said. "We won't play matchmaker and the pair of you won't play detective."

"Not a bother," Ron said. "But if we hear anything?"

"Or see anything?" Grace added.

"Our eyes and ears work just fine. You two concentrate on your jobs, how does that sound?"

Siobhán could tell her husband was growing irritated, and she for one was here for it. Normally, they did want people to come to them with anything they saw or heard, but these two were already stepping over lines, and encouraging it would only make it worse. Siobhán thought about the Lucky Book. Grace's harp was quite a distance from where Liam was killed. The killer was already working with an extremely tight timeline. If Grace's account was correct and the Lucky Book was stolen the moment she left her harp to see what the screaming was all about, they should try to find any CCTV cameras that were pointed in the direction of the harp. It was possible the thief and the killer were not one and the same, and it was equally possible that instead of looking for one killer they were looking for a pair. "Let's go speak to the crowd, shall we?" Siobhán said. She was eager to get this investigation started. Murderers always had the head-start advantage, and it was maddening.

"Does the Lucky Book have any value?" Macdara asked. "To anyone but yourselves?"

"It's priceless." Ron's eyebrow shot up. "Any matchmaker would die to get his or her hands on it." He gulped. "Or kill."

"Why don't you try putting a price on it," Macdara suggested.

Ron whistled. "Fifty years' worth of matchmaking observations? Like I said. Priceless."

"If only I hadn't been playing the harp," Grace said. "I probably would have been by Liam's side. Maybe I could have saved him."

"Or maybe," Ron said, "you would have taken an arrow through the heart."

"Why does murder always seem to follow you around?"

Siobhán stared at Chris Gordon, wondering whether or not it was a rhetorical question. They stood on the footpath in front of his comic book shop, watching as people filed into Fitzgerald's Pub across the street. For some reason, Chris had flagged her down when he saw her passing by, and of course she'd obliged, but whatever the reason was, it seemed he was going to work his way up to it. When Chris had first arrived, he'd looked like a movie star. And although he was still undeniably handsome, he had become somewhat relaxed in his appearance. No longer a clothes horse, he more often than not wore comic-book-themed T-shirts, and his dark hair was often uncombed.

"This used to be a quiet town," Siobhán said. "I believe the murders all started shortly after *you* arrived."

"Touché."

Siobhán laughed. She had to hand it to Chris, it wasn't easy to integrate into this small town, and when he first arrived, she thought for sure he wouldn't stay long. But here he was, all these years later, and for the most part everyone accepted him as a local.

"Where were you when the murder happened?" she asked.

Chris arched an eyebrow. "Why, Detective Sergeant O'Sullivan, are you asking me for my alibi?"

"I hardly think you'd have reason to murder our matchmaker. Unless you asked if he could find you a match and he shot you down?" The moment it was out of her mouth, she winced at her choice of words. But Chris either hadn't heard how Liam had been shot with a bow and arrow or he was polite enough not to mention it.

"If you must know, I'm seeing someone."

"Do tell."

"It's a long-distance thing. A girl from home."

"Any chance she'll be visiting soon?"

"I'm working on it."

"I was asking where you were because someone in the crowd might have seen something before the lights cut out. Were you there?"

"Funny you should ask. I hadn't planned on going out there, but when I heard laughter and clapping, it drew me out of the shop." He paused, and Siobhán waited. She had learned not to interrupt people when they were collecting their thoughts, as sometimes an interjection could cause them to forget what they were going to say. It worked especially well for suspects: the more someone ran their mouth, the higher the chance they'd blurt out something they hadn't intended. It probably worked for marriage too, but she'd yet to perfect it with Macdara. "I headed straight to the square and crossed through the underpass of the castle." That would have brought him directly to the cutout Cupid, the exact spot where Liam had been murdered. This was more than she could have hoped for. "But then my phone rang, and you know how it echoes in there—and I didn't want to ruin the session—so I turned around and went back the way I came, so I could at least see who was calling." Then again if you let a person go on too long, they might put you to sleep before they got to anything good. "But then they hung up, and so I turned back around, and I was about to go through the underpass when the lights went out."

"Meaning you didn't see anything that will help me."

"I saw a figure in the underpass. But it was dark—I cannot tell you if it was a man or a woman, but they seemed to be practicing tai chi or karate or something because their right arm was pulled back and the left was sticking straight out, at least the best I could see in the dark."

He saw the killer about to strike. "You could see all that but you couldn't tell if it was a man or a woman?"

"It happened so fast—the streetlights on Sarsfield stayed on, so I could see what I thought were arms—and the position struck me as odd—but right after, I heard a scream and I hightailed it out of there."

"You ran *away* from the scream?"

"I like my drama between the pages of a comic book," Chris said. He held up a finger. "But I might have *heard* something that will help you."

"Go on, so."

"I heard a man's voice. And he said something a bit ominous." This time Siobhán simply waited for him to continue. "He said, 'What do you think you're doing?' "

What if Liam saw his killer? "Are you sure?"

"How could I forget something like that?"

"Did you hear anyone reply?"

Chris shook his head. "I heard a gasp, and then a swish of air, a thud, and finally a scream."

Was the male voice Liam's? If so . . . Siobhán followed the thread. Liam saw his killer and said, "What do you think you're doing?" He must have seen the killer holding the bow and arrow. Next, he sees the killer preparing to shoot the arrow and gasps. The arrow flies through the air (the swish), he's struck in the heart and falls to the ground (thud), and the final scream must have come from someone near the body when it fell. All the while the killer must have hid in the underpass. The passage was a great way of studying the castle's foundation, but apparently it was equally great as a killer's hiding place. "When Liam fell did the figure you saw run to the town square or away from it?"

"What?" He shook his head. "I didn't see the figure again."

"When you 'hightailed it out of there,' did you go into your shop or stay on the footpath?"

"I went into my shop."

"So, you didn't see anything after that?"

"I did look out the window and there were a lot of people on the street—all moving toward the scream—but no, I did not see anything in particular."

The information was only slightly helpful. The comment wasn't one you'd say to a stranger—*What do you think you're doing?*—was it? Maybe if the action was odd enough one might say it to a stranger. An action such as pointing a bow and arrow at one's heart . . . Maybe this wasn't that helpful, after all. Siobhán had already surmised that Liam had been killed by someone he knew. If there was a stranger running around shooting random people in the heart with an arrow made from the bow of a bass, they had even bigger problems on their hands.

"Thank you," Siobhán said. "And please—keep this to yourself."

"Do you think I heard the man's last words?"

"I don't know, but the less information circulating the better." It wouldn't be safe for Chris if the killer knew he was an ear-witness. She did not say this bit out loud. There was no use freaking him out.

"I understand," Chris said. "I won't say a word."

"To *anyone*," Siobhán said. "No chatting with customers about murder."

"Why Detective O'Sullivan, are you calling me a gossip?"

"Let's just put it this way—you've become a local." Siobhán slapped him on the back and left Chris with that thought. She headed back to the square and found Macdara and Aretta standing near the white tent they'd erected around the body.

"Aretta is going to escort the musicians and Liam's staff to the Kilbane Inn," Macdara said, as soon as he saw her. "I thought maybe you'd like to accompany them." He wasn't wrong—it would be a chance to watch their suspects when they didn't think they were being watched.

"Absolutely. Chris Gordon might have heard something." She filled him in on their conversation.

"He knew his killer," Macdara said.

"That's what I think," Siobhán said. "And whoever it was, it seems that Liam Noone had finally met his match."

Chapter 10

Siobhán and Aretta were in the squad car, and nearly to the Kilbane Inn, when Siobhán spotted a large tire rolling down the middle of the street, directly toward her vehicle. She managed to swerve just in time before slamming on the brakes.

"Close one," Aretta said, breathing heavily.

"Are you alright, chicken?" Siobhán asked.

"That's Garda Chicken, and I'm still in one piece."

Siobhán laughed. As the newest member of the team, Aretta had taken a while to warm up, but these days her humor was on point. The tire was still on the move. Siobhán pulled over, got out of the car, and chased it down. It was a spare tire from the looks of it—for a truck or SUV, or some such. She threw it in the boot, and soon they were pulling into the car park where a neon sign showed NO VACANCY. No doubt Emma and Eileen Curley were thrilled to have every single one of their rooms booked with lovebird musicians.

The identical twins, who were expecting them, were waiting in front of the rooms. The musicians were here too, ferrying instruments from Grace's van to their rooms.

Siobhán and Aretta approached with a wave. "Has anyone reported missing a spare tire?" Siobhán asked.

They shook their heads in stereo, their brunette curls bouncing. "But people are always driving too fast on that road," one of them said.

"We need something done about it," the other added. She eyed Siobhán. "Maybe you could do something about it. Now that you're a detective sergeant."

Siobhán sighed. "I'll bring it up at the next department meeting."

"How is it going with the musicians?" Aretta asked. "Did you know there's another set of identical twins?"

As they drew closer, Siobhán was able to tell the twins apart. It had taken Siobhán ages to see the differences in them, but as they aged it became easier. In their early forties now, Emma's face was slightly thinner than Eileen's and her hair just a tad shorter.

"Of course we know," Eileen said. "We're chuffed."

"They're adorable," Emma said. "We're mad about them."

Eileen nodded, her face beaming. "We love twins, and we love musicians."

"They've all promised to play music every night in the garden," Emma exclaimed. "It will be lovely."

"Lovely," Eileen echoed. "They've just returned with their instruments, all but Grace's harp, which was too big to lug around."

"But it's safely inside Fitzgerald's Pub," Emma added. From the sounds of it, they had taken a keen interest in all of their guests.

"I'm sure you heard of the tragedy this evening," Siobhán said. She hated to ruin the moment, but they did have a murder to solve.

"We did," Emma said, instantly sobering up.

"And we have concerns," Eileen added.

"Safety concerns," they said in unison.

"We're way ahead of you," Siobhán said. "Macdara has assigned a garda to the inn. He'll be here shortly, and he'll be on watch all night."

"We would prefer if someone stayed watch all week," Eileen said.

Siobhán nodded. "Let's take it a day at time."

From their expressions, the answer wasn't satisfactory, but at least they didn't put up an argument. "They're very efficient," Emma said, pointing to the musicians unloading the van. Grace stood off to the side, watching them, and Ron was headed to the edge of the car park, where he began pacing near the road, his phone glued to his ear.

Eileen and Emma drew close to Siobhán and lowered their voices. "A little birdie told us you're having twins," Eileen said.

"It sounds like that little birdie has a big beak," Siobhán replied.

The identical twins laughed in stereo, brunette waves bouncing again. "Identical or fraternal?" Emma asked.

Eileen leaned forward. "Boys or girls?"

"We don't know yet," Siobhán said. "We prefer to be surprised."

Like Róisín and Helen, Emma and Eileen sported the same hairstyle and often dressed alike. Today they wore T-shirts that read TREBLE MAKER, complete with a treble clef. Emma saw Siobhán staring at them.

"We bought them just for the occasion."

"You don't say."

"We want to put our hats in the ring as babysitters," Emma added. "Two for one!"

"Actually, two for two," Eileen said. They laughed again in perfect harmony, even the crinkles in the corner of their eyes identical.

"I'd give them to you now if I could," Siobhán said, resting her hand on her belly. "I'm keeping them out past their bedtime."

"Twins are the best," Eileen said. "And we simply cannot wait."

"Are you going to dress them alike?" Emma asked eagerly.

"We will see," Siobhán said.

"Consider us your personal consultants on anything twins," Eileen said.

"I appreciate that."

"Not only that," Emma said, "but we want to throw you a baby shower."

"That is so sweet, I mean it, but Gráinne is organizing one in Lahinch." Siobhán had resisted at first, but a getaway to the sea sounded like heaven, and everyone who had been invited seemed thrilled to have an excuse for a mini holiday. James and Gráinne had made the effort to come here this week, and Siobhán wanted to return the favor.

"We love Lahinch," Eileen said. "We can plan it with her!"

"And we could give her tips on running an inn."

"I'm sure she'd love that," Siobhán said, while simultaneously imagining Gráinne's overreaction. When it came to certain things, like staging parties, Gráinne was a lone wolf. "I think she's already decided on everything. But of course, you're invited."

The twins nodded, but their disappointment was palpable. Siobhán hesitated, for she knew what she was about to ask would make them uncomfortable. "I'd like you to let me into Liam Noone's room."

For a moment the twins simply stared at her. "Don't you need a warrant?" Emma asked.

"If you give me permission, I do not need a warrant."

The twins looked at each other for several seconds, communicating telepathically for all Siobhán knew.

"We'd prefer to wait for the warrant," Eileen said.

"Under normal circumstances, I understand," Siobhán said. "But a man has been murdered, and it's perfectly legal for you, as the proprietors of this inn, to allow me access."

"Especially, if you care about the safety of your other guests," Aretta added. Siobhán imagined fist-bumping her—it was the perfect thing to say.

"I'll get the key," Emma said. Eileen opened her mouth to speak, but Emma shut her down with a shake of her head.

"Thank you," Siobhán called out, as Emma headed for the small house situated next to the inn.

Siobhán studied the musicians who had finished unloading and were conversing in front of their rooms. "I was told by one of the other guests that they saw Liam Noone—and someone else they couldn't identify—coming and going at all hours this week."

"We don't have a curfew," Eileen said.

"Of course not. But I know you keep a quiet establishment. Did you notice their comings and goings?"

"We heard cars come and go. But it's always like that when musicians are in town. They're all night owls."

She had a point there. "Did anyone complain, did any arguments break out, anything of the sort?"

"Nothing of the sort."

Emma returned dangling the keys. Siobhán reached to take them, but Emma pulled them back. "About that baby shower . . ."

"I would let you, I swear, but Gráinne has already put so much work into it. I couldn't do that to her."

"Luckily, we have the solution," Eileen said.

"You're having twins, so Gráinne will throw you a baby shower for one, and we'll throw you a baby shower for the other."

"Hard to argue with that," Aretta quipped, flashing a cheeky smile. Maybe she was fitting in too well.

Emma continued to dangle the keys at they stared at her.

"Brilliant," Siobhán said. "Double the fun."

Macdara arrived in time to help search Liam's room. Aretta stayed on the footpath, quietly observing the group. One look at Liam's disorganized room and it was immediately apparent why the matchmaker relied so heavily on Grace. His bed was unmade, the covers twisted and shoved aside, empty beer bottles lined the bathroom counter along with five bottles of cologne, and his suitcase was tossed on a chair, clothes spilling out and trailing along the floor. The rooms at the Kilbane Inn were arranged in a horseshoe shape, and Liam's room was the first room in a grouping: if one was standing outside facing the rooms, his was to the left. According to the twins, Grace's room was next door. Siobhán and Macdara began to quickly sift through the scattered contents of Liam's room. "I found something," Macdara said. He stood by one of the night stands holding up a piece of paper. Written in capital letters was a single message handwritten in blue ink: YOU OWE ME!!!

"Is he the writer or the receiver?" Siobhán wondered out loud.

"Once we find his Lucky Book we can compare the handwriting—the way the *E* curls should be a dead give-away." He dropped the note into an evidence bag.

"Let's check the other stand." Siobhán hurried to the one on the other side of the bed. There was a single calling card on top from a local printer.

"Something to check out," Macdara said.

"Maybe he needed to print something for one of this weekend's activities."

"We shall find out."

Siobhán tucked the card into her notebook. Ten minutes later, they were almost finished. "He was worried about going bald," Macdara said, emerging from the bathroom. "At least according to his shampoo."

"He had a full head of hair, but I suppose he was future minded." *Or a narcissist.*

"Between the cologne, the three different skin creams, and the number of outfits he brought—I'd say he was expecting a little romance alright," Macdara said.

"Did you see this?" Siobhán moved over to the dresser situated next to an open closet. She pointed at a pile of ties. "He wasn't wearing a tie," Siobhán said. "But it looks like he tried on every single one."

"I don't see any signs of a female staying here," Macdara said.

"That's because he didn't plan on bringing her back here. I mean, look at the state of the place." Siobhán knew of one person staying in Charlesville. "If only we had his mobile phone or something to tell us whether or not his secret paramour was Helen."

Siobhán turned to the last place they needed to check, his closet. "Interesting," she said as she faced it. The clothes were either pushed all the way to the right or all the way to the left, leaving the space in the middle open. Siobhán edged in closer. At first, she wasn't sure if she was imagining things, but once she was only an inch from the wall, it was definitive. A hole had been drilled. Siobhán looked through it. It had a clear view to the bed next door. Grace's room.

"What are you doing?" Macdara asked.

"See for yourself." Siobhán stepped out of the closet, and Macdara took her place. "That's his assistant's room?"

Siobhán nodded. "Grace Collins."

"This is extremely disturbing."

"We're going to have to tell her." Maybe she'd finally knock him off of the inexplicable pedestal she'd put him on.

"And the twins," Macdara said. "They'll want to reinforce this wall so that the next time a perverted guest takes a notion, he won't be able to follow through with it."

"We have to make sure there isn't any chance this hole wasn't here before," Siobhán said. "But I have a feeling we already know who drilled it."

Siobhán stood outside Grace's room, waiting for Macdara to return from the main house. Siobhán knew that Grace was going to try to find any excuse for Liam she could, so Macdara was checking in with the twins to see if there was any possibility the hole had been drilled by a previous guest. Perhaps Liam had even pointed it out to them. Siobhán doubted it, but when it came to investigations, the possibilities were endless. Failing to follow through on even one permutation of the options could easily lead a detective down the wrong path. On telly and in films, cases were usually solved with DNA or some high-tech forensics. But here in Kilbane, they still had to roll up their sleeves and solve cases old school. Unless, of course, they wanted to wait several weeks or even months for any kind of forensic results. That type of evidence helped in court, no doubt, and they always made sure to collect it and send it off, but more often than not the key to catching the killer came down to the grunt work. Macdara was now exiting the house and making his way toward her.

"They were mortified," he said on approach. "And the closets were all scrubbed clean and organized for the arrivals of these guests, so they are one hundred percent sure the hole was not there."

"Interesting," Siobhán said. "Where do you suppose he got the drill?"

Macdara copped on. "That's right. You searched the van. No tools?"

"No tools."

He sighed. "This is why you should have come with me. Shall I go speak to the twins again?"

"Yes. I believe they keep tools in the garden shed. It would be worth checking to see if there's a drill."

"Does it really matter though? They were setting up the stage in the town square—he could have easily nicked a drill and then returned it."

"That's true. We can put a pin in it for now." She glanced at Grace's door. "This isn't going to be fun."

"I'll let you do the talking," Macdara said. "It's a bit delicate."

Siobhán knocked on Grace's door. She opened it straightaway. Her eyes were red and swollen, with mascara smudged on her cheek. In her hand, she held a bottle of whiskey, and from the look of things, she'd already made quite a dent in it.

"Don't judge me," she said.

"I'm not here to judge." She resisted the urge to advise her to drink water, eat something, and have headache tablets on the ready. "I need to speak with you for a moment."

Grace stood back and gestured with the bottle for Siobhán to come in. "I'd offer you a glass, but I'm afraid I haven't been using one."

"No worries, I think my bosses, and especially my doctor, would frown on it."

Grace gasped. "You *are* pregnant!" She hugged the whiskey bottle to her chest. "I was wondering, you've got that belly bulge, and of course the puffiness in your face."

Siobhán touched her cheek. Was she puffy? Why hadn't anyone mentioned it? "It's twins," she said, hoping that might justify some of the puffy.

Grace curled up into a corner armchair. Unlike Liam's train wreck of a room, here everything was in its place. "I was playing his favorite song when he died," she said. "'Inisheer.'"

"I didn't know what it was, but I remember it was lovely," Siobhán said.

"I keep thinking that I need to speak with Liam," Grace said, her voice hitching. "It doesn't seem possible that he's gone."

"It takes a while," Siobhán said. The truth was, grief never really went away; it just ebbed and flowed, but that wasn't the news she wanted to impart in this moment.

"The matchmaking community is going to be devastated," Grace said. "That is, before they all rush to take his place." At this, her glance flicked to the window, out onto the front of the inn. Ron strode by the room, then veered off into the car park.

"He likes to smoke by the road," Grace said. "As if we can't see him."

"He seemed to really look up to Liam," Siobhán said.

"Who?" Grace seemed startled.

"Ron."

Grace frowned. "He was his shadow." The sentiment sounded positive, but the tone did not.

Siobhán moved to the wall and located the peephole. "Listen, Grace. There's something I need to tell you, and I'm afraid you're going to find it upsetting."

Grace shot out of her chair, sloshing whiskey. "Did you find the killer?"

"No." She pointed to the peephole. "We were just processing Liam's room, and we discovered that he had drilled a hole in the closet. It looks directly onto your bed." She pointed at it. "You can come see for yourself."

Grace advanced, her gait wobbly. She went right up to the peephole and put her eye through it. She then backed away and stared at it as she swayed slightly. Perhaps Siobhán should have waited for a sober moment. Then again, bad news was never convenient. "It could have been someone else. Another guest." But the look on her face proved that she didn't believe her own words.

"We checked with the proprietors. They did a thorough cleaning of the closets and insist it was not there prior to your arrival."

Grace began to wring her hands as she paced. "What was he playing at?"

"Unfortunately, I think the answer is probably simpler than we wish to admit."

"I can't believe it. How could he? I mean—" She came to an abrupt stop and stared at Siobhán. "Do you think?" She swallowed hard. "Is it possible?

"Do I think what? Is what possible?" She was babbling and not making an ounce of sense.

"My original room was on the opposite side of the horseshoe—the very last room to be exact."

"You switched rooms?"

Grace nodded. "They asked me to switch. Róisín wanted to practice her drums but she was worried she'd disturb Liam. And so, we switched."

"Róisín Doyle? You switched rooms with Edward Kavanaugh and Róisín Doyle?" Grace nodded.

"How long were Róisín and Edward in this room before you switched?"

"Two days."

Siobhán mulled it over as Grace began pacing again. It was a crude thought, but Liam hadn't shown any kind of obvious attraction to Grace. Instead he spoke to her like a servant. Róisín, on the other hand, as distasteful as it may be, was young and beautiful. And it wasn't that Grace wasn't attractive for an older woman, but between the two of them it did seem more likely that it was Róisín he was peeping on.

"What if one or both of them found out about this peephole?" Grace said. "What if that's why they wanted to switch rooms?"

"You don't think they would have warned you about it—or reported it to Emma or Eileen?"

"I don't know. But it's possible, isn't it?" Grace moved toward the peephole. "What if—I'm not trying to point fingers—but what if they knew what was happening but decided to take matters into their own hands?"

"And by take matters into their own hands you mean—"

"Revenge. I mean revenge. And what they decided was to get even and tie it up with a bow."

But not just any bow. This one came with an arrow.

Chapter 11

"I need to emphasize that you are not to share this information with anyone." Siobhán and Grace were now standing outside Grace's room. "Not a word about the peephole, or the fact that you switched rooms with Edward and Róisín. I don't want them to have any kind of heads-up before I speak with them."

Grace nodded. "I swear on me life I won't say a word."

It was getting late, and the best thing to do might be to bring them into the station in the morning. She would check in with Aretta and Macdara, bring them up to speed, and put it up for consensus. Ron was no longer by the road smoking. Presumably, he'd gone into his room.

"Liam seemed a bit harsh earlier when he was addressing Ron," Siobhán said. "Was there often animosity between the two?"

"As you may have noticed, Ron was obsessed with Liam. I'll leave it up to you to figure out whether or not it was to a healthy degree."

"Obsession usually has a dark connotation," Siobhán said.

"Ron admired Liam, but it wasn't reciprocal," Grace

explained. "Then again, Liam might have felt threatened by Ron."

"Threatened?"

"Yes. A young man, biting at his heels, wanting to take over as matchmaker? I'm sure it drove him mad." Siobhán could concede that. But mad enough to provoke the man to murder? "He was a wonderful man and fierce talented," Grace continued, "but his ego often got in his way. He would have despised anyone who called themselves his protégé, especially if he perceived a coup. . . . Liam simply couldn't fathom anyone doing his job but him."

"Are you saying that Ron was actively trying to oust Liam?"

"Trying?" Grace shrugged. "I have no proof of that. But did he want to? I'd say that much is obvious."

They were interrupted by a squad car pulling in. Macdara was here. "We'll pick this conversation up again," Siobhán said.

"You won't repeat anything I said to Ron, will you?" Grace's voice was edged with worry.

"We're conducting one-on-one interviews for a reason," Siobhán said. "Everything you say is private." *Unless and until it needs to be divulged.* Siobhán was ready to head off, but Grace seemed like there was still something on her mind. "Anything else?"

"Liam liked the ladies," Grace said. "Even before the peephole, we all knew he liked the ladies."

"What exactly does that mean?"

"I've worked with him for twenty years. There hasn't been a single festival where he didn't find a pretty young woman to keep him company."

"I see."

"And it often didn't even matter if they were single."

"You're saying?"

"I'm saying, what if the partner or spouse of his latest dalliance discovered the betrayal?"

Love was often a motive for murder, but Siobhán kept this to herself as she studied Grace. "Do you know for sure if he was seeing anyone here?"

"I do not," Grace said. "But if he wasn't, it was only a matter of time."

"As much as I'd like to call it a night, I think we should interview the rest of them while the events of the evening are still fresh in their minds," Macdara said. "And before they have time to consult with each other."

"I was thinking the same," Siobhán said.

"But if you're tired—"

"I'm grand." Macdara didn't push it—he knew she didn't want to be treated with kid gloves. She had filled in Macdara and Aretta on the development with the peephole and her conversation with Grace.

"We should be able to knock this out pretty quick," Aretta said. "At least take down everyone's movements during the time period when Liam was murdered."

"There aren't any empty rooms to conduct the interviews in," Siobhán said. "Apart from Liam's."

"I've already sorted something out." Macdara gestured toward the field behind the inn. "Follow me."

When they passed the rooms to head out to the back garden, the gazebo was aglow. Emma and Eileen had been kind enough to place a heat lamp in it, along with a pot of tea and three mugs. The twins had also lined the seating with soft blankets. Maybe they wouldn't be so bad at organizing a second baby shower. Luckily, the wind had died down, and there were no sounds other than the rhythmic chirping of crickets.

"Who should we start with?" Macdara asked.

"Edward and Róisín, then Saoirse and Aisling, and finally Tara, Niall, and Ron," Siobhán said. "I've already spoken with Helen and Grace."

Macdara nodded his agreement while Aretta headed off to knock on doors.

Róisín perched on the end of one of the built-in benches while Edward stood off to the side. Macdara gestured for him to sit down. He did so reluctantly, his knees bouncing. After a moment, Róisín reached over and placed her hand on the knee closest to her.

"Sorry," Edward said. His legs stilled.

"We'll make this first session brief. We need to know if there is anything we should know about the meeting you had with Liam, and what you did during the thirty minutes between the time he dismissed you up until your sister discovered the body."

"There wasn't much to the meeting," Róisín said. "Liam lectured us all a bit."

That caught Siobhán's attention. "Why would he lecture you?"

"In case reporters or anyone else asked us about our relationships," Edward said. "He wanted us to assure everyone we were still happily matched."

"Even if we weren't," Róisín added.

"She's not talking about us," Edward quickly interjected. "At least, I don't think you are."

"Of course not." Her hand went back on his knee. Siobhán could have been reading into things but from the raise of his eyebrow, and the way Edward stared at Róisín's hand, she got the distinct feeling that the intimate touch wasn't something commonplace for them. "Not us," Róisín was saying. "But I have the feeling there are other participants who aren't exactly on cloud nine."

Edward nodded. "Some of them aren't even on cloud five."

"Which couples do you think are struggling?" Macdara asked.

"It's just a feeling," Edward said. "Tara and Niall, for one. All you have to do is look at the expression on their faces when they're around each other. Very pained expressions, I might add."

"Don't forget Saoirse and Aisling," Róisín said. "I saw Saoirse take Aisling's hand before they walked out on stage this evening, but Aisling yanked it away."

"That's right," Edward said. "She did."

"Did anyone seem particularly annoyed by Liam's lecture?" Siobhán asked. Unless they found it somehow related to his murder, she wasn't as interested in the state of everyone's romance. In addition, they had failed to admit to their own disagreement after the session, that is, if Helen's observation had been correct.

"You mean, did someone seem so annoyed that it looked as if they wanted to shoot an arrow through his heart?" Edward said.

"Something like that," Siobhán said.

"We've been around each other all week," Edward said. "It's been mostly tame."

"Mostly?" Macdara pressed.

"There was a bit of a dustup on the first night we arrived," Edward said.

"At Fitzgerald's Pub," Róisín interjected. "Between Niall and Liam."

"What happened?"

Edward rolled his eyes. "We came in during the middle of a session. We figured we were the guests of honor, so we joined the circle. Apparently, that rattled some of the other musicians."

"Is it protocol to wait?"

"Normally, yes," Róisín said. "Jumping in in the middle can disrupt the flow."

"But we were the guests of honor!" Edward repeated.

The guests of honor didn't seem too honorable. "And then what happened?"

"It started a bit of a row, and we were asked to leave the circle," Edward said. "Can you imagine?"

"She just wants the facts," Róisín said. "We took a bit of revenge, music-style."

"What does that mean?"

"Niall spotted someone's double bass lying near the pile of instruments," Edward said. "It's a bit unorthodox to play one in a trad session. He decided to 'borrow' it for our musical coup."

"Musical coup?" Siobhán asked.

"We started our own session on the patio," Róisín said. "It browned off a fiddler, and he stormed out and grabbed Niall's bow and broke it in half."

"But as we've stated, it *wasn't* Niall's double bass, which means it wasn't his bow," Edward said. "It was a random one lying in the back."

"It was a cheeky thing to do, but it's not like he was damaging it," Róisín said. "That is until the little man snapped it in two."

Edward nodded. "And the wee fiddler probably didn't know he was breaking someone else's bow—I don't know that for sure."

"Do you know whose double bass it was?"

"That's the thorny part," Edward said. "It belonged to the session leader, Jim McVeigh."

"And it was a pricey one," Róisín added. "He doesn't bring it to sessions, but he's played it for a few recordings of Irish music."

Siobhán and Macdara exchanged a quick look. Jim was a local musician, and he owned a music shop in nearby Bruree. He was good folk, but Siobhán couldn't imagine he would have been too happy about someone messing with one of his instruments. "Do you know what the outcome was?"

Edward tilted his head. "What do you mean?"

"How did Jim McVeigh take it?"

"Liam stepped in and settled the matter," Róisín said. "But how exactly he settled it? I have no clue."

"At least everyone lived," Edward said. He froze. "At least, no one died over a damaged bow." He stopped talking but seemed to be mulling it over. "It couldn't have been over that—could it?"

"That should do it for now," Macdara said. Edward and Róisín stood up to go.

Siobhán waited until they'd taken a few steps to stop them. "I understand you changed rooms here?"

They stopped and turned. "Is that a problem?" Edward asked.

"Not at all. I'm just wondering if there was any particular reason?"

The pair of them exchanged a glance. "Liam requested it," Róisín said.

Sometimes asking a question that you thought you already knew the answer to paid off. This was such a time. "Did he say why?"

"If I had to guess? He wanted Grace nearby," Róisín said. "She was always at his beck and call."

"That's putting it mildly," Edward said. "He was always barking orders at her."

"She had a sense of humor about it," Róisín said. "She always knew when Liam was calling her, because her ringtone for him was a barking dog." The pair of them laughed.

"Good on her for being a good sport," Edward said. "But if I were her? I would have never let him get away with it."

Chapter 12

Aisling and Saoirse sat on opposite ends of the built-in seating, and neither of them looked too happy as evidenced by their pose: mouths set, arms crossed, slouched.

"Are the two of you in a row?" Siobhán asked. Sometimes you had to address the obvious.

Aisling looked away. "She's browned off with me," Saoirse said. "But if you don't mind, we'd rather not talk about it."

Siobhán gave it a beat, as she pondered whether or not to push the issue. "Does this have anything to do with Liam?"

"No," Saoirse said.

"Yes," Aisling said.

"It's a yes, then," Siobhán said. "Now that Liam has been murdered, I am afraid you will have to talk about it."

"You just had to say something, didn't you?" Saoirse shook her head.

"I'm sick of your lies," Aisling replied. "I can say whatever I like."

"Brilliant. Because now they're going to think that we had a motive to murder him."

From the look on her face, this hadn't occurred to Aisling. Unfortunately, it meant that whatever came out of their gobs next could be lies. Normally they would talk to people one-on-one, but it was so late that they'd opted to start off the conversation with the couples, knowing they could split them up later, if necessary. In this case, it was definitely going to be necessary.

"It's really not a big deal," Saoirse said. Her long blond hair was flowing out of her cap and she began to twirl a strand around her finger.

"Are you joking me?" Aisling was fuming. "And yet minutes ago, you were apologizing as if your life depended on it."

"I know I hurt you, and yes, that's a big deal. And I am sorry. But it certainly doesn't rise to a 'I'm going to murder him' level. That's all I meant."

"You're the one who messed up, so you tell her."

Saoirse sighed. "I had no intention of participating in a matchmaking festival. Apparently, Liam wanted to represent the LGBTQ community—I'd bet anything it was some kind of publicity motivation rather than out of any kind of heartfelt motive—but yes, he paid me to participate. But then, after I truly fell in love with Aisling . . ." She turned and stared at her. Aisling refused to make eye contact. "He blackmailed me, alright? He wanted me to repay the five hundred euro he paid me with another five hundred on top of it."

"She refused to pay," Aisling said. "So Liam sent me Saoirse's page from his Lucky Book." She gestured toward the inn.

This caught Siobhán and Macdara's attention. Siobhán thought of the card from the printer they found in Liam's room. Was that what he had been photocopying? Pages from his Lucky Book? "What do you mean—he sent it to you?"

"I found it tucked into the case of my squeeze-box," Aisling said. "Monday evening, at Fitzgerald's."

It seems quite a bit had gone on in that pub that Monday evening. "Do you still have it?" Macdara asked.

Saoirse let out a snort. "Are you joking me? She's practically taped it to the bathroom mirror just to torture me."

Aisling rolled her eyes. "That's an exaggeration. It's in me room."

"We need to see it," Siobhán said.

Aisling stood. "I'll fetch it."

"I'll accompany you," Macdara said. They left to collect it.

Had Liam been printing pages from his Lucky Book in order to blackmail his clients? And if they refused to pay up, he was exposing them? However, Saoirse's secret had already been exposed. Was there still a strong motive to murder him?

Macdara returned without Aisling, the page clutched in his hand. "That's all for now," he said to Saoirse.

"I really do love her," Saoirse said glumly, as she headed off. Macdara handed Siobhán the page. She glanced at it. Liam had detailed notes on Saoirse, including the fact that he had paid her to participate. He'd added a personal note: *Message Saoirse—either she returns the five hundred euro—(on second thought, double it)—or Aisling will find out her lover was paid to be with her . . .*

"He was diabolical," Siobhán said. Had anyone else received pages?

Macdara nodded. "Let's see if we can catch Ron Gallagher. I just saw him go into his room."

But by the time they knocked on Ron's door, there was no answer. Macdara caught the twins just before they headed to bed and learned the make of his car. It was no longer in the car park, and he wasn't answering his mobile phone. They would have to interview him in the morning. With only Tara and Niall left to speak with this evening, they decided to interview them separately. Mostly because it was obvious Niall loved being the center of everyone's attention, and they figured they would get more out of him in a spotlight environment. Siobhán was once again seated in the gazebo when he arrived with Macdara.

Niall spread out on the circular bench across from Siobhán and Macdara, his confidence on full display. "This must be devastating for your group," Siobhán said, mainly because he didn't look at all bothered.

"A bow and arrow," he said slowly. He stopped there as if that was a satisfactory answer.

"What about a bass? Own one?" Macdara asked.

"Yes," Niall said. "I own one. But I barely play it, and I didn't bring it with me."

"Is it a double bass?" Siobhán chimed in.

" 'Tis." He crossed his arms. "Strange question, unless you were thinking I owned a bass guitar." He paused. "Which I do. I dabble in everything."

"And if we were to ask permission to search your vehicle and your room," Macdara asked, "would you have a problem with that?"

Niall's mouth dropped open. "Yes, I would have a problem with that."

Macdara arched an eyebrow. "And why is that?"

"You'd be calling me a liar." Niall dropped his arms and crossed them. He'd started the interview all spread out and open, and one little request and he'd completely closed up. *Interesting.*

"If we showed you the bow, would you be able to ascertain anything about the bass it pairs with?" Siobhán asked.

"No." He paused. "I'd be able to tell if it was made of Brazilian wood." He shrugged. "But most of them are."

"That's something," Macdara said. "We might take you up on it." Siobhán knew they would be getting a professional who wasn't a suspect to weigh in on the bow they'd found sticking out of Liam's heart, but Siobhán knew Macdara wanted Niall to feel less like a suspect and more like a confidant.

Niall dropped his arms to his side. "I'm not the only one who owns a double bass, you know."

"Oh?"

"Edward Kavanagh has at least one, and I believe Saoirse O'Reilly does too."

"Good to know," Siobhán said. "Did either of them bring them along?"

"I helped load Grace's van," Niall said. "She transported our instruments. I didn't see any double basses other than Ron Gallagher's—"

Most likely the killer would have snuck it in another way. . . .

"Ron Gallagher!" Niall said, snapping his fingers. "I forgot about that one." He shook his head. "Most trad musicians play more than one instrument, but not many would think to bring a double bass to an event like this. What a pain to carry around."

The same could be said for the harp, but neither Grace nor Ron seemed to mind the lugging around bit.

"Why don't we go back to earlier this evening," Macdara said. "Where were you when the lights went out?"

"Róisín and I were in line for a hot cocoa."

The drink booths were in the opposite direction of where Liam was found. If Niall was telling the truth, there was no way he could have made it to the underpass of the castle in time for the killing. Then again, he could be lying. But something else Niall had said was piquing her interest at the moment. "Róisín?" Siobhán asked. "As in Róisín Doyle?"

Niall frowned. "What about her?"

"You just said the two of you were in line for a hot cocoa."

"Did I?" Niall's face flushed red. "Tara," he said. "I meant Tara." He looked around as if he feared Tara might be lurking in the bushes, listening.

A Freudian slip. Why had he said Róisín? Sure, people

made mistakes, but calling your girlfriend by another woman's name was notable. Someone else had mentioned Niall and Róisín . . . *Helen.* She said they would have made a better match. Was there more to it? It was hard to imagine the "little rose" with the "big ego," but objectively speaking—both dark-haired and gorgeous—she could see them together. Siobhán filed it away for later. "Do you know anyone in your group who had any problems with Liam?"

Niall tilted his head. "Even if someone wasn't happy with their match, none of us are being forced to stay with each other—so I can't think of anything that would incite any of us to murder, if that's what you're asking."

"Do you know of anyone unhappy with their match?" Siobhán asked again. He seemed to be avoiding the question.

Niall squirmed. "It's hearsay."

"Opinions are fine," Siobhán said. "You're not in a court of law."

"If I had to guess, I'd say Edward and Róisín aren't well matched." Once again, his face flushed red.

"Have you heard about either one of them being unhappy?"

"I really don't want to talk out of school." He leaned forward, a glint in his eye. "But if I were you, I'd ask Helen if Róisín ever confided in her about her relationship with Edward."

Noted. Róisín again. Niall seemed almost gleeful.

"Did you like Liam Noone?" Macdara asked.

"I thought he was a character," Niall said. "And I was happy with my match, so all's well that ends well." He seemed to register what he'd just said. "For us, anyway."

Macdara jotted down a few notes and then looked at Niall. "Was this past week the first time you've seen Liam since you were matched?"

"Absolutely," Niall said. "What reason would I have to see him?" Macdara's answer was in the form of a stare. "It's the first time we've seen him since we were matched," Niall confirmed.

"And that was a year ago?"

"Yes, sir."

"Is there anything else we should know—either about the events of this evening or the week leading up to it?" Siobhán asked.

Niall looked up as if he were pondering it. "The only thing I can think of is the way he spoke to his staff."

"Grace and Ron," Siobhán supplied.

Niall nodded. "The way he spoke to them was pretty demeaning. But neither of them stood up for themselves, so maybe they didn't mind." He shook his head. "He wouldn't dare speak to me that way." His tone sounded threatening. He must have realized that himself, for he dropped the grimace and smiled. "But he didn't, so I never had a problem with him."

"I see." Siobhán had heard his treatment of them for herself, so there was no need to ask him to elaborate. "You teach people how to treat you."

Niall grinned and pointed at her. "Exactly."

"Anything else?" Siobhán asked. "Say from Fitzgerald's Pub last Monday evening?"

Niall crossed his arms. "I suppose Edward ratted me out."

"Any reason why you didn't think to tell us about it?" Macdara asked.

"It was embarrassing. A nothingburger that escalated quickly. I'm not a thief. I planned on returning that bow. I'm not the one who broke it in half, you know?"

"Do you know the name of the man who did?"

"Oscar something," Niall said. "He's a little person." He shook his head. "And surprisingly strong."

"We were told that Liam 'dealt with' the situation," Siobhán said. "Do you know what that entailed?"

"I only knew that Liam was going to make me pay somehow," Niall said. "I guess now I'll never know what he had in mind."

"And why do you think he was going to make you pay?" Macdara asked.

"Because Liam always made people pay. He wasn't some happy-go-lucky man. Not at all."

"Did he ever . . . *ask* you to pay?" Siobhán didn't want to come out and ask if he had received a Lucky Page or a note from Liam—such as YOU OWE ME!!!—so she kept her question vague.

"It was a figure of speech," Niall said.

"I see." He had an annoying way of not answering questions.

Macdara handed Niall his card. "We will probably circle back to you at some point."

"I'm assuming the event is canceled?"

"We've decided to go ahead with it," Siobhán said.

Niall raised an eyebrow. "You're joking me."

"It's the only way to keep everyone in town while we try to figure this out," Macdara explained.

Niall gulped. "Are we *required* to stay?"

"No," Macdara said. "But it will make me think you have something to hide."

Niall stood. "I have nothing to hide."

"One more thing," Siobhán said. "Have you ever had a look at Liam's Lucky Book?"

Niall sat back down. Crossed his arms. Looked at his feet. "You two seem to know a lot in a short amount of time. Who told you? Was it Edward?" He shook his head before they could answer. "Typical. Pipers never can keep their gobs shut."

Chapter 13

"They know," Niall said to Tara, as he ushered Siobhán and Macdara into their room. Tara was digging through her luggage bin, throwing contents onto the bed with wild abandon.

"Who told them?" she asked. "Róisín?" She shook her head. "Drummers have loose lips."

"Let's pretend nobody told us a thing," Siobhán said. Next to her, she could see her husband trying to contain a smirk. "We want to hear it from you."

Tara stopped digging in her bag. "Give them yours," she said to Niall. "I'm still looking for mine."

Niall walked over to a leather jacket slung over a chair. He reached in the pocket, pulled out a sheet of paper, and tried to hand it to Macdara. It wasn't until Macdara made no move to take it that he handed it to Siobhán. "Hold on," Siobhán said. Just in case, she reached into her pocket, pulled out a pair of gloves and slipped them on. She held the paper up to the light. It was another photocopy of a page with handwritten notes all over it. At the top of the page someone had written: *Niall and Róisín would make a fantastic match*. Siobhán felt her heart rate tic up. *Another page and another reference to that particular pair.* And not that she was condoning blackmail, but why would Liam give away his leverage? Had someone else been distributing these pages? She glanced at Macdara. "It's a page from Liam's Lucky Book."

"Is that so?" Macdara asked.

"I presume so," Niall said. "What else would it be?" Tara shot him a look. "I'm sorry if I sounded disrespectful," he added. "This whole murder business has me on edge."

Siobhán had no interest in correcting Niall's behavior, so she focused on the page in front of her. "Where did you get this?"

"Someone, I suppose Liam himself, slipped it into the pocket of my jacket at the beginning of the week. Tara has her own page."

Macdara lifted the leather jacket. "Did they slip it into the pocket of this jacket?"

"Yes," Niall said. "That's the one."

"Let's take one step at a time," Siobhán said. "When might someone have slipped it into your pocket, and when exactly did you discover it there?"

"I discovered it Monday night after the session," Niall said. "My jacket was thrown into a pile on top of my instrument case."

Siobhán nodded and turned her attention back to the page. Somewhere in the middle Liam had written: *Edward came to see me, he wants to be matched with Róisín. I named my price. . . .*

Underneath that, another note: *Edward's deposit is complete, agreed to pay monthly.*

"Liam took a bribe in order to change his mind about a match?" She held it up so Macdara could read all of the notes.

"That's what it says," Niall said. "It came as quite the

shock." He flicked a glance at Tara whose face was impossible to read. "Not that it pertains to me in any way."

"It does pertain to you," Siobhán said. "Liam noted that he was thinking of matching you with Róisín."

Tara didn't open her mouth, but her face was a portrait in jealousy.

"I'm sure it's just part of his process," Niall said. "Mulling through combinations of matches. But in the end, he made the right choice." Sweat broke out on his brow, and this time he seemed to be looking everywhere but at Tara.

Siobhán studied Tara. "You received a page out of his book as well?" Tara nodded. "What did yours say?"

Tara gulped. "I paid Liam for some extra coaching," she said. "It wasn't a big deal—just his coaching notes." Siobhán could tell there was more to the story, but it seemed she wasn't going to talk in front of Niall.

Macdara, no doubt sensing the same thing, turned to Tara. "Let's take our chat out to the gazebo," he said. Tara nodded, and the two headed out the door.

Siobhán gave it a beat. "Do you have any idea as to who might have slipped the page into your jacket?"

"Liam," he said. "Why would anyone else do it?" He stopped to think about it. "Unless one of his worker bees did it for him. You'll have to ask them."

"Did you notice anyone lingering around the area?"

"I wasn't paying any attention to the jacket and we were nowhere near it," he said. "You should ask the session leader. His group was seated closest to the table, and as the session leader he was facing in that direction."

"Who was the session leader?"

"Jim something," Niall said. "That's all I know."

Jim McVeigh. "And which direction were you facing?"

"I wasn't anywhere near my jacket. We had decided to hold our session on the patio."

Siobhán would have to ask every musician who played the session that evening if they saw anyone lurking around the cases. "Did this page come with any kind of demand?" As Siobhán examined it again, she noticed another note in the margins. *Spoke with Niall—he would be thrilled to be matched with Róisín.* And here Niall had said it didn't pertain to him. Had he also overlooked this note? More likely he did not want Tara to know that she hadn't been his first choice.

"No demands," Niall said. "Just that page." His eyebrows furled. "Why would anyone have demands?"

"Perhaps whoever left this thought it contained secrets you wouldn't want to get out," Siobhán said.

"He didn't have any secrets on me."

He left Siobhán with no choice but to point out the obvious. "There is another note written on this page," she said. "*Spoke with Niall—he would be thrilled to be matched with Róisín.*"

"So what? That was at the beginning of the process. He was interviewing me after our date and asked me what I thought of Róisín. I thought we got along alright. That's all. But then he matched me with Tara. Case closed."

"You weren't at all upset that your first choice went to Edward simply because he paid Liam to make the switch?"

A look of anger flickered over Niall's face for a moment, but just as quickly, it was gone. "I ended up with the right match, so I couldn't care less." The set of his jaw said otherwise. Niall slumped down on the edge of the bed and put his head in his hands. Siobhán was starting to see what a dangerous game Liam had been playing—toying with people's emotions. And emotions were never higher than when it came to love.

"Earlier when you spoke about getting hot cocoa you accidentally mentioned Róisín's name instead of Tara's."

"And that means I'm a killer, does it?" Niall's reaction was one of fury, and it took Siobhán by surprise. She had to make a concentrated effort to stay calm.

"No. But it could suggest that you did prefer Róisín." Niall looked in the direction of the door. "Tara isn't listening," Siobhán said. "And I'm certainly not judging you. The heart wants what the heart wants."

Niall scoffed. "I mean if Edward wants to *pay* for his match and live with that knowledge for the rest of his life—I guess that's his decision." He shook his head. "But Róisín has a right to know, don't you think?"

"I do believe in transparency," Siobhán said, "but let's put that aside for the moment."

Niall shrugged. "What then?"

"It says right here that *you* preferred Róisín as well." She was not going to let him wriggle out of this. "I'm just curious why you refuse to admit it."

"That was a year ago."

Siobhán waited for him to say more, something along the lines of how in love he was with Tara, but he did not. "Do you and Tara plan on getting married?"

"It's only been a year," he said.

In the span of a few moments a year was both a long time ago and not long at all. Niall certainly was good at twisting words to suit him. "If I were in your shoes, I would find this very upsetting. And if you still have feelings for Róisín, I'm certainly not going to mention it to Tara." Niall remained silent. "Have you shown this page to Róisín?"

"No," he said. His head shot up. "Do you think I should?" For the first time he sounded chipper.

"Since I am investigating a murder case, I will have to ask you not to show her the page at this time."

"You really think one of us killed Liam?"

"Someone did. And if he was blackmailing his clients that points to motive."

Niall began to blink. "If I'm angry with anyone, it's Edward."

"Is that so?"

Niall jumped up and walked to the window. He pulled back the curtain and stared into the car park. "This little maneuver exposed Liam as disingenuous, that's for sure. All he cared about was money. Some matchmaker! But Edward knew I liked Róisín, and I promise you she liked me back. When all of this murder business is over, I do plan on having a chat with Róisín. Not for me but for *her*. What do you imagine she'll feel when she hears that Edward *paid* to be matched with her?" Niall stopped. "Wait. Do you think something like that will turn her off or impress her?"

"I think you should forget about Róisín for the moment and tell Tara the truth." It was the age-old struggle, the femme fatale versus the girl next door.

Niall glared. "And what 'truth' is that?"

"That you're in love with Róisín."

"I already know," Tara said, startling Siobhán as she appeared in the doorway. "Because of this." She was holding several photocopied sheets in her hand. "I found them."

"Found them? I thought you were going out to the gazebo with Detective Sergeant Flannery?"

"We made a detour to a rubbish bin," Macdara said, popping up from behind.

"You *found* them," Siobhán said. "In the rubbish bin?"

Tara sighed. "I forgot I tossed them in there, alright? I was so angry I nearly set them on fire."

"When did you toss them in there?" Siobhán was truly perplexed.

"Monday evening. That's when I received the pages. Same as Niall." She huffed. "I guess it's a good thing the owners haven't emptied the bins yet."

"That's done once a week," Siobhán said, feeling surprisingly defensive for Emma and Eileen.

"You did not find your pages slipped into a jacket pocket," Macdara said. "Correct?"

"Correct," Tara said. "Someone slipped them into my flute case."

Just like someone slipped them into the case of Aisling's squeeze-box. Did Tara really forget she had thrown it away, or had she been debating whether or not to tell them about the page? "Let's take this outside." Siobhán turned to Niall. "Please don't speak to anyone about what we've discussed here this evening."

"I won't say a word."

Once outside they examined Tara's sheet. Liam had handwritten notes all over this page as well: *Indicated her preference was Niall McCarthy. Niall is adamant he wants Róisín. See who is willing to pay the most.*

"Apparently Niall was too cheap to pay up," Tara said. Her freckled face hardened. "I knew a man like that couldn't be in love with me."

"Are you in love with him?"

Tara crossed her arms and looked away. "Not anymore, I'm not. I mean he's good-looking and all, and he's an excellent musician, but he's full of himself. At first, his confidence was sexy. But now that I know he didn't want me in the first place? I think he's pathetic."

"Both you and Niall discovered these pages Monday evening. When did you discuss them with each other?"

Tara shifted uncomfortably. "We waited until last night. I guess that's something we had in common. Neither of us knew what to make of it or how to bring it up."

"What changed last night?"

Tara looked stricken. "What do you mean?"

"Who was the first to bring it up, and what do you think prompted it?"

"I was the first." Tara looked away. "I saw him flirting with Róisín, alright? I suppose my jealousy got the best of me. Later that night I confronted Niall about it. He denied it, and that's when I showed him the page."

"When did you see him flirting with Róisín?"

"All week, if I'm being honest. He can't keep his eyes off of her."

"And when you told him you'd received a page from Liam's book, did he come clean about his straightaway?"

"Yes. We realized that it wasn't our fault—someone was trying to stir the pot. Get us all worked up."

"I see."

"But I was suspicious of Niall before we admitted to the pages."

"Suspicious?" Siobhán asked. "Why is that?"

"This whole week he's been acting strange. I had no doubt it was because of seeing Róisín again."

"Acting strange, how?"

"Glaring at both Edward and Liam. Staring daggers at them, like. Can you believe he was more furious at Edward for paying off Liam than he was sorry about keeping this secret from me? No woman wants to play second fiddle." Her fists curled at her side. "No pun intended."

"It must have been very hurtful." Jealousy was often a motive for murder.

"Liam's been parading us around as success stories when it's all rigged. Imagine if that got out? Anyone one of us could have ruined him."

And one of you did.

It was getting late, and even though Siobhán wanted to question Tara further, she'd be of no use to this investigation without a good night's sleep. Macdara exited Niall's room and glanced at his watch—he was thinking along the same lines.

"It's been a long day, and we're going to pick this up in the morning," Siobhán said. "I'm going to say the same thing to you that I said to Niall. Do not discuss this with anyone—not even Niall."

"There's nothing to discuss anyway," Tara said. "You can't make someone love you, can you?"

"Tensions are high right now," Siobhán said. "And we don't want to add to them. So, if you think you and Niall stand a good chance of arguing this evening, I would suggest you find another place to stay."

"I don't know of any other places."

"The Charlesville Hotel. It's the next town over, but I can drive you. Róisín's sister is staying there."

"Róisín," Tara said in a tone that suggested there was a bad taste in her mouth.

"I called ahead and they have rooms. I can drive you, but you have to let me know right now."

"Yes," Tara said. "I don't even want to look at Niall right now." She hurried into the room to pack a bag.

Niall leaned against the wall outside the door. "I would have taken the room," he said.

"Why? Because you can look at Róisín's twin and pretend it's her?" Niall frowned but didn't respond. "Whatever," Tara said. "We don't have to pretend anymore, and I want to go."

"You can't possibly think we're the only ones to receive pages," Niall said. "I won't say a word to the others, but I'm guessing they already know."

"Be that as it may," Macdara said, "we do not want all of you comparing notes."

"I still can't believe that you think one of us killed Liam," Niall said. "In the history of trad music, I think you'll find the only thing we kill is our sessions."

Tara came out rolling her luggage bin. "Ready."

"I can leave instead," Niall said.

"Stop pretending to be a gentleman." Tara scoffed. "Besides, I've already packed." She headed straight for the squad car without a glance back. Niall stormed into the room and slammed the door. Tara was right about one thing. If the information in those pages had gotten out, it would have ruined Liam Noone's reputation. She could imagine the headlines about the King of Matchmakers being a fraud. *Mismatched* . . . There would have been legal ramifications for his blackmail endeavor as well. Yet another reason Siobhán couldn't help but think that someone other than Liam had been distributing those pages, purposefully destroying all of Liam's leverage. That would have riled him up on several fronts: One, he would have been livid that someone had been accessing his Lucky Book. And two, this person was interfering in a big way with his blackmail scheme.

Did Liam figure out who was distributing his pages and that's who he met with this evening? Is that why he wasn't as paranoid about keeping ahold of his Lucky Book—because he knew someone had already infiltrated it? It was one thing to peek at his book—but someone had actually copied pages from it. For all Siobhán knew they'd copied the entire book. They would have to stop by that print shop. Whoever this killer was, they were methodical. Someone had come to Kilbane knowing that this festival was going to be anything but a music and love fest. The only question was who.

Chapter 14

Tara was silent on the drive to Charlesville, which suited Siobhán just fine. It had been a long day, and she was ready for bed herself. When they arrived at their destination, Siobhán parked in front of the hotel, walked Tara inside, and charged the room to the garda station.

"I knew there was something off." Siobhán stopped. She'd been heading for the exit when Tara spoke. Siobhán turned around and waited. "I told people that Niall didn't love me, and they said I was imagining it." Siobhán could hear the pain in her voice. Once again, Siobhán was reminded how Liam's actions had been truly despicable. People were the most tender and vulnerable when it came to love, and he had deliberately exploited that. "I've actually known for a long time," Tara said. "I just didn't have the proof."

"Life is complicated," Siobhán said. "It is possible to have feelings for two people at the same time. And unrequited crushes aren't based on reality. Róisín is a fantasy for Niall. You have a real relationship with him. But if he had feelings for someone else, he should have been honest with you. You have a lot to think about, but try to get some sleep. You won't solve anything tonight."

"Who do you think sent us those pages? Was it Liam? Before he died?"

"I don't know. We're only at the beginning of our inquiries. I'll see you sometime tomorrow."

Siobhán strode for the exit, already dreaming of her bed. But the minute she was outside, she smelled cigarette smoke wafting through the cold night air, and there on the footpath was Helen Doyle, puffing away and speaking to someone on her mobile phone.

"You cannot say anything to anyone," Helen was saying. "Not a soul. Do you understand?"

Was she talking to her twin? Helen didn't even glance at Siobhán as she walked by. Siobhán's options were few. She had no reserves left to interview even one more person this evening, and even if she called Macdara or Aretta to do it, it was likely that Helen wasn't going to tell them the truth. If she was Liam's secret lover, admitting it would make her the prime suspect. She would have no motivation to tell them the truth. Not unless they had evidence to back up their suspicions. Speaking with Helen could wait until an official interview.

But there was something she could do before going home. Siobhán went straight for her car and rooted around the cubby bin until she found an evidence bag and gloves. She watched until Helen flicked her cigarette to the curb and disappeared into the hotel. A litter offense to be sure, but Siobhán was more interested in the lipstick forming a ring around the cigarette stub. She slipped on her gloves, exited her vehicle and dropped the stub into the evidence bag. Satisfied, she began the drive home. Dorothy Gale got it right. Siobhán didn't need a Good Witch of the North to tell her there was no place like home.

The next morning, after a fitful night's sleep, Siobhán awoke with a start. It wasn't the alarm that shook her awake, but rather the absence of one. The sun streaming through the window was her first clue that she'd slept in. She fumbled on the nightstand for her mobile phone. It was nearly nine in the morning. The other side of the bed was empty. She called Macdara.

"How ya, pet?" he said. "Sleep well?"

"Too well," she said. "Are you at the station?"

"You caught me," he said. "I'm at the bookshop café and then I'll be at the station."

The bookshop café. That mean that at this very moment her husband was standing in front of a case full of pastries. He did love his sweets. It was usually her first stop as well. She once heard a financial guru explain how much money one could save by not buying coffee or pastries, and it made sense, but the guru didn't understand that the benefit wasn't just a cup of coffee. First of all, the café made an excellent cappuccino, but secondly, that little cup of heaven was a sweet buffer against the possibility of a very stressful day ahead. A little cup of comfort, sharing a connection with the sweet employees, and once in a while, or—who was she kidding?—*always*, getting a delicious baked good or three to go along with it. It was the simple pleasures in life that made getting out of bed just a little bit easier. Then again, she was now reducing her caffeine and her sweets intake during her pregnancy, so she should probably enjoy a bit of oversleeping. "Why didn't you wake me?"

"No need. Musicians are not early birds, and there's no sense questioning them when they're hungover and sleep deprived."

She felt her shoulders relax. "Why didn't my alarm go off?"

"It did," he said, his deep laugh warming her through the phone. "You sawed logs right through it."

"Macdara Flannery, are you accusing me of snoring?"

He laughed. "I'm sure it was the twins," he said.

Poor babies. She'd lost count of the number of things

they were already blaming them for. She rubbed her belly in apology. "I'll be in as soon as I can shower and dress."

"Don't forget to eat something."

"You mean besides the lemon bar you are going to buy me from the café where you just happen to be at this very moment?"

He hesitated. "I believe Mam is waiting to make you breakfast."

Siobhán made a concerted effort not to groan. "Brilliant," she said. *Oatmeal, fruit, egg whites* . . . or whatever other torture Nancy Flannery could think up. If she had it to do all over, she wouldn't tell Nancy about the pregnancy—they would just show up at her door one day with the twins. *Surprise!* "What she doesn't know won't hurt her," Siobhán said. She really wanted that lemon bar.

Macdara laughed, knowing full well that Siobhán was ready to have their space back. Nancy had yet to mention when she was planning on returning to her home. These babies weren't coming for another five months—she wasn't planning on staying until then, was she? "Fitzgerald's opens at eleven," Siobhán said, "and the print shop at one. Why don't I go straight to the pub after brekkie and see if I can get the scoop on that bow incident that occurred Monday evening?" If sessions were underway, she could probably find Jim McVeigh and ask about the fiddler who broke the bow. Was it the same bow that was used to craft the murder weapon? When one was at the beginning of an investigation, one had to keep all possibilities open and on the table.

"Perfect," Macdara said. "I'm lining up our official interviews and securing enough guards for the start of this festival."

"Right." Siobhán had nearly forgotten that they were continuing with the festival. "I also snagged a cigarette stub of Helen Doyle's last night."

"Because?"

"Lipstick stains."

"Good thinking."

"Is Dr. Brady arriving today?"

"She said she'd be here by two, but the coroner will be here any minute to pick up the body."

Often, if the state pathologist couldn't arrive straightaway to designate the area a crime scene and examine the body before removal, they would permit a local coroner to do it. Siobhán was grateful the coroner was on the way. It would be nearly impossible to hold a matchmaking and music festival with the matchmaker himself lying dead in the town square. "Are we meeting Jeanie at the hospital morgue?"

"She said she's willing to examine the body at the morgue herself and meet with us in Kilbane for her preliminary findings. I'll let you know when she reaches out to me."

"Perfect, I'll present the cigarette stub to her then."

"Brilliant. It's the perfect gift for a state pathologist."

It was exciting to see dancing in the streets early in the morning with trad musicians set up underneath makeshift tents along Sarsfield Street, filling the air with lively tunes. Although everyone was free to join the festivities, the actual singles looking for love had their red hearts pinned to their shirts. Siobhán stood in front of Fitzgerald's taking it all in. Ciarán was amongst the dancers, but she was trying not to stare at him, or his current dance partner. The young woman was taller than Ciarán, making it impossible to see his face anyway. Siobhán basked in the moment before entering Fitzgerald's. The familiar scent of bleach and ale greeted her, made even stronger now that her sensitivty to smells had increased. There were more patrons in the pub at this hour than usual due to the festival. Siobhán squeezed up to the bar and waited several minutes until the publican arrived.

"Mineral?" he asked. "Sparkling water?" In a town of this

size everyone knew your business. Or maybe he was simply suggesting nonalcoholic beverages because she was on duty.

"I'm actually here to speak with you in an official capacity," Siobhán said. "Were you the publican on duty last Monday evening?"

"*On duty*. Sounds so formal, like." He nodded, threw a dishtowel over his shoulder, and called to another bartender that he was taking ten minutes. "I can speak with you out on the patio," he said. "Can I bring you something? An orange juice?"

A lemon bar and a cappuccino. Hopefully, Macdara had one waiting for her, but she wasn't counting on it. When a mother-in-law was pitted against a daughter-in-law it was often a losing battle for the latter. "An orange juice would be grand, thanks a million." Siobhán headed for the patio, aware that the patrons were openly staring at her. Whether it was because they knew she was a detective or they were trying to figure out whether or not she was pregnant was an open question. Possibly it was a mix of the two. This morning Nancy had done her best to convince Siobhán that she should take time off work immediately. Could Siobhán say with one hundred percent certainty that all this talk of murder wasn't working its way into her womb? Siobhán tried to talk Nancy into coming out to the festival to let loose and enjoy a good trad session, but she'd refused. Church was the only activity she condoned. To each his own.

Siobhán was passing the middle of the bar when she spotted a petite woman with short, wavy black hair. She probably wouldn't have looked twice at the woman, but as Siobhán passed, she downed a shot, plunked the glass on the bar and immediately called for another one. That was when she realized it was Aisling Byrne. Had her troubles with Saoirse escalated? Was that why she was pounding shots before noon? But the publican was already headed for the patio, orange juice in hand, so Siobhán would have to catch her on the way out. She continued on her way.

"How are you, Barry?" she asked as she lowered herself onto the bench of the picnic table. The patio was enclosed but not heated, and with a chill in the air, Siobhán found herself wishing she had ordered a cup of tea instead.

"I'm grand," he said. "And yourself?"

"You know yourself." They exchanged a smile as she pulled out her notebook. "I do have a few specific questions, but I'd like to start with something more open-ended." If she asked straightaway about someone missing a bow to their double bass, she might miss something she didn't even realize was important. It was better to get an unprompted firsthand account.

"I'm all ears."

"Why don't you take me through last Monday evening—I believe that was the first session after the matchmaker arrived?"

"That's right," he said. "The craic was mighty." Siobhán sipped her orange juice and waited. "It was a big crowd, I'll tell you that. Musicians came in from all over—I'd like to see more of that in the future."

"There's nothing like a good session," Siobhán said as she brought out a notebook and biro.

Barry launched right in. "The first thing I did as the musicians started filing in was designate a space for their belongings. Instrument cases, jackets, those sorts of things. We needed the floor space so I cleared out a section at the back of the bar. Then I helped arrange the chairs, but after a while they had to set up a sign-up sheet and rotate musicians—there just wasn't enough room for them all. They played, people drank—it was tight in here but not over capacity, mind you."

"I'm not looking into any minor infractions." Siobhán

set her biro down on her notepad. "Do you remember interacting with Liam Noone?"

Barry crossed himself. "May he rest in peace." He rubbed his chin. "He came in late. I only remember that because the musicians were playing a softer tune and he came in like he was the star of the show—barking orders at a man and a woman trailing in after him and announcing himself."

"Announcing himself?"

Barry nodded. "He said, 'Hello, Lonely Hearts. Never fear, the Matchmaking King is here."

"That is quite the entrance."

Barry grimaced. "That's just the beginning," he said. "Wait until you hear the rest of it."

Fitzgerald's Pub, Last Monday evening
Account by Barry Guy, Publican

As you know, I've been a publican here for a long time, but it had been ages since I felt that amount of energy in Fitzgerald's. It was electric. People jammed into the pub without a care in the world, and you could see the joy on the faces of musicians, who up until now had been playing for small, unappreciative crowds. That night, the audience was there for it.

By the time Liam Noone, his two employees—the man with the slicked-back hair in the oversized suit and the blondie harp player—along with the three musical couples walked in, there was already a session in full swing. I should have known it would be a stellar night when Jim McVeigh walked in. He was one of the best session leaders around. If you don't know, a session leader has to be a bit of a mediator: they have to make sure they include everyone's song ideas, weed out aspiring musicians who don't yet have the skills to keep up, or negotiate with folks if too many rhythm players try to sit in—as you may know, sessions tend to lean heavily toward melody instruments.

The first problem with the lovebird musicians was that each of them brought multiple instruments and piled them on a table in the back. Even while playing "Morrison's Jig," I could see the look of dismay on Jim's face when he took in the jumble of instruments haphazardly thrown down on the table. The session already had a bodhrán drummer and guitar player, and any more would ruin the balance. That didn't mean the newcomers couldn't play, but they would have to wait their turn and Jim would have to figure out the rotation. Then again, everyone knew this week and approaching weekend was about this matchmaking event, so I had no doubt that Jim would welcome the newcomers into the circle at the right moment.

That was the first mistake these newbies made—they didn't wait for Jim to do his thing. They grabbed chairs from me storeroom and inserted themselves into the circle. Two bodhrán players, two guitars, a banjo, three squeeze-boxes, a handful of whistles and flutes, a concertina—don't even get me started on the number of fiddles. No bones, spoons, or eggs, so I was a bit disappointed about that, but I digress.

The whistles and flutes can get drowned out by too many fiddles, and Jim was a great session leader because he was always paying attention to the delicate musical ecosystem. I suppose it was Jim McVeigh's worst nightmare. But the one who looked ready for a fight was the Wee Stringman.

"The Wee Stringman?" It was about time Siobhán learned who this man was.

"He's a little person," Barry said. "And he plays a mean fiddle. Have you not met him?"

"I've heard of him from a few of the others, but no, we haven't met."

"You really need to come to more sessions."

"I won't argue with that. Where's the Wee Stringman from?"

"He's a Galway man. But he moved to County Cork some years ago for a business opportunity. He also doesn't let anyone play him for a fool—and if you must know, he's a bit of a hot kettle."

"What's his actual name?"

Barry scratched his chin. "Oscar O'Brien. But as long as I've known him, everyone's called him the Wee Stringman, including himself."

"Got it. Please, go on, I'll save any further questions until the end."

> Jim looked a bit stressed when the Wee Stringman walked in, because tensions were already high with the newbies, and if anyone was going to start the fight with them, it was him. Now, Jim gave a quick shake of his head when he saw the look on the Wee Stringman's face. Well, don't you know, these six newbies shoved their way into the circle and just started playing like they were the cocks of the walk. Luckily, they had the skills, so I really thought everything was going to calm down. How could it not? The guiding principle of all sessions, as you know, is *ceol agus craic*. Music and a good time. Traditional Irish music is an oral tradition, you know yourself. It's a thriving tradition, passed through minds, hearts, and hands. What could be more uplifting than that? There's a power in that, you know?

It would go against the grain of everything in Jim if the session devolved into fisty-cuffs. Jim did the only thing he could, he let everyone finish the tune and then he called for a break. He asked the newbies to stay for a moment so he could school them a bit in the etiquette of the evening. Sure, the weekend was going to be all about them, but not that night. And he wouldn't be a great session leader if he just let folks barge into the circle when it was already full.

He was polite but firm. He told them they were welcome to join eventually, but there was an order, a hierarchy if you will, and if they could just wait until they finished another few rounds, he would rotate them in.

Barry stopped for a moment and shook his head. "Jim couldn't have been more polite. But do you know what these six musicians did?"

It was only when the silence stretched on as Barry stared at her that Siobhán realized he was waiting for her to respond. "No," she said. "What did they do?"

"Would you believe they moved their chairs to the patio and they started their *own* session? Like dueling pianos, only it's dueling sessions. Which would be fine if they were like, taking turns, you know? But no. They were just playing on their own. You could hear 'Galway Girl' belting out from the back." Barry's eyes widened as he remembered the evening. "That did not sit well with Oscar. And that was before he realized Jim McVeigh's double bass had been stolen. Now, I wasn't back there to see it, mind you, but rumor has it Oscar snuck out back, stood in front of the double bass, and yanked the bow right out of the thief's hands before breaking it on his knee. He might be little, but he's as strong as an ox, he is."

This was the same tale she'd heard from the others, but it was always good to get confirmation.

"Ciarán mentioned he heard someone asking where his bow had gone that Monday evening—I'm assuming it was Jim?"

"I haven't a clue." He shrugged. "Could have been a fiddler."

Siobhán was starting to regret that she'd missed all of this and couldn't believe Ciarán hadn't filled her in on the rest of the drama. "How did Niall react to Oscar breaking the bow?"

"The other five had to hold him back, that's how. Can you imagine hitting the Wee Stringman? But to their credit they did manage to hold him back. And that's when the matchmaker walked in. Boy, oh, boy. When he saw all the trouble his lovebirds were causing?" Barry gave a low whistle. "Let's just say it wasn't all flowers and butterflies."

"Wait," Siobhán said. "I thought Liam Noone was already in the pub."

"In a sense," Barry said. He rubbed his chin. "He was walking in and out of the pub, constantly going out to the footpath. Not sure if he was having a smoke or making phone calls. It was rather loud inside."

"Then what happened?"

"He promptly rounded up his musicians and left. From the look on his face, he wasn't too happy with them."

"Do you know what happened to the broken bow?"

"I haven't a clue." Barry shrugged. "I suppose Jim took it back to his shop."

Visiting Jim's shop was already on Siobhán's ever-growing to-do list. "And the Wee Stringman? Where might I find him?"

"Ask Jim. If anyone knows where to find him, it's him."

Chapter 15

Siobhán and Macdara stood outside the garda station, waiting for the matchmaking activities to begin. The singles were ready to mingle. At the moment they were free from the wind and rain, but according to the forecast it would be back late this afternoon. Ron and Grace had been advised to move all of their events indoors, and they were currently visiting the shops that would host the activities to make sure everything was ready. Grace had agreed to provide them a schedule and locations when they had it all sorted out. Siobhán planned on attending as many of the events as she could—it would be a good way to get to know their suspects. Macdara handed Siobhán a cup of tea from the bakery. She eyed it warily. "Out of lemon bars, were they?"

Macdara laughed. "I thought you'd be full from Mam's breakfast."

"Oatmeal, egg whites, and fruit," Siobhán said. "It's like she's never met me at all."

"If you're still dying for a lemon bar this afternoon, we'll have a wander back to the café," Macdara said.

"Now you're talking."

"What's the story?"

"I spoke with Barry Guy this morning at Fitzgerald's. First of all, Aisling Byrne was already in there doing shots."

Macdara raised an eyebrow. "Did you ask her why?"

Siobhán shook her head. "By the time I finished speaking with Barry, she was gone."

"I'll keep an eye out for her."

"Barry confirmed what we already know, but let's go through it again." Repetion was always helpful in an investigation. "Jim McVeigh was the session leader last week. One of his fiddle players—Oscar O'Brien—got into it with our previously matched musicians. Specifically, Niall O'Malley. As we know they barged into a session already in progress, which wasn't well-accepted, especially by Oscar. Jim McVeigh stopped the session and schooled the newcomers that they would have to wait their turn. But instead of doing that, they started their own session on the back patio."

Macdara nodded. "Bold move."

"Very. Next, Oscar marched up to Niall, grabbed the bow, and snapped it over his knee. Apparently, he's strong for a little person."

"So it seems. He's called The Wee Stringman, is he?"

"Barry says he calls himself that, but before I know it for sure I'll stick to Oscar."

"Wise plan."

"This is all to say that it was Jim McVeigh's bow because Niall nicked Jim's bass from the table." She paused. "Or, as he put it—'borrowed.' "

"When you borrow something without asking it's called stealing."

"Exactly." The sky began to mist, covering them with light rain. "I doubt Jim McVeigh was too happy about this. I'm surprised he didn't report it to us."

"You're not thinking Jim McVeigh is our killer?"

Siobhán shook her head. "Unless we find some kind of connection between himself and Liam, I simply want to find out why he kept the information about the damaged bow to himself—and what he did with it."

"Sounds like a plan. Aretta and I are going to start arranging the interviews with our main suspects."

Siobhán sighed as she looked around. The dancing seemed to be over, as participants were hanging out in clumps listening to the trad music. Heads craned to the skies, everyone was waiting to see if this misting would stop or morph into a heavy rain. Food carts were showing their optimism by setting up despite the weather. The smell of coffee and pastries wafted by. "In an alternate universe this would have been such a fun weekend."

Macdara nodded. "Text me when you're back from the music shop, and maybe we can have a dance in the streets." He winked.

"That sounds lovely," Siobhán said. "Especially, if it's with a lemon bar."

Jim McVeigh's music shop, The Mad Session, was located in Bruree's small downtown, on a forgotten corner street. A bell dinged as Siobhán walked in, and before she could softly close the door, a gust of wind slammed it shut. It smelled like a combination of wood and oil, which Siobhán found surprisingly pleasant. The rain was heavier now, drumming on the roof of the cozy shop. A plethora of guitars and fiddles hung on the wall behind a counter littered with musical paraphernalia: sheet music, a single drumstick, guitar picks, and a metronome. Larger instruments—a double bass, a drum set, and a squeeze-box took up considerable floor space, and a glass case beneath the counter housed harmonicas, flutes, and pipes.

Jim McVeigh was planted on a stool behind the counter. A middle-aged man with curly whitish-gray hair down to his shoulders, he had a guitar in his hands and a tuner in his mouth. He sounded a note on the tuner, then fiddled with the guitar until they matched. He nodded to her as he continued to pluck the notes. Finally, he seemed to reach a stopping point, for he set the tuner on the counter and gently laid the guitar into the case by his feet. "How ya?" he asked. "Are you here to finally come over to the musical side?"

Siobhán laughed. "I truly wish that's why I was here."

"Let me guess. You're here about the ruckus in Fitzgerald's last Monday eve."

"You guessed it."

"Someone's been chin-wagging about me, I see." He sighed. "What would you like to know?"

"I'd just like to see how your perspective of the events squares up with the others."

"Let me first say that I'm appalled by the murder of that matchmaker," he said, shaking his head. "Terrible business altogether."

"Murder always is."

"In retrospect, the entire incident seems petty. But I don't see how I could have reacted any other way. It never occurred to me that our invited guests—all fine musicians from what I've heard—wouldn't be familiar with the protocol of a session. You can't just nose your way in when we're already vibing. Trad music is a delicate ecosystem of instruments, heavy on the melody, and if there are too many guitars, more than one percussion, or one-offs like autoharps, the system could collapse, you know? If they had simply waited for our set to finish, they would have been rotated in."

"That sounds reasonable. It's a lovely way of working."

He nodded. "Music is a language, and language is a back and forth, is it not?"

"I would say it is."

He flashed a smile over the top of a pair of eyeglasses that slid down his nose. "I can go on about this all day long, but I know you're not here to learn the protocols of a good session."

"I wish I were, to be honest."

Jim held up a finger, then rose and fetched a chair from the corner of the room. He placed it in front of the counter and gestured for her to take a seat. She did so.

"Cup of tea?" he asked.

"I'm grand," Siobhán said. "But thank you." She was already running to the jax more times than she could count.

"How's Ciarán's love quest coming along?" He grinned.

"I wish I knew. He doesn't appreciate me nosing in."

Jim laughed. "He's a mighty fine fiddle player. He'll go far—if that's what he wants."

"I'll tell him you said so. It's a mighty compliment coming from you."

Jim gave a nod and a smile. "So, what else can I tell you?"

"I'd like to know more about the incident between Oscar and Niall that evening." Jim had mentioned the trouble with the session protocol but not a word about Niall's thievery and his broken bow. Her interest was piqued.

For a moment, Jim looked confused. "Right," he said, "the Wee Stringman—sorry. I'm not used to anyone calling him Oscar."

"He prefers the Wee Stringman?"

Jim nodded. "He insists on it. And it's been a brilliant marketing strategy. Nobody forgets the Wee Stringman. When he's not running his other business, he travels all over Ireland joining sessions."

Barry had said something about Oscar having a business. She'd ask about it later. She wanted Jim to focus on the bow-breaking incident. "Was it unusual for Oscar to react that way?"

Jim stroked his beard. "He does have a bit of a temper, but he rarely loses it like that."

"Why do you think he did?"

"He has high standards. And there is no doubt about it—first interrupting a session and then starting their own on the patio?" Jim shook his head. "It was shockingly bad behavior." He sighed. "I'm a bit perplexed, though. He should have copped on that it was my bass and bow."

"Why is that?"

"Because he's the one who asked me to bring it."

This got Siobhán's attention. "Wait. Who asked you to bring it?"

"The Wee Stringman."

Siobhán had no idea what to make of this. "I'm going to need some context."

"It was a recent acquisition. The bow was a Francis Xavier Tourte. Late eighteenth-, early nineteenth-century. French, if the name didn't give it away."

"And they're rare?"

"Made from fine Pernambuco, crafted by a master, and complete with provenance? One of the finest bows you could acquire. I was thrilled to get it."

"Pernambuco?"

Jim nodded. "It's a gorgeous Brazilian wood. Excellent for articulation, a stunning reddish-brown hue." He gave it the chef's kiss.

"Normally, I wouldn't pry, but I need to know its approximate value."

"Ten thousand euro."

"For the bow alone?"

"Absolutely."

For a moment Siobhán was stunned. She never knew a bow could be worth so much. "And how did it come about? Why did Oscar ask you to bring it?"

Jim stroked his beard. "I was doing a bit of bragging about it alright."

"When was this?"

"Early Monday afternoon. We were all in Fitzgerald's setting up for that evening's session. Normally, we just roll in at the last minute, but we told Barry we'd help fancy the place up a bit with the decorations. He had hearts and whatnot he wanted to put up."

"And who all was around?"

"It was most of us musicians, including the matchmaker and crew."

"But I thought they came in at the last minute?"

"That evening they did. But earlier, we all helped set up and then had a few hours before the start of the session so folks had a few hours' break in between." He sighed. "We told them to be on time that evening. It's another reason they should have been patient. Wasn't our fault they were late."

"So, when you were bragging about this bow—did anyone else hear you?"

Jim shrugged. "I was within range of everyone, so I suppose it's possible." He grinned. "My vocal cords aren't shy, if you know what I mean."

"I'm just curious why you never reported the damaged bow, especially given its value."

Jim sighed. "I suppose I didn't think it mattered anymore."

"Why wouldn't it matter? A rare, expensive bow like that?"

"Liam Noone approached after the bow was snapped in two and apologized for Niall's thievery. He offered to pay me for it on the spot."

"Offered to pay you for it?" Siobhán was paying attention now. Liam seemed more the type to collect money rather than hand it out.

McVeigh nodded. "First he tried giving me five hundred

euro." McVeigh chuckled. "You should have seen his face when I told him the price. But he made good on it."

Siobhán was pretty sure her face sported the same look when he told her the price. "How did he make good on it?"

"He gave me *that*." Jim extended a finger to a far corner of the shop. Siobhán turned to see a large harp. It had beautiful rich brown wood mixed with natural wood—an elegant harp, if Siobhán ever saw one.

"A harp?" Siobhán asked. "He gave you a harp?"

"Not just any harp. That's a Lyon and Healy Chicago Petite 40."

"I see." She paused. "And it's worth?"

"Thirteen thousand, five hundred euro."

"And did Liam ask you for three thousand, five hundred back?"

"It sounds like you have his number." Jim winked. "But I decided to play his game instead."

"Meaning?"

"Instead of cash, I gave the petite blondie woman an autoharp."

"Grace Collins," Siobhán said. "Did the Lyon and Healy harp belong to her?"

"I know she plays it, and planned on playing it this week, but whether or not she owned it, I couldn't say."

"Did Liam bring it to the shop himself?"

"You bet he did."

"And I take it Grace was with him?"

"Aye. As I said, I gave her a chord zither."

"A chord zither?" Siobhán was starting to get a headache. Music, in its various parts, was a language all to its own.

"A chord zither is in the harp family. An autoharp." He nodded to the large harp. "And even though the zither I gave her is about six feet tall, it's a lot easier to wheel around than that yoke would have been." Once more he gestured to the larger harp.

Something tickled at the back of Siobhán's mind. "You said it's an autoharp?"

"That's right."

"Does that mean it plays on its own?"

Jim stared at her for a moment. "You mean like a player piano?"

"Yes. Just like that."

"What true musician would want the instrument to play itself? Sacrilege." He shook his head. "No, don't let the name fool you. The autoharp still requires the musician to operate it. It simply allows one to automatically play chords with one hand by depressing buttons with the other that either mute or stimulate certain chords. In other words, it allows the harpist to quickly switch between chords—and maybe save a blister or two on their fingers."

There was so much she didn't know about this world, but it was fascinating. "Why do you think Liam went to all that trouble to pay for Niall's negligence?"

"I dunno." McVeigh shrugged. "Perhaps he didn't want me chin-wagging about the vandalism. It wouldn't have been good publicity. And there's no doubt he wanted good publicity for this event."

It was true that Liam had seemed hypervigilant about his reputation. But it hardly seemed likely that he would have let Niall off the hook. Was there some kind of deal cut between the men? If so, depending on what this agreement was, it could be a motive for murder. And even more troubling, Niall hadn't uttered a single word about the incident. It seemed that to many of these players, notes came easier than words. "Did you have any other interactions with Liam?"

"That was the one and only."

"Did you ever speak with Niall himself about it?"

"Only because Liam insisted on it. Niall shuffled up to me, head down, eyes anywhere but on me, and mumbled an apology." Jim pulled a face. "I feel sorry for the young woman he's matched with. If I were her, I would have had a bone to pick with the Matchmaking King."

Siobhán took her time jotting down notes. "If I wanted to meet the Wee Stringman, how would I go about it?"

"Just stop into any session at Fitzgerald's this weekend. He'll be there."

That was good to hear, it would save her some running around. "What were your impressions of Liam Noone?"

"I appreciated his intervention . . . but if you ask me, he was a bit of a Wild Rover."

"And by that you mean . . . ?"

"That his main interest in being in the pub that evening was to scope out the fairer sex." Jim shrugged. "Perhaps he's always on the lookout for singles to match. But I doubt it. It was only the women he was eyeing."

"Any woman in particular?"

"Now that I couldn't tell ya. The rest of my mind was on the music."

"I have to ask. What did you do with the broken bow?"

"They basically paid me for it, so I couldn't very well keep it. Liam Noone kept it."

Siobhán had not been expecting this. For a moment she was at a loss for words. "You gave the bow to Liam?"

"You seem shocked," he said. "As I mentioned, he paid for it."

She was shocked, but not for the reasons he was thinking. Liam might have been in possession of the bow that killed him. It was an eerie thought. "Would there still be value in the bow?"

"Absolutely. Once he had it repaired, he would get a good deal of his money back."

"Would you recognize the bow from a photo?"

"If it's a decent photo, I would." He either hadn't heard about the murder weapon or he had an excellent poker face.

"This stays between us," Siobhán said, taking out her mobile phone and bringing up a close-up photo of the arrow. The minute Jim laid eyes on it, Siobhán no longer needed verbal confirmation. One look at his face and she could tell it was his precious bass bow. And the last person known to have it was dead.

Chapter 16

By the time Siobhán arrived at the print shop, there was a note on the door: GONE FISHING. It was typed with a computer-generated picture of a fish, winking and pointing one of its fins—as if to say, *See ya*. Siobhán peered in the dusty windows, but apart from several old photocopiers, there was nothing to see.

How long had the shop been closed? It was owned by an elderly man who ran it with his wife until she died. Then one of his grandsons took over and ran it for a few months before growing bored, at which point the old man realized he needed something to do all day, and he took back the helm. Only this time, his hours varied, and the shop was open whenever he damn well felt like it. The establishment was squeezed in between Liam's Hardware Shop and Sheila Mahoney's hair salon, Curl Up and Dye. The print shop was probably a service whose time had come and gone. The wind had picked up, rattling the sign, and animating the fish—as if he was wiggling on a hook.

"He's not really fishing, you know," a female voice said from behind. "The old goat." Siobhán turned to see the owner of the hair salon, Sheila Mahoney, hanging out in front of her shop, chewing on a licorice stick. Her platinum blond hair was spiked, her long nails were painted deep purple, and her makeup, as usual, had been applied with a heavy hand.

"How long has he been closed?"

"All month."

The pages from the Lucky Book hadn't been printed here after all. They could have been copied long before this trip. It was a dead end. "I'd offer you one," Sheila said, waving her licorice sticks around. "But I'd say you don't need it." Her gaze fell to Siobhán's stomach.

"Not a bother."

"Been eating at your brother's restaurant every day, is that it?"

"You caught me," Siobhán said. "It will probably take me another, say, five months to get my shape back." Sheila wasn't a slim woman by any means, so the dig cut extra deep.

"Just as well. I'm not in a sharing mood." She wagged the licorice in the air. "I'm in mourning."

Mourning? Had something happened to Pio? Her husband, tall and skinny as a rail, was a local trad musician—and her better half, in Siobhán's opinion. Siobhán would much rather be having a conversation with him. "Is Pio alright?"

"Pio? You think I'm mourning Pio?" Sheila threw her head back and laughed. "What, like? You thought he was dead?"

"You said you were in mourning."

"I bet you thought I murdered him." Now the licorice stick wagged in Siobhán's direction. "Are you suspicious of everyone, like? Now that you're a fancy detective and all?"

"I wouldn't say that."

"I can see the probing question in your eyes, so I'll tell ya why. I quit smoking, that's why." Sheila twirled the licorice. "Saw this on TikTok. Every time you want a smoke you stick one of these in your mouth instead. I've probably got a stone worth of licorice in me, and I only started this morning." Sheila wasn't Siobhán's favorite person in the world. Truthfully, she was a bit of a bully—albeit one who often wielded pink scissors—but at least she was trying to do something for her health. And now maybe her clients wouldn't come out of the salon with their new hair styles smelling like smoke.

"That's wonderful," Siobhán said. "Good for you."

"And bad for everyone else," Sheila said. "I'm ready to rip me some heads off. Just ask me very-much-still-alive husband." Sheila put her fingers between her lips and let out a piercing whistle. Moments later, the window above the salon creaked opened, and Pio Mahoney poked his head out.

"Yes, boss?"

"Tell her. Tell her I quit smoking, and it's turned me into a beast."

"She's telling the truth. I'd cross the street if I were you, Siobhán."

"She thought I'd murdered you, can you believe that?" Sheila threw her head back and cackled.

"Still alive," Pio said. "But thanks for checking."

"How ya, Pio?" Siobhán called. "I thought you'd be at the trad sessions."

"Yer one won't let me. Me ankle is chained to the bed."

Sheila rolled her eyes and tore into another piece of licorice. "He wishes. He's on bed rest."

"Are you still baking that brown bread?" Pio asked. "I sure could go for a slice."

"I've been a bit busy," Siobhán said. It had been a while since she'd made her famous brown bread. "When things quiet down, I'll bring you a tin or two."

"Brilliant." He retracted his head, and the window slammed shut.

"Is he okay?"

"He'll be fine."

"What's the real reason he isn't mingling with the trad musicians?" Siobhán realized she was being nosy, but she was too curious not to ask.

"Eejit. He tore his rotator cuff playing cupid."

"Playing cupid?"

Sheila nodded. "Bow and arrow, you know? Someone left a flier for a free archery lesson on the door of me shop. Pio was mad for a lesson. I told him he was going to poke somebody's eye out. I was wrong. He tore his own shoulder instead."

Free archery lessons. "Do you have the flier?"

Sheila eyed her. "What? Should I hang it in full view of everyone? Like a punishment?"

"What? No . . ."

"That would serve him right. You've become wise since you tied the knot. I should have kept it and put it on the bathroom mirror. See if he ever shoots a bow and arrow again."

"I actually wanted to look at the flier for other reasons. Where was this archery?"

"I dunno. You can go up and ask Pio if you like." Sheila gestured to the door. Siobhán headed for it but Sheila stepped in front of her before she reached it, blocking her way. "If you want to talk to me husband, it will cost you," she said, eyeing her like a lion stalking its next victim. "Fancy a new hairdo?"

By the time Siobhán was done getting tortured hairstyle-style and had climbed the stairs to Pio and Sheila's bedroom, he was fast asleep. Siobhán had somehow convinced Sheila that instead of a cut or color, that a styling would do. Siobhán's hair was now pulled back into a French braid, which wasn't too bad, apart from the fact that it was so tight, it was as if she'd gotten a face lift along with it. Whatever drugs Pio was on were making him sleep like the dead. It had all been for nothing.

"Try the bookstore café," Sheila called cheerfully to Siobhán on her way out. "They had one of those archery fliers on their bulletin board."

Lift the Cup, the café Macdara was at this morning when she called him, and the same one mentioned by Sheila, just happened to be Siobhán's favorite coffee shop. Located behind Turn the Page, Kilbane's beloved bookshop, owned by Oran and Padraig McCarthy, the addition had only been open a few years, but Siobhán couldn't imagine Kilbane without it. She loved its cozy feel, amplified by exposed brick, comfy seating, local art on the walls, and plenty of thriving plants. Customers could wander between the bookshop and the coffee shop through an arched doorway, although the coffee shop also had an entrance off an alleyway, in case someone in a hurry for caffeine and sugar needed to avoid the temptation of the bookshop or vice versa.

The rich smell of coffee hit Siobhán the moment she walked in. Normally, that was a good thing—there was nothing more comforting than the smell of rich coffee. But today, her stomach instantly turned, and all thoughts of a lemon bar immediately evaporated. Her pregnancy had brought a few odd cravings, such as cheese and jam toasties. And the list of smells she was sensitive to was growing; apparently, she now had to add coffee to the list. At least it would quell the urge to scale the bar and wrestle a cappuccino away from an unsuspecting barista.

A small crowd was gathered in the café for the next matchmaking event, a "Love Quiz" that would start in ten minutes. A row of chairs had been set up in the center of the shop, where, presumably, the singles would sit and answer questions pertaining to their ideal partner. Based on the agenda Grace had provided to the guards, the single women would answer the questions first, then they would file out of the coffee shop before the men filed in and answered the same exact questions. Ron had the idea to involve the audience in the event: he would encourage them to vote on which couples they thought would make the best matches. The suggestion had made Grace cringe. "Liam would be rolling over in his grave," she said. "Perhaps Ron isn't up to this job after all."

"I have to be free to be me," Ron called after her. "And I'm not saying I'm going to listen to them, I'm just going to let them chime in!" Grace responded by playing what sounded like a funeral dirge on her harp before striding away. Siobhán had the feeling that the minute this week was over, the two of them would part ways and never see each other again. It was probably for the best. Shaking Liam's ghost would be easier for each of them without the other serving as a constant reminder of the past. Siobhán was dying to corner Grace about the sale of the harp and whether or not she resented Liam for it, but that would have to wait.

Ron was nervously straightening the stools and testing the microphone. Siobhán approached and waited until he noticed her. "How will this work?" she asked.

Ron lifted a finger and then ran and fetched his clipboard. He read from the top sheet. "Róisín Doyle will be interviewing the women, and Edward Kavanagh, the men." At this, Siobhán glanced at the counter. Róisín was leaning against it, intently staring at a sheet of paper—no doubt the questions she would be asking. At that very second, Siobhan received a very urgent call. From mother nature. A bout of nausea had snuck up on her, and it wasn't messing. She was going to be sick. Her mind whirled with panic, while outwardly, she tried to pretend everything was fine.

"Are you alright?" Ron asked, studying her. "You look as white as a ghost."

She shook her head and held up a finger. As the doctor had promised, the morning sickness had eased up after the first trimester, but it still snuck up on her. The jax was located just around the corner. She made a mad dash for it, praying all the while for two things: one, that it would be unoccupied, and two, that it was soundproof. She had been hoping that her morning sickness was behind her, but it seemed the Dynamic Duo were not fans of coffee, even if it was just a whiff. Adverse to coffee? She was going to have to have a word with them eventually.

She reached the bathroom to find that her first wish had not been granted. The indicator on the door was turned to occupied. What if one of the single women was in there, putting on makeup, brushing her hair, and staring forever into the mirror? She had to get in. Siobhán pounded on the door.

"Welcome, everyone," she heard Ron say from the other room. "Love is in the air."

Siobhán pounded again, too afraid to open her mouth and speak. "Occupied!" a woman's voice yelled. Siobhán gave it one last try. "Feck off! I said it's occupied!"

Siobhán whirled around, frantic for a solution. She spotted a potted plant at the end of the hall, situated next to the entrance to the bookshop. At present, she was shielded from the main coffee shop via the hallway wall. But if she had to throw up in the potted plant, she would be in full view of *everyone*, including any unfortunate souls wandering around the back of the bookshop.

Her retching in the background probably wasn't the mood Ron wanted for his first event as a matchmaker. Then again, he would also never forget it. Who was she kidding? This was the one of the worst moments of her life. Not a great impression—the local detective sergeant barfing into a potted plant. *Beggars can't be choosers.* . . . It was either there or on the floor. But just as she had turned to make a beeline for the potted plant, the bathroom door flew open and Aisling Byrne stormed out. From the look on her face, she was enraged.

Siobhán didn't have time to care. She rushed past Aisling and slammed the door shut, as Ron began introducing the single contestants. Siobhán made it to the commode and by the time she was expelling the contents of her poor stomach, it was to the background sound of cheers and applause. She could only hope the twins wouldn't take it as encouragement or expect such adulation the next time she got sick. Soon, she felt much better, especially after brushing her teeth and rinsing with mouthwash. It had actually been Nancy's suggestion to carry them in her handbag, and today, Siobhán was grateful for the advice. Maybe she needed to ease up on thoughts about her mother-in-law. What was it they said? *It takes a village* . . .

Siobhán finished brushing and gargling, and was just about to exit, when pink smudges on the mirror caught her attention. Upon closer look, the smudges were words and they had been written with pink lipstick. Was it the exact shade as the lip prints on Liam's neck? They were vastly different surfaces, it was hard to tell. However, it was the word written on the mirror that had Siobhán transfixed: *Traitor.* Aisling, their day drinker, had just fled the bathroom. She had to be the one who "tubed" rather than "penned" it.

Who was she calling a traitor? Was it just a way of venting, or was she expecting the recipient of the message to walk in and see it? Or did she not care who saw it, for she fully expected that regardless of who walked in next, that person would start the rumor-mill grinding?

Siobhán snapped a photo, and pondered her options. Leave

it? Wipe it off? She could hardly cordon the area off and declare it a crime scene, especially after she was the one who ran in and got sick. But if she didn't wipe it off, she would have to explain to the employees that she had not been the one to write *Traitor* on the bathroom mirror. They might think she was talking about her unborn babies, now that they had just made their presence loudly known. She had no choice but to leave it. She would ask the employees to cover the mirror, and if they weren't willing to do that, she would have to threaten to cordon off the bathroom. By the time she emerged from the restroom, her stomach was actually growling for a lemon bar. These drastic ups and downs were disorienting. Pregnancy was making her feel insane.

Heads swiveled Siobhán's way as she walked out, but she did her best to ignore them. She approached the counter and signaled for an employee to come over. It was a young woman with large glasses and curly hair. After Siobhán explained the situation, the employee agreed to cover the mirror. Siobhán promised her they would be back as soon as possible to conduct an investigation, and she texted Macdara. He texted back that they would send a garda over as soon as possible to remove the mirror. The girl groaned when she heard this, no doubt worried about what Oran or Padraig would say. "Tell them you had no choice, and if they have any questions they can call Detective Sergeant O'Sullivan. Alright, pet?"

"Not a bother," the girl said, as a look of relief washed over her.

Siobhán scanned the crowd before situating herself onto a stool at the counter, but there was no sign of Aisling Byrne. Was the "traitor" amongst them? She turned her attention to the event panel. All the single women were sitting in a row on their stools, with Róisín standing to the right of them with her cue cards. Siobhán expected to see Saoirse—her best guess as to the person the message was intended for—but she was nowhere in sight. Maybe Aisling made a habit of writing *Traitor* on every mirror she saw. Maybe it was the reverse of positive affirmations. Either way, it was sus.

"Pretend it's a lovely Saturday afternoon," Róisín Doyle said, as the wind howled and rattled the windows. "You and your love have the day to yourselves. In an ideal world, how would you spend it?" Róisín beamed at the first contestant, a petite young woman with wavy honey-colored hair. Her lips were shiny and pink. It wasn't a given that Aisling had written the word on the mirror. But if she didn't write it, why did she hightail it out of the shop before the start of the panel? And she had been drinking shots earlier this morning, another factor that led Siobhán to believe she was the lipstick writer.

"I would spend it with breakfast in bed," the young woman answered.

"Nice," Róisín said. "Are you receiving breakfast in bed or delivering?" she asked with a wink.

"Receiving, of course," the young woman answered. A few women in the audience hooted at this. She grinned and pumped her fist. "And ideally, he delivers it to me with roses and champagne." More hoots and whistles followed.

Róisín snorted, and then slapped her hand over her mouth as a ripple of laughter filtered through the crowd. "She's a diva, Ron," Róisín said, as she gestured to him. "I hope you're writing this down."

"I've got it," Ron said, his face reddening, as if he didn't approve of Róisín's cheeky response. "And why shouldn't she be treated like a queen?"

The young woman beamed. Róisín frowned. "Maybe because that's not real life?" Róisín answered. She stared intensely at the young woman who was already squirming in her seat. "Is it your birthday, like?"

"What?" The woman's eyes widened. "No."

"Then why do you expect him to bring you breakfast in bed with champagne and roses? Is it your anniversary?"

"No." The young woman crossed her arms and glared at Róisín.

"Christmas?"

The woman shook her head.

"Did you just get engaged?"

"Róisín," Ron hissed from the corner.

"Well?" Róisín put her hands on her hips and stared at the poor young woman.

"You said in an 'ideal world,'" the young woman answered. "I thought we were fantasizing."

"Do you really want a serious match, or do you want to set your expectations so high they can never be met?" Róisín demanded.

The girl looked horrified. "I want a real match."

"Then you'd better change your answer."

"Róisín," Ron stage-whispered once again. "Do not censure them. They can answer however they like."

Róisín shook her head. "She's never going to be happy if she goes into this with such unrealistic expectations."

The woman chewed her lip. Ron jumped up from his chair. "Ladies, ladies, feel free to answer the questions *however* you would like. Fantasize away." He glared at Róisín. "Is that clear?"

A wistful string of notes drifted out from a harp. Siobhán hadn't noticed, but she turned to see Grace in the corner with her—what did Jim McVeigh call it? Chord zither? Whether Grace was trying to drown out Róisín or distract from the debacle, the gentle music was effective in momentarily forcing Róisín to shut her gob. Róisín waited until Grace was finished and then turned to the second woman on the panel. "What about you?" she said. "Why don't you take us through *your* ideal Saturday."

"I would make *him* breakfast," the second woman said, beaming. "Every morning."

"That's even worse!" Róisín threw her arms up. "Why would you do something so insane?" The harp began to strum again, this time over the sound of nervous chatter.

"Thank you, Róisín, I will take it from here," Ron said, snatching the questions out of her hand and nudging her away.

"Whatever you do in the first year of your relationship, ladies, he's going to expect the rest of his life. Do you hear me?"

"Maybe we should take a little break," Ron said.

"You know how you're really going to spend a Saturday?" Róisín continued, whirling on the panel. "Your boyfriend—and yes, I said boyfriend because if you think these 'eligible bachelors' are marriage material despite still being single at this age, you've got another think coming. Your *boyfriend* is going to sleep in—not quietly, mind you—he'll be snoring away, his dirty socks will be on the floor, and if you didn't clean up last night's dinner, well, that's how you'll be spending your Saturday morning, because his filthy dishes are probably still sitting on the table. And the stove. And the countertop. Or even worse, his wet towels on the floor and his big smelly shoes wherever he felt like flinging them. And if you nag him about any of it, he'll whine that he's a musician and he was out late, and you don't understand him. Did you hear what I said? *He's* a musician? Because, guess what, ladies—he certainly won't consider *you* one. Your musical talents are just a little hobby. He's the *real* musician. Drums? Who needs the drums? One could just bang one's head against the wall instead. And do you think he'll start out like this? So you can go into this relationship with the full knowledge of what you're getting yourself into? Of course not. He's going to be Mr. Charming. Everyone will tell you that pipers are quiet. It's shite.

And breakfast in bed? Only if he fell asleep eating his late-night fish and chips. Meanwhile, you'll be waiting for these grand gestures, like surprise holidays and little planes that write your name in the sky. You'll think you're in love, and nobody will be able to tell you otherwise. It will be the best drug you've ever taken. But one day, you're going to wake up and realize that Dr. Jekyll has turned into Mr. Hyde, and if you're really unlucky—or lucky, depending on your state of mind—you'll find out that he's fallen madly in love with your sister!"

Mouths around the coffee shop had dropped open, including Siobhán's. Róisín tossed the sheet of questions into the air and stormed out the door as they came billowing down. Ron snatched the questions from the floor, apologized to everyone, and continued the love quiz as if nothing had happened. Siobhán groaned and slid off her stool. The lemon bar would have to wait.

Chapter 17

"Róisín," Siobhán called, as she watched her race-walk down the alley. "Róisín!" She finally stopped, whirled around, and if her face was any indication, she planned on letting Siobhán have it. But when she realized she was about to bite the head off of a detective sergeant, her expression slowly went from anger to anxiety. Siobhán was breathing hard by the time she caught up to her. She needed to get back to her jogging routine.

"Let's go somewhere and talk," Siobhán said. Róisín glanced at her watch. "It won't take long."

"Is there anywhere private we could go?" she asked. "I've already embarrassed myself in front of people enough for one day."

"Do you feel like a walk?" The wind had picked up slightly, but otherwise things were relatively calm at the moment.

"As long as it's away from here," Róisín said.

"Follow me." Siobhán turned, and soon they were walking in the direction of the abbey. The alley would end at a car park, and they would have to navigate through a few fields and streets before they reached the path leading to the ruined monastery, but it was the perfect place to have a private chat.

"I didn't mean to make a fool of myself back there," Róisín said. "I looked at all those eager women, and it was suddenly so clear." She paused, and Siobhán allowed for the silence. Early on in her garda career, she would have jumped in with something, *anything,* as silence could feel painful. But she'd learned to let it exist, and more often than not, the person would resume speaking. Sure enough, Róisín didn't let it stretch out too long. "Once upon a time I was them," she said. "Last year. I was so convinced that some matchmaker could do what I hadn't managed to up until then. Find the perfect man for me." She shook her head. "None of it has worked out the way I imagined."

"There's nothing wrong with wanting to find the perfect man for you. As long as you aren't actually expecting him to be perfect."

Róisín stopped. "That's just the thing. And this is going to make me sound like the worst woman ever. But Edward wasn't my type in the first place. Niall was the kind of man I usually went for. But a nerdy piper? I almost refused the match."

Did she know that Niall would have been her match had Edward not broken out his wallet? "Why didn't you refuse the match?"

"Friends and family made me realize that maybe it was time I listened to someone who knew what they were doing instead of falling for the same type over and over again. You know the type. Extremely handsome. Cocky. Fierce talented."

It sounded like she was describing Niall O'Malley, alright. "I know the type," Siobhán said.

"And so, against that little voice in my head saying he

wasn't the man for me, I went with it. I trusted Liam." She stared off into the distance. "That was a mistake."

"But you are still dating Edward, are you not?"

Róisín bit her lip. "This is going to sound bad."

"Go on, so."

Róisín sighed. "I didn't want to come to this event. In fact, I told Liam that if I did come, I might have to drop some major truth bombs. But then he said our entire group had agreed to come, and that the point was to help Kilbane find the next batch of single lovebirds. It was hard to say no to that. Especially, if it meant Liam would stop holding us up like his shining achievements."

"Liam seemed like he was good at getting his way," Siobhán said. "It seems he convinced you to attend."

"He did much more than that," Róisín said, as a troubled look came over her face. "He made it impossible for us to say no."

It had been a while since Siobhán had toured anyone around the remains of their astounding Dominican priory, and every time she did, she felt a fierce sense of pride in her town. She knew the history of the ruined abbey, which was built in 1291, as if she'd lived it. The magnificent cloister, with stunning five-light east windows, was added in the fourteenth century, and the Franciscan bell tower was added in the fifteenth century. Originally, the priory had been donated to the Dominicans but cared for by the White Knights. And even though it was now a ruined abbey, it was still a sight to behold.

Stone carvings of heads and flowers still adorned the ancient structure, and Siobhán could spend hours gazing at them. Laid out in front of the abbey was the river where the monks used to brew beer, surrounded by green fields. It was a genuine source of inspiration to Siobhán no matter how many times she laid eyes on it. The thought of bringing the twins here for the first time made her stomach give a little flip—there were so many good times ahead of them. And although of course it made her heart ache that her parents would never meet their grandchildren. But the twins would certainly learn all about Naomi and Liam O'Sullivan. They would know how much her parents would have adored them. Macdara too had lost his father a long time ago. Despite Nancy Flannery's faults, Siobhán was gripped by a sudden love for her. She was the granny—or "nana," as she wanted to be called—the only would they have. Siobhán needed to work on her attitude and show her some appreciation. And Siobhán had no doubt that her parents would be smiling down at them, watching them grow.

Róisín didn't comment on the abbey, and Siobhán tried not to take it personally. But there was a noticeable calming effect: her shoulders relaxed and her breathing slowed down. Maybe after all this time, the quiet energy of the monks still resonated with folks, even if they didn't know it.

"Where do you want me to start?" Róisín asked.

"The beginning," Siobhán said. "Whatever that is for you."

"As I mentioned, I didn't want to participate in the matchmaking festival in the first place," Róisín said. *Saoirse had essentially said the same thing.* "But our mam said that it was extra hard for female drummers to meet men. As if they all think we'd beat on them if we got the chance." A smile tugged at the corner of her lips, as if there was a bit of truth in that statement. "I didn't expect to get matched." As Róisín talked they continued to walk through the interior grounds of the priory. There was no longer a floor or ceiling, just grass and sky. "But I certainly didn't expect to get *played.*"

"And who was it that played you?"

"Several people, but I won't lie. The biggest player of all was Liam Noone. If he was still alive, I would have exposed him for the fraud that he is. *Was*. I'm sorry, I don't mean to disrespect the dead." She crossed herself.

"Tell me exactly how he played you," Siobhán said.

Róisín reached into her handbag and removed a folded sheet of paper. "I don't want you to think I'm keeping any secrets." She handed the paper to Siobhán. It was another photocopied page from Liam's Book. However, this one had Edward's name at the top. "It's Edward's interview form. Someone slipped it inside my bodhrán case last Monday."

Siobhán began to read through the page. It confirmed Niall's revelation that Edward had paid Liam to be matched with Róisín, despite Liam first choosing Niall as her match. Five hundred euro. "Would you rather have been matched with Niall?" Siobhán asked. She was genuinely curious.

"No. Fiddle players are way too cocky. However, I also don't buy this 'pipers are always so nice and quiet' perception. You can see for yourself that Edward is as sneaky as they come. Five hundred euro! On top of what we already paid him for his matchmaking services? And he was supposed to be the real deal. A third generation matchmaker—the King of Matchmakers. Hogwash. And here it is a year later, and Edward has never owned up to what he did." She let out a sound that resembled a growl. "Not to mention Liam. I'm just sorry I never got the chance to give him a piece of my mind."

"Let's put all that aside for a moment, if you can. Before you learned about his betrayal—how was your relationship with Edward?"

Róisín sighed. "He wasn't the love of my life, but I was just wrapping my head around the fact that it was nice to be with a man who was crazy about me. And he was—in the beginning—he doted on me. We played sessions together, and if we arrived at one where the other musicians didn't want percussion involved, he always stood up for me. And everything was going fine. All the way up until the moment he fell in love with my sister."

Helen had already told Siobhán as much, but she wanted to get Róisín's version. "Why do you think he's in love with Helen?" But before Róisín could answer, a streak of lightning lit up the skies, and a loud crack of thunder followed. "We'd better head back," Siobhán said. "That doesn't look good." The darkening sky cast an eerie glow across the fields.

Róisín glanced at Siobhán's belly. "Can you run?"

"I used to do it nearly every day," Siobhán said. She thought she was barely showing but other people were starting to notice. Did Róisín know she was pregnant, or like Sheila Mahoney, did she think Siobhán was eating too many sweets? They began to jog across the field toward town. The river that ran through the field was shallow, and never anything too wild, but now, as it swelled with rain, small waves rippled on the surface, sloshing onto the grass. A nearby horse whinnied, and the smell of a storm permeated the air. Róisín pulled ahead, running faster and faster, and as she picked up speed, an object fell out of her pocket. Siobhán bent to pick it up, and nearly shouted at Róisín to stop. That is, until she saw what it was.

A tube of lipstick. Siobhán quickly uncapped it. *Hot pink*. The shade looked like an exact match to the lipstick mark on Liam's neck. Maybe this drummer didn't just like beating things; maybe she also liked shooting things with bows and deadly arrows. Siobhán shoved the tube of lipstick into her own handbag—Róisín was already far ahead. Siobhán picked up her pace, fighting the howling wind.

Just after she crossed the little bridge, the skies opened up and the rain came down in buckets. Within seconds she was thoroughly soaked. Siobhán could already hear Nancy lecturing her about catching a cold, getting the babies sick.

Everything she did now had a consequence for two other living beings. It was intense.

When Siobhán reached the road leading back to Sarsfield Street, she ducked underneath the overhang of the Kilbane Museum. Róisín was already out of sight. Now at least Siobhán had a tube of lipstick to present to Jeanie Brady. She also had an additional photocopied page from Liam's book. Every one of the musicians had received a page, but now she knew they hadn't necessarily received their *own* page. Liam had come here with the intention of increasing the pressure on those he felt owed him. And knowing him, he was never going to let them off the hook. Every one of them had a motive to murder him.

But if Liam wasn't the one who distributed the pages, someone else had beat him to it. Someone who did not like the secrets they held and intent on spilling each and every one. To what end? The pages had been distributed last Monday *before* Liam was killed. Had someone done it to stir up trouble? Or put an end to Liam's blackmail? Were this person's intentions innocent or evil? Was the messenger the killer? Or had the messenger simply triggered the killer?

The streets were beginning to flood, the water already past Siobhán's ankles. This storm was going to drive everyone indoors—scratch that—no doubt it already had driven everyone indoors. On the other hand, the wind was starting to loosen her too-tight braid, and was there a better way to spend a stormy day than inside an Irish pub listening to trad music? Not in Siobhán's book, but this time, there was a distinct disadvantage. This time, they might all be shut in with a killer. And there was no doubt about it, whoever this killer was—he (or she) was intent on playing to his own tune.

Chapter 18

Siobhán continued to battle the wind and rain all the way to the garda station. By the time she arrived, she was so soaked, she had no choice but to put on her garda uniform—at this point, if she wanted to breathe, she couldn't button the trousers. She pulled the shirt down as far as it would stretch and wrapped the blazer around her before heading into the evidence room. Once there, she grabbed an extra bag for the lipstick tube, and after signing the checkout sheet for the evidence bag with the cigarette butt, she continued to Macdara's office, where she would be meeting himself and Aretta. When she walked in, they were already there, and soon they were staring at Siobhán openmouthed.

"What?"

"Your hair," Macdara said. "And . . . why are you in your garda uniform?"

She pointed to her hair. "Sheila Mahoney. Long story." She then indicated her garda uniform. "I was at the abbey with Róisín Doyle," she said. "We got caught in the storm." She sunk into the seat next to Aretta. Even with her promotion there was no separate office for Siobhán. This garda station was too small for two detective sergeants. Macdara had been looking into transferring to either Bruree or Charlesville, but they were small too, and the most likely place for one of them to transfer was to Cork city. It would be a forty-minute commute. For now, Siobhán was technically still serving under her garda pay. She'd be taking maternity leave in five months, they had time before they figured out all the logistics. Both of them would like the challenge of a bigger city, but there was no way with newborn twins that when Siobhán did go back to work she was going to be that far away. They'd both agreed that Macdara should take the position in Cork city. Maybe, with him there, Siobhán would drive up sometimes and they would visit Kinsale and Cobh. The thought of pushing around a double-pram in either of those gorgeous towns by the water was appealing.

Siobhán set the two evidence bags on the desk along with the photocopy Róisín had received from Liam's Lucky Book. "The page doesn't tell us anything new. But Edward certainly has some things to answer to."

"Agree," Macdara said, jotting down a note.

"How did Róisín take that news?" Aretta asked. "It couldn't have been easy knowing the man she was with manipulated the entire system. Paid for her, like she was a product."

"She certainly let off some steam about it. Especially since, after of all that, he fell in love with her sister—and that's according to both herself and Helen." Siobhán pushed the two evidence bags forward. "Róisín dropped this lipstick tube. You'll find the color is a match to the lip prints on Liam's neck, and of course, here is the cigarette butt, also with a lipstick mark, the one Helen discarded outside the Charlesville Hotel." Macdara and Aretta leaned in. Aretta brought out the photo on her phone, enlarged it, and held it near the lipstick marks.

"That definitely looks like a match," Aretta said.

"I agree," Siobhán said. "We'll have to wait for Jeanie Brady to confirm it, but I think we can comfortably assume they are a match."

"What are you thinking?" Macdara said. "To which sister does the lipstick belong?"

"Sisters share things—or nick things off each other. Either Helen borrowed the lipstick from Róisín or vice versa. Or maybe they bought identical tubes."

Macdara stared at the evidence bags. "Where is Róisín now?"

"I dunno. She gave me the slip."

Macdara frowned. "Why would she give you the slip?"

"She could simply have been running from the storm, or she may have regretted everything she'd told me—or a little bit of both. I'm a bit slow these days, so I did tell her to run ahead. She has no idea she dropped the lipstick tube."

"This means one of the Doyle sisters could have been sleeping with Liam," Macdara said.

"And often where there's love, there's murder," Aretta added.

Macdara grimaced. "It's a sad tale but a good lead."

"We still need to speak with Edward," Siobhán said. "I'd like to see how he reacts when we confront him with the news that Róisín was given his page out of Liam's Lucky Book." Was Edward given one too? According to the pattern—the answer would be yes. And yet, when they'd spoken to the pair of them at the gazebo, neither had mentioned anything about receiving a page.

"Liam was collecting money from them then, is that correct?" Aretta asked.

"He was certainly *asking* every one of them for money," Siobhán responded. "We'll have to pull his financial records to see who actually paid up." Maybe the killer would be one who hadn't paid. One who made sure that Liam would stop collecting on the debt. *Permanently.*

"It could have been done in cash," Macdara said. "There may not be a record." Siobhán nodded—there was always that. "But you're right. In light of these revelations, let's make sure we circle back and interview all of them again. See what shakes up this time."

"I wonder if this storm is going to delay Jeanie Brady," Siobhán said.

"I would think so," Macdara said. They all paused to listen to the rain still pounding on the roof. "For her own safety, she should wait until tomorrow. The streets are flooding."

"I'll call her," Siobhán said. "Let her know we would rather she pull off and check into a hotel. We can wait another day for her."

"I was thinking I would start sifting through the photos people have been sending in from that night," Aretta said. "Along with CCTV footage from the surrounding pubs."

"Excellent idea," Macdara said. He stood and grabbed his car keys.

"Where are you off to?" Siobhán asked.

"I'm taking you somewhere," Macdara said.

"Home," she replied. "To change clothes."

"Let's grab a brellie on our way out."

Once they were in the car, it became obvious they were not going home. They were headed in the direction of Charlesville. "Is there something you haven't told us?" Siobhán asked. "Are we going to the hotel?"

"No," he said. "I think it's time." He sounded cryptic.

"You think it's time . . ." The lightbulb went on. She opened her mouth to protest, then shut it. If her work pants didn't fit, the rest of her wardrobe was soon to follow. Kilbane did not have a maternity store, but Charlesville did. "Do we have to do this in a storm?"

"The distance to the house would have been about the same."

He wasn't wrong. "I suppose it is time," she said. "But I don't like it."

Macdara held his hand out, and she finally took it. "You're beautiful," he said. "I just want you to be comfortable."

Siobhán sighed. "Sheila Mahoney thought I'd been eating too much, and Róisín asked me if I could run." Macdara laughed. Siobhán shook her head. "It would be funnier if I had actually caught up to her."

Siobhán called Jeanie, who informed her she had already decided to check into a hotel and hit the road again in the morning. It was a relief to know she was safe, and if Mother Nature calmed down, she would be here tomorrow. Macdara pulled into a parking space near the maternity shop. "After we're finished, let's stop at the Charlesville Hotel and ask to look at their CCTV," Siobhán said.

Macdara nodded. "I was thinking along the same lines."

"It's ironic. One minute we're having a matchmaking festival, the next we're watching CCTV footage to see who was cheating with whom."

"All in a day's work, Mrs. O'Sullivan-Flannery. All in a day's work."

The hotel clerk led them to a back office, then pointed out a rack where they could hang their wet jackets. Siobhán hesitated, and for a moment pondered keeping it on before finally giving in and hanging it up. A monitor sat on a desk, and the clerk set up the camera footage. "These are from both the front of the hotel and the lobby," she said. "You'll find the dates along the side. Just click on the date and the location, and the footage will play." She hesitated as Siobhán and Macdara took seats in front of the monitor. "May I ask what you're hoping to see?" she asked. "We haven't had any reports of trouble."

Siobhán had no doubt that she had heard about the murder. In fact, she would be surprised if Helen Doyle hadn't mentioned it. "We're just double-checking on something," Macdara said. The clerk nodded. She turned to Siobhán.

"Cute outfit."

"Thank you." Siobhán felt her cheeks heating up, and she just knew Macdara was stifling his laughter. There had not been much to choose from in the little maternity shop, and so, Siobhán was wearing maternity trousers and a white blouse covered in images of strawberries. She looked ridiculous. But at least she was dry and her pants were no longer cutting into her stomach, so she'd take the win. She'd ordered two more pairs of pants and tops for casual use and both a gray suit and a black one for work. They would be shipped to her. Until then, she would try and configure old suits of Dara's to wear—after all, who would take her seriously as a detective sergeant if she showed up covered in strawberries?

Once the clerk left, pulling the door shut behind her, Macdara clicked through the dates. "They arrived Monday last, is it?"

"Yes," Siobhán said.

"We might as well start there."

The first "hit" they got was Helen Doyle entering the hotel on Monday afternoon, pulling her roller bag. She checked in at the desk, and there was nothing unusual in her expression or with the interaction. The next shot was her rolling the bag to the lift. Hours later, she emerged in the lobby sans roller bag, and she had changed her outfit to something a tad fancier. "She's probably going to the first session," Siobhán said.

She stood in the lobby, looking at her watch and pacing the floor. Macdara leaned forward. "She's waiting for someone."

"Maybe her sister and Edward." Eagerly they both leaned forward, waiting to see who was going to show up. But no one did. Helen eventually made a phone call, then strode outside, looking none too happy.

"Someone stood her up," Macdara said.

Siobhán nodded. "It could still be her sister."

The third clip showed Helen returning that evening. This time she wasn't alone. Róisín was with her. They stood in the lobby, and from the expression on their faces and their hands flailing, it was obvious they were arguing. Siobhán wished there was sound. "So much for a fun session," Siobhán said.

"Maybe too much drink," Macdara guessed.

Róisín jabbed her finger at Helen, then whirled around and strode out. Helen waited a minute and followed. Macdara quickly switched to the outside footage. Róisín was no longer in the frame, she must have gone straight to her vehicle. Helen was smoking, and scrolling through her phone. Once again, she made a phone call. "Awfully late to be calling someone," Siobhán said. "That is someone other than a lover."

She stayed there long after finishing her cigarette. "She's waiting for someone again," Macdara said. Her head popped up and her expression changed. The camera gave no view of the street.

"I think that someone just pulled up," Siobhán said.

"Only we can't see who it is." Sure enough, Helen walked straight out of the frame.

"Let's see when she returns."

"What time was it?" Siobhán squinted until she could read the time stamp. "Two in the morning," she said. "I don't remember the last time I was up at two in the morning."

"I do," Macdara said. "You were yacking into the commode."

Siobhán laughed. "I forgot about that."

"I wish I could."

She gave him a playful shove. He grinned, and they focused once again on the screen. Helen returned at five in the morning. "Three hours," Siobhán said. "Where did she go for three hours? And with whom?"

"We can ask her," Macdara said.

"We should check out footage from the Kilbane Inn," Siobhán said. "See if Róisín's or Edward's movements match this timeline."

"Good idea. I'll ask Aretta to look into it."

The next few days showed Helen returning and leaving, but once she returned to the hotel, they didn't see her again until the next morning. It was Thursday evening that something different occurred. Helen had already returned—it was nearly one in the morning. The doors opened at half one and in walked none other than Liam Noone. Siobhán literally gasped.

"The lipstick Róisín dropped," Siobhán said. "I bet it either belonged to Helen or Helen borrowed it."

"We can't be sure he's there to see her," Macdara said. "But Helen is the only one from the festival staying there."

"Let's see what he does."

Liam passed the check-in counter and walked straight to the lift. The clerk on duty didn't even look up. "Security is a bit lax," Macdara said.

"I don't think it's often that anyone causes trouble here." This was the double-edged sword of small towns. Things were fine until they weren't. They continued watching. Liam did not emerge until the morning. *Alone*. Thirty minutes later Helen exited the hotel.

"I think we've found his lover," Macdara said. "Question is—is she also his killer?"

Chapter 19

"Welcome, single musicians and guests." Jim McVeigh grinned at the crowd gathered in Fitzgerald's. He stood at the top of the circle, surrounded by his fellow musicians, who were ready to start the session. "I was asked to say a bit about traditional Irish music sessions for those who need a little education. You may have noticed that we play sets of tunes. Usually three tunes in a set. We have categories of tunes as well. Dance tunes—or reels. Jigs. And polkas. All this music is handed down—it's an oral tradition. Although there is a session leader, we often go around the circle in a clockwise direction, asking each musician if they have a tune. Tonight, I'm going to start us off with three reels. And although we don't normally announce the titles, we're doing that for you tonight. So sit back and enjoy 'Lizzie Picking Cockle,' 'Pigeon on the Gate,' and 'The Bride in the Bed.' "

Jim McVeigh sat back down and seconds later the pub filled with the first reel. Siobhán loved learning a bit about trad music—Ciarán so rarely shared things like that with them. Would one or both of the twins be musical? She loved the passion musicians embodied, the drive to express themselves through tunes, to communicate with one another without words. The storm was taking a brief respite, but the weatherman warned there was more to come. For now, everyone seemed prepared for whatever the skies decided to bring. Siobhán was so lost in the moment, she nearly missed Aisling Byrne slipping out the front door. *Again*. This time Siobhán hurried after her. But before she could call out to her, the door opened behind her and Saoirse flew past Siobhán calling out to Aisling. "Wait," she said. "Please." Aisling kept walking. "Why are you so browned off?"

Aisling whirled around. "Because I know what you did." Siobhán ducked underneath an awning, despite the fact that neither of them seemed to register who she was. Maybe the strawberries weren't so terrible after all.

"What did I do?" Saoirse asked, her tone pleading.

"Why don't you tell me?"

"Because I have no idea what you're on about."

"What about your secret little deal with Liam Noone?"

"This again?" Saoirse said. "We've been through this." Siobhán didn't dare move but she could see their reflections in the storefront window. "You're never going to get over this, are you?"

"The others don't think I should."

"The others? You've been talking about me behind my back?"

"I've been *processing* your betrayal."

"You know what? You can stop. Because I'm done." Saoirse whirled around and headed back to the pub. This time she looked straight at Siobhán. Maybe staring into the window of a closed shop hadn't been the best idea after all. "Not here," Saoirse said, flicking a glance at Siobhán. "Let's go somewhere private."

Siobhán had no choice but to turn around. "Brilliant idea," she said. "Aisling? That included you."

"What?" Aisling stammered.

"I said, *Let's go somewhere a little more private*."

* * *

Siobhán held open the door of The Six for Aisling and Saoirse, and they walked in like prisoners headed for their cell. But it didn't take long for the beautiful atmosphere of her brother's new restaurant to calm them. There were times you had to play hardball with suspects, but there were other times when you had to feed them. Eoin was in the kitchen along with Gráinne, James, and Nancy. Ann was away at university and Ciarán was no doubt hanging with the other single musicians. It was getting late, but Siobhán had called ahead and asked Eoin if he could prepare some appetizers and drinks for their guests, and he'd happily obliged.

Siobhán watched as the women took in the large converted dairy barn. Thick wood beams, stone walls, communal tables, and a three-sided fireplace gave the place its charm, along with its large windows overlooking their fields. And when you added in Eoin's cooking, The Six felt downright magical. But today the view was obscured by the rain—the storm was dancing in and out, and seemed to be here for the long haul. Siobhán loved hearing the rain drum on the roof, and she was grateful for the warmth of the fireplace.

"This would be an amazing place for a session," Aisling said.

"You're right," Siobhán said. "We'll have to make that happen." She gestured for them to sit at the nearest table before going into the kitchen to say hello to the gang.

Gráinne was the first to come up to Siobhán, and she circled her like a shark. "You look berry nice," she said. "Strawberry fields forever, eh?"

"Hilarious," Siobhán said. "It's a temporary solution."

"Which field did you pluck it out of?"

Siobhán laughed and gave her sister a playful shove.

"If you wanted help with maternity outfits, why didn't you just say so?"

Siobhán sighed. "Can we discuss my wardrobe another time?"

"Not a bother. Can we discuss your hair?" She walked up and sniffed. "No smoke, but I would have sworn you were captured by Sheila Mahoney."

"She quit smoking," Siobhán said. "And I needed to speak with Pio." Just then it hit Siobhán that she'd forgotten to check the bulletin board at Lift the Cup to look for the archery flier. *Pregnancy brain times two* . . . Hopefully, she'd remember tomorrow. She texted herself a note just in case. When a ding rang out, Gráinne tilted her head.

"Did you just text yourself?"

"Yes. I text myself all the time."

"Do you answer?"

"Ha ha. I just leave myself little reminders."

Gráinne peered into the dining room. "Do you think either of them is a killer?"

"Or both?" James said, coming up from behind and poking Gráinne, making her shriek. "A murderous couple?"

They were interrupted by someone slamming down a pan. Nancy Flannery. "I cannot fathom why you're all so obsessed with murder," she said. "You'll want to stop all that business once the twins are born."

James made a face at Siobhán the minute Nancy wasn't looking. Siobhán shook her head—she couldn't help but laugh. "I appreciate you all chipping in," Siobhán said. "Subjects tend to divulge more information when they're in a comfortable atmosphere." *Ply them with warmth and good food, and they might just lower their guard.*

"Suspects," Gráinne said. "I knew it."

"Everyone is a suspect at this point," Siobhán said. "You know the drill."

"Shall I ask if they'd like a glass of wine?" Eoin was the consummate professional.

"No," Siobhán said. "I need them sober."

"I'll be right out with appetizers," Eoin said. "And sparkling water."

"Perfect."

"Have you been sticking to your diet?" Nancy asked. "Taking good care of my grandchildren?"

"Everything is just fine," Siobhán said. She faced her mother-in-law. "And if I haven't said it lately, thank you for being here for me."

Nancy blinked rapidly and Siobhán didn't have to turn around to know her siblings all had their mouths hanging open. But if Nancy registered the compliment, she didn't let it show. "I'd hardly say everything is fine," Nany replied. "I bet they can feel you thinking about murder."

Siobhán sighed. "We don't focus so much on the murder, we prefer to focus on getting justice."

Nancy pursed her lips.

"I think you'd better get out there," James said. "Sounds like trouble is brewing." Siobhán turned her head just in time to see that Aisling and Saoirse were now standing face-to-face, screaming at each other.

"What do you want me to say?" Saoirse said. "Tell me, and I'll say it!"

"I don't know."

"I can't change how it started—and I'm sorry. But I truly fell in love with you."

Aisling shook her head. "How can I believe that? For all I know, he paid you to say that."

A look of exasperation came over Saoirse's face. "If that were true, why would I continue the farce now that he's dead?"

Siobhán hurried out. "Have a seat, ladies."

The fighting stopped, and the pair slunk into their seats.

Siobhán couldn't help but notice that Saoirse was looking at Aisling but Aisling was refusing to make eye contact.

"What's the story?" Siobhán asked, standing next to them. She didn't want to sit, and standing might remind them that she was the one who held the power.

Aisling shook her head. "You tell her."

Saoirse folded her arms across her chest. "Why don't you give her the article?"

Aisling reached into her handbag and handed a newspaper to Siobhán. Siobhán took in the headline:

Matchmaker Embraces the LGBTQ Community.

Love is in the air, and at this year's matchmaking festival, Saoirse O'Reilly will be matched with Aisling Byrne, making them the first lesbian couple that Liam Noone can add to his impressive love roster . . .

Siobhán stopped reading. "Is this new information?"

"It is to me," Aisling said. "Saoirse picked me to be matched with, and Liam just went along with it."

Saoirse put her head in her hands. "First you're mad that he paid me to participate, and then you're mad because I chose you?" She looked at Siobhán. "I'd seen her at numerous trad sessions, but I'd never worked up the courage to speak to her."

"Funny how easy it came to you when you were being paid to seduce me."

"When did you receive this article?"

"I found it inside the case to my squeeze-box," Aisling said. "I don't know who put it there or exactly when. It fell out this morning, when I was taking the instrument out of my case."

"Can you narrow down the timeframe?"

Aisling pondered the question. "It definitely wasn't in

there yesterday morning. But it's possible I put my squeezebox away without noticing it. It was left sometime in the past twenty-four hours."

In other words, unless Liam's ghost had figured out how to photocopy articles and slip them into musical cases, it wasn't Liam Noone. And it probably wasn't Liam who distributed the Lucky Pages. They needed to get the CCTV footage from all the pubs. Going through endless hours of footage was time consuming, but sometimes it could crack a case wide open.

"I gave Liam his money back," Saoirse said. "After I fell in love with you. That's when he tried pressuring me for more."

"Had Liam been blackmailing anyone else?" Siobhán's suddenly asked. The women's heads swiveled Siobhán's way.

"Sausage rolls and curried chips coming up," Eoin said, as he entered with two large platters. *Saved by the appetizers.*

"And sparkling water," Gráinne said, as she entered with the bottle and two glasses. "But I'd be happy to also get you a mineral or tea."

"I told you," Saoirse said to Aisling. "Don't let the environment fool you. This is an official interview."

These two were sharp. Siobhán was going to have to start paying closer attention to them. "You're free to have a drink soon," Siobhán said. "After a few more questions."

Saoirse jabbed a chip at Aisling. "Told you."

"She's investigating a murder," Aisling said. "She should be questioning you."

"You're just as much of a suspect as I am," Saoirse said.

"How do you figure that? I'm not the one he was blackmailing."

"As far as we know."

"What's that supposed to mean?"

"How do we know he wasn't blackmailing you too? For all we know, he had secrets on everyone."

"Please don't shout," Nancy said, emerging from the kitchen. "It's not good for the babies."

"Babies!" Aisling and Saoirse cried out at the same time. They stared at Nancy as if she had grown two heads.

"Not me," Nancy sputtered. "*Her.*" She pointed to Siobhán. Their heads then pivoted to Siobhán.

"Is that why you're wearing fruit?" Aisling asked.

"I'm having twins," Siobhán said. "But they will not be here for another *five months.*" She snuck a look at Nancy, hoping she would realize that meant there was no reason to harass her right now.

"These next five months are vital," Nancy said. "I don't think you should be stressing them out."

This time Siobhán gave Eoin the look, and he copped on straight away. "Nancy," he said. "Let's check on your apple tarts."

Nancy pursed her lips, gave a nod, and followed Eoin back to the kitchen.

"Congratulations," Aisling said. "I can't wait to have children someday."

"Me too," Saoirse said.

"Really?" Aisling crossed her arms and glared. "It that an honest opinion or were you paid to say that?"

Saoirse stood. "I can see the damage I've done is permanent. But I have been beaten up enough. Do you hear me? Consider us over. I cannot stand to be berated over this anymore."

"Of course you're giving up."

Saoirse shook her head. "I cannot win. I just cannot win." She stood. "Do you swear on your life that Liam wasn't blackmailing you too?"

"On what grounds?"

"I don't know. You tell me."

Aisling chewed on her lip, then shrugged. "It's late," she said. "I'm knackered."

"I'll drive you both back to the inn," Siobhán said.

"No, you won't," James piped in, as he entered the dining room. "You get some rest. I'll take them back."

"This is my older brother," Siobhán said. "He's a good egg."

James laughed. "A bit cracked and scrambled sometimes, but I'll get ye there safely."

"Please do not discuss this with any of the other musicians," Siobhán said to the young women. "Not until we know what's what."

The three of them exited the restaurant. Siobhán sat down, and soon Gráinne brought her an apple tart with ice cream and a glass of milk before sitting across from her. "You're the best," Siobhán said. It was a bit of a dairy overload, but she kept the criticism to herself.

"Eat it quick, I told Nancy it was for me."

Siobhán laughed. "Why don't you invite her to Lahinch? She can organize the inn for you."

Not a chance, Gráinne mouthed. They smiled at each other as Siobhán dug into the apple tart. "Besides, she'll be there for the baby shower."

Siobhán began to choke as a piece of tart went down the wrong pipe. Gráinne shoved the milk closer and Siobhán drank.

"It was an accident," Gráinne said. "She asked if anyone was having a baby shower. What was I supposed to do? Play dumb? She would have thrown you another one."

Siobhán thought of Emma and Eileen. "Another one," she said. "Imagine that."

"Nightmare," Gráinne said. "How many times can you play pin the tail on the diaper?"

Siobhán grimaced. "That's not really a thing, is it?"

"Don't worry," Gráinne said. "You're going to love it."

"Maybe we could all just walk by the sea. We don't really need to do the typical baby shower stuff."

"Are you joking me? We're doing it all. You only get one baby shower."

Or two. "Right, so." Siobhán finished the apple tart and pushed the plate away. "That was so good."

Gráinne slid the plate to herself, clinked her fork on the empty plate. "Wow," she said loudly. "It's too bad you didn't want any of this apple tart, Siobhán. It was delicious." She glanced at the kitchen and grinned. "How much do you want to bet she heard that?" Gráinne whispered.

She was probably right. "Thanks."

"Don't mention it." They settled into a few minutes of silence. "Do you suppose Ciarán has met anyone?" Gráinne asked. "Or will he be loveless in Kilbane?"

"Liam's protégé Ron has taken over, and they're having matchmaking events. But there's certainly a different feel to the entire festival now." Siobhán studied her sister. "I've been expecting you to say that you wished you could participate. Are you dating anyone?"

A sly grin came over Gráinne's pretty face. But before she could spill the beans, the door opened and Aretta walked in with Macdara. One look at their faces and Siobhán knew that something was up.

"What's the story?" Siobhán asked.

"Before we get to that," Macdara said. "We just saw James with Aisling and Saoirse. Anything to report there?"

Siobhán handed him the newspaper article. "Not only was Saoirse paid to participate in the festival, she also told Liam she wanted to be matched up with Aisling."

"And that was a problem?"

"I'm sure Aisling feels like she was a pawn."

"Liam certainly did a lot of damage."

And he'd paid for it with his life. . . .

Nancy Flannery emerged from the kitchen with another

apple tart, this one piled with ice cream. She beamed at her son. "Dara," she said. "I have an apple tart for you, fresh from the oven. With a double scoop of vanilla ice cream."

"Wow," Siobhán said. "It's like you're eating for two."

"Thanks, Mam." Macdara grinned. "I'll have it in a moment."

"Nonsense. It's going to melt." Nancy set the tart topped with ice cream on the table. Macdara shrugged and sat in front of it. Nancy began massaging Macdara's shoulders. "Aretta, would you like an apple tart with ice cream?"

"No, thank you," Aretta said politely.

"Just a small piece then," Nancy said. She patted Macdara on the back before turning back to the kitchen. Aretta looked stricken. Siobhán knew she did not eat sweets.

"Don't worry," Siobhán said. "We'll cover you."

Aretta laughed.

"Where were we?" Macdara asked between mouthfuls.

"I was wondering if Saoirse had paid Liam?" Aretta asked.

"She did not," Siobhán replied. "But Liam was certainly pressuring all of them to pay."

Eoin emerged from the kitchen and beamed when he saw Aretta. She smiled at him and held up a finger.

"I'll get you a cup of herbal tea," Eoin said. Aretta thanked him with a smile. He hurried off. Their discussion turned to the festival for a few minutes, and they all took bets on whether or not Ciarán had found love. It was a good sign that they'd hardly seen him since it started, they had high hopes.

"Are we thinking Liam is the one who distributed the pages before he was murdered?" Aretta asked. Eoin quickly slipped in carrying a cup of tea and an apple tart with ice cream. He set them in front of Aretta. Then he took the fork and stood there eating the apple tart and ice cream until it was gone. He left the empty plate and fork in front of her before winking and going back to the kitchen.

"Now that's love," Macdara said, making Aretta blush.

Aretta asked again if they thought Liam had been the one to distribute the Lucky Pages.

"Did you learn anything at the print shop?" Macdara asked.

"He wasn't open. Apparently, he's taken up fishing." She sighed. "However, I did learn that Pio strained his shoulder doing a little archery practice."

This got their attention. "What in the world?" Macdara said.

"It seems Lucky Pages and newspaper articles aren't the only things that were passed around that week. Someone passed out fliers for free lessons at an archery."

"Well, I'll be damned," Macdara said. "What archery?"

"I hit a bit of a snag—Sheila had thrown the flier away, and Pio was in a drug-induced sleep by the time she finished turning me into Pippi Longstocking."

Macdara laughed. "Didn't she have two braids?"

"I love a man that knows his children's books," Siobhán said. "That's going to come in handy very soon." They shared a smile.

"Ah, right," Macdara said, "so Pio had an archery experience, and you were going to have a chat with him about it. That's how you ended up with the Sheila special."

Siobhán touched her head. "I cannot wait to take this down, it's giving me a headache."

"I suppose tomorrow we can call the archeries nearby and see which one was the culprit," Aretta said.

"Sheila mentioned that Lift the Cup had a flier, but by the time I was there, I discovered the message on the mirror, and then I was chasing Róisín down and I forgot to check."

"I'll check the board in the morning," Macdara said. "So

what are we thinking? Liam did or did not distribute those pages?"

"I've been considering every possibility," Siobhán said. "But I don't think it was Liam. First, if he was the one who disturbed them, I bet there would have been an 'ask.' A certain amount of money to keep the secret, or some such. But why would he kill the blackmail plan he already had in place? Some people were given *other* people's pages—i.e., whoever distributed them wanted to expose the secrets, and thus, Liam would have lost his leverage. It just doesn't make sense that he's the one who copied and distributed the pages."

"Then what is this person's motive?" Macdara asked. "They simply wanted to ruin Liam?"

"Maybe," Siobhán said.

"Or," Aretta said, "this person wanted someone else to murder Liam and decided to rile everyone up."

"Yes," Siobhán said, "or this killer wanted to make sure they weren't the only one with a motive."

"It would be cheaper than hiring an assassin," Aretta said. It had taken her a while, but Aretta was starting not only to catch on to their dry humor but be able to dish some out as well.

Macdara pushed his empty dessert plate away and crossed his arms. "Doesn't it seem a bit of a stretch to think that any of these 'secrets' would actually incite someone to murder?"

"I believe it is too much of a stretch," Siobhán said. "Which is why I think this person wanted *everyone* to have a motive so they, as the real killer, could hide in plain sight. Nobody makes a bespoke arrow on impulse. This murder was planned in advance."

"Supposedly the Lucky Book was in Liam's possession until hours before his death," Aretta pointed out. "If it wasn't Liam distributing the pages, then how did the killer make copies without him realizing it?"

"I don't know," Siobhán said. "But several people pointed out he'd been distracted this week. And there's also the matter of his secret lover . . ."

"Which we now know is Helen," Macdara said. "At least the CCTV from the Charlesville Hotel heavily suggests it."

"We're making progress," Aretta said. "Baby steps."

Siobhán eyed Macdara and Aretta. "I feel as if you two have discovered something."

"We cannot get anything past you," Aretta said with a smile.

"Even with pregnancy brain," Siobhán quipped. She turned to Macdara. "Well?"

"Aretta's been going through the photos folks have sent in from the opening night of the festival," Macdara said. "But that's enough for tonight. I think we should get you out of that hair straitjacket and into bed. But bright and early tomorrow morning, there's something you have to see."

Chapter 20

The next morning, bright and early, as promised, Siobhán and Macdara sat in the kitchen in front of her laptop.

"I thought you were going to the café to see if you could find the archery flier?"

Macdara pointed at the screen. "It might not be necessary."

"I'm listening."

"Aretta went through hundreds of photos," Macdara said, as he brought up the screen. Sure enough, each frame was filled with shots of the town square jammed with people. He scrolled down past numerous photos until he found what he was looking for. "Here." He pointed to a person walking down Sarsfield Street. It was a man but his back was to the camera.

"I don't understand," Siobhán said. "There's no way of knowing who that is. And what's suspicious about him?"

Macdara zoomed in. There was writing on the back of his jacket: FÁINNE NA SAIGHEAD.

"The Ring of Arrows," Siobhán translated.

"We looked it up. It's an archery just outside of town."

"That is a great catch," Siobhán said. "Well done, Aretta," she said to the air. She would repeat it in person later. Siobhán brought her attention back to the photo. She spotted a little person walking next to the man in the archery jacket. He had a violin case in one hand. "I think that's Oscar O'Brien. The Wee Stringman."

"The one who snatched the bow from Niall and snapped it in two?"

"The one and the same." Jim McVeigh had mentioned something about Oscar's business. She should have followed up on it earlier. "I think Oscar owns the archery."

"Interesting."

"Isn't it?" This was most likely the archery that was passing out the flier for free lessons. It would be easy enough to find out.

"Jeanie Brady is coming today. She's going to pick up the lipstick tube and sample you collected first—she thinks it shouldn't take long to compare the tube to the markings on his neck. And then after our visit with her I say you and I visit this archery."

"I could stand to do a little shooting," Siobhán said.

"Shooting?" Nancy Flannery called out from the other room. "Around the babies?"

"A bow and arrow, Mam," Macdara called. "The sport of archery."

"She could get stuck with an arrow," Nancy said. "It's too dangerous."

"You could put someone's eye out with it," Macdara teased. "Thank you for your concern, Mam. If any arrow comes flying at her, I'll gladly step in front of her."

Nancy appeared in the doorway. "I know you'd do anything to protect my grandchildren."

"And me," Siobhán said. She turned to Macdara. "Right?"

He grinned. "I'd gladly take an arrow for all of ye."

* * *

Jeanie Brady was due to arrive any time now. Siobhán was currently in Blooms, the local flower shop where three single men and three single women were putting together flower arrangements. Ron would then pair each arrangement made by a single woman with each made by a single man—whichever two looked like they would make a nice match. Then, the singles would pair up in the same way. Ron was holding a clipboard and walking among the participants. They were all set up in their own corners, with vases, ribbons, and cut flowers on the work spaces in front of them. They were spread out to give each privacy as they put together their arrangements.

"Why does making similar floral arrangements make them good as a couple?" Siobhán asked Ron. She was genuinely curious.

"Impulsivity, choices, and favorite colors," he said. "You'd be surprised what you could learn about a person—are they lavish or simple? Manicured or wild? Dark or light?"

"Interesting," she said. It seemed they were going to be at this for a while. It was a good time to have a longer chat with Ron. "No sign of Liam's Lucky Book?"

His eyes widened. "Why are you asking me?"

"We need to have a chat. It can either be here, and we keep our voices low, or you'll have to find someone to take over this event." She hardly thought they needed to be micromanaged while placing flowers in a vase.

Ron sighed. "Everyone," he announced. "I'm going to step outside. You have twenty minutes to complete your arrangements." He nodded to Siobhán, and they proceeded to the back patio. Blooms had done a magnificent job staging the area, and even though it was a relatively small patio, it was covered, making it more like a small greenhouse, and filled to the brim with blooming flowers and decor. A fountain in the center of the patio stole the spotlight. Ron gravitated to it, then stared into the water. "Fire away."

"I need to know if you or Grace are aware that several of the matched musicians received photocopied pages from Liam's Lucky Book last Monday evening."

Ron turned to her, a look of surprise stamped on his face. He shook his head. "Why would Liam do that?"

"I don't believe Liam did. I think someone managed to get ahold of the book while he was still alive."

Ron frowned. "Normally I would say that's impossible—"

"But?"

"But he'd been funny that last week. Distracted. If there was ever a time to snatch the book, that would have been the week."

Siobhán waited a few seconds, but Ron asked no follow-up questions. "You don't want to know what the pages said?"

"If you want to tell me."

"Why don't you take a guess?"

"Detective Sergeant, I mean no disrespect, but I do not think it wise for me to guess. This is a murder inquiry after all."

"Did Grace mention anything about this to you?"

"Grace knew about this?" His face hardened. "I'm going to have to fire her."

"Slow your roll. I haven't spoken with Grace yet." It was also interesting how Ron just promoted himself to Grace's boss. "I was just curious if she mentioned anything."

"If she had, then I would have been lying, when I said I knew nothing about it."

Ron was both evasive and slick. He would have made a good politician. "I never understood why Liam needed to keep Grace around. Other than have someone who adored him and would answer his beck and call."

"Do you really think you have the right to take Liam's

place? Aren't there family members who will now want control of the business?"

"None of the remaining members of Liam's family have ever shown any interest in the business. I suppose I will have to start my own—with a new name—so technically, it would be all mine."

"In that sense, one could say you stood to benefit from Liam's death." It was a rather harsh thing to say, and if this were anything other than a murder inquiry, as Ron himself pointed out, she would never have been so blunt. But sometimes you had to stir the pot and see what rose to the surface.

"You said the musicians found these pages Monday evening. At the session, was it?" Ron hadn't reacted to her comment at all. He was either so absorbed in his own thoughts, he didn't register what she said, or he simply refused to take the bait.

"Yes. It was Monday at the session." A look flickered across his face, as if he'd just thought of something. Once again, Siobhán waited, but he did not say another word. She found this behavior odd. Most people, if innocent, wanted to tell the guards everything they knew so that they wouldn't seem suspicious. It took effort not to talk. Ron was monitoring himself. He looked at his watch.

"I'd better get back in there."

"Right. Thank you for your time."

He hurried away from her. She took out her mobile phone. It wouldn't hurt to have Aretta tail him the rest of the day. With a little luck, they would find out why Siobhán had just triggered him and what he was going to do about it.

"We can meet with the archer tomorrow morning," Macdara said. "It was his soonest opening."

"That works," Siobhán said. "Jeanie texted me, and she's here."

"Is she in the square?"

"No. She's at a session."

"Work and play, is that it?" Macdara said. "After driving through yesterday's storm, I can't say I blame her."

"She also wanted to speak with Jim McVeigh about the murder weapon, and she added that she wouldn't want to miss a chance to see the Wee Stringman."

"We've been missing our chances to see him as well."

"Two birds, one stone?"

"Just don't tell Jeanie you're including her with that stone."

Siobhán laughed. "She'd understand my meaning."

"You go ahead—I'm bringing Edward Kavanaugh in for questioning. Confront him about the Lucky Pages and see how he changes his tune." Macdara grinned. "See what I did there?"

Siobhán laughed. "Are you bringing him into the station?"

Macdara nodded. "So far, we've kept it casual. I think it's time to go official."

"Will you be calling all of the suspects in for a formal interview?"

"That's the plan."

"Brilliant. Good luck."

"Thanks," Macdara said. "With this lot, I'm going to need it."

Siobhán found Dr. Jeanie Brady at a booth in Fitzgerald's. She sat in front of a pint, fingers tapping on the table, lost in the music. "You just missed the Wee Stringman," she said. "He was brilliant."

"We are two ships that pass in the night," Siobhán said as she took a seat across from her. "You're looking well."

"Ah, stop. You're the one who's glowing." Jeanie winked.

"I'm downright radioactive," Siobhán quipped. They

laughed. Jeanie did look good, and she was as cheerful as ever with her bright eyes and brown curls. "Are we good to have a chat here?" Jeanie asked. "Or is the music too distracting?"

"It's grand," Siobhán said. "And no one will be able to hear us." They were tucked away in a back corner, and everyone else was focused on the music.

"You were right about something," Jeanie said. "It *was* glow in the dark lipstick." She leaned forward. "And the shade in the tube you supplied is an exact match."

"That's huge," Siobhán said. "There are only two people who might have shared that lipstick."

"It's not advisable to share makeup," Jeanie said. "But then again nobody asked me."

"They're twin sisters," Siobhán said. "It's possible one nicked the tube from the other."

"Twins," Jeanie said, eyeing Siobhán. "How interesting." Jeanie knew all about Siobhán's pregnancy but was too polite to ask her outright if she was now worried that this was some kind of bad omen. And although Siobhán was not prone to superstition, there was a big part of her praying that one or both of these twins were not murderers.

"In order to see the lipstick in the dark, how close would our killer have been standing in relation to Liam?"

"Only a stone's throw away."

"I figured as much, especially with how precise the arrow hit."

"You're not wrong. Direct to the heart."

Just thinking about it gave Siobhán goose bumps. "Am I safe in concluding that the killer purchased the lipstick for that very reason? To orientate them in the dark before they let the arrow fly?"

"I see why you're thinking that way, but there is an issue."

"A matter of timing, isn't it?" Siobhán said. Jeanie nodded.

"If the killer were the wearer of the lipstick, there wouldn't be enough time to kiss him on the neck, and then rush to retrieve the bow and arrow from wherever they hid it, and then shoot."

"Exactly," Jeanie said. "We did a fade test with the lipstick. After just five minutes, it begins to fade on the skin considerably."

"That's puzzling."

"It could be seen for as long as thirty minutes—it just grows fainter after five."

"I saw Liam at least thirty minutes before he died. I didn't notice any lip prints on his neck." He'd been wearing a T-shirt and his neck had been clearly visible.

"You may think you would have noticed it, but remember it glows in the dark. You saw him when the lights were still on."

"That's true. I could have missed it." Siobhán mulled it over. "But it's not definitive either way. The killer might have been the one to kiss him on the neck—in which case our killer is a woman—or the woman who kissed him is not our killer at all, she's simply a lover being affectionate with her man."

"Or," Jeanie said. "The killer kissed his neck after he was already dead."

Siobhán gasped. "Why would someone do that?"

"If our killer is a man—he did it so that you would only suspect women."

"Could you tell anything by the shape of the lips?"

"Unfortunately, it was only a partial, smudged print. I cannot draw any conclusions from it."

"Can you identify the lip prints? DNA? Ridges?"

"Lips, like fingerprints, do have unique ridge patterns. But I would have needed a clear enough impression. In that situation I could photograph it under magnification, then enhance the image with forensic filters and then compare it to a suspect's lip pattern. But it's not an accepted form of ID in court, I'm afraid. At least not yet. But all that is moot. The print is smudged."

"What about DNA?"

"Lipstick can trap epithelial cells from the kisser's lips—and yes, that means DNA. Even if the glow-in-the-dark pigment is present, it shouldn't prevent collection of biological material underneath. If we swabbed the lipstick mark carefully and ran it through the system, we might get a hit. But only if the suspect is already in the database."

"The chances of that are slim."

Jeanie nodded. "And the process would take time. But I've already gone ahead and submitted a swab, just in case."

Siobhán wasn't surprised to hear that Jeanie was on the ball. "If the lipstick wasn't used as a shooting guide, how did the killer plan on hitting his or her target in the dark?"

"You see—this is why I'm glad that part of the job is yours to handle. There was nothing on the shirt in the area of the heart that could have guided the killer. So your original theory about the lipstick acting as a guide could be correct. Or if the killer and the kisser are not the same person, the killer got lucky."

"All might not be lost. Just because *we* know that the findings cannot point to our killer, our killer doesn't know that."

"There's the Siobhán O'Sullivan I know and love," Jeanie said, raising her pint. They took a moment to share a laugh.

"Anything else?"

"I was hoping you'd ask. While I was waiting for you, I had a chat with your man there." She nodded to Jim McVeigh, who was currently playing in the session.

"About?"

"The murder weapon." Siobhán took out her notebook and waited. "It was a hybrid. The killer used the bow of the double bass but attached an arrowhead to the end. *An instrument of death.* "I spoke with Jim about what it would have taken to craft, and it wouldn't have required much. The killer removed the frog and the horse hair"—

"Frog?" Siobhán knew the strings were made of horse hair, but she'd never heard of a frog.

"It's the little part you hold on the bow."

"Got it. I've learned something new."

"You and me both." She took a moment to watch the session and spoke as she did. "The bow was already shaped much like an arrow and configuring it would have taken minimal tools and less than an hour."

"Is it something that could have been done in one of the rooms at the Kilbane Inn?"

"Easily. The arrowhead was attached with epoxy and the killer even added a small weight near the arrowhead for the right balance. This tells me they knew at least a little bit about archery. And really that's a given—from the accuracy of the shot and all. And the tools needed? Screwdriver, knife, pliers, and the glue. That's it."

"The bow belonged to McVeigh but there were also reports it was broken in half. I'm surprised it still worked."

"The killer glued the pieces back together, then used duct tape, cloth, and a few feathers to bind it."

"Feathers?"

"Attached to the back end. Helps it fly—gives it stability."

"Unless the killer had back-up arrows, he or she was confident enough in him or herself that he or she only brought one arrow."

"And he or she was correct."

"So we're talking about an experienced archer?"

"Either that, or the killer did plenty of homework and then just happened to get lucky."

"If that's the case," Siobhán said, "we better hope their luck has run out."

Chapter 21

Bright and early the next morning, Siobhán and Macdara headed off for the grand manor house that now served as a luxury hotel complete with archery lessons. It was a two-hour drive, which gave them time to discuss the case. "What did Edward have to say for himself?"

"He canceled. Said he had a stomach bug and was staying in the motel room all day."

"I wonder if that was a lie."

"He said it was something he ate."

"I wonder if it was really something he *did*." Was this a guilty conscience?

"I wasn't going to test the theory, but he's definitely on my radar." Macdara reached over and took her hand. "When this case is over, we should have a little weekend away."

"We have the baby shower coming up. In Lahinch."

"I forgot about that. Grand."

"And Emma and Eileen coerced me into letting them throw me one here."

"How did Gráinne take that?"

"I'll let you know when she finds out."

"How are you feeling?" Macdara had been judicious about asking her, and Siobhán appreciated that.

"I haven't felt sick since the time I almost fertilized the plant in the café," she said with a laugh.

"Brilliant," Macdara said. "Personally, I'm having cravings for ice cream, so we'll have to rectify that today."

"I'll join you," Siobhán said. "Just so you don't have to suffer through it alone."

The rest of the way their conversation switched to the twins and all the challenges and joys ahead of them. They'd only started tossing names at one another, but so far none of them had resonated. Macdara liked Ronan and Nolan for boys, and Siobhán liked Ronan but not Nolan. She was partial to Aidan as an additional boy name. For girls they liked Ciara and Quinn or maybe Orla. Middle names would be Naomi and Liam after Siobhán's parents. The two hours flew by, and soon they were pulling into a long winding drive to the manor house.

Oscar O'Brien was expecting them, but when they arrived, he was still teaching an archery lesson. A horizontal line of people stood with their bows and arrows aimed at targets about ten meters away. From the looks of terror on their faces and the awkward way the students were holding their bows and arrows, this was definitely a lesson for beginners. Today was the last day of the weekend festivities and Siobhán felt they were no closer to solving the crime. She felt anxious to return to Kilbane and hoped they could get the information they needed from Oscar in a timely manner. For now, they stood off to the side to watch the lesson.

"Everybody check your stance. Stand sideways to the target, feet shoulder-width apart. Pull back, concentrate on the target, and let her fly." The line of people standing with bows and arrows followed the Wee Stringman's commands, and soon multiple arrows were flying through the air toward their targets. Most of them missed. Oscar had a makeshift stand from which he stood watching over his students. When they caught his eye, he acknowledged them with a nod and held up a finger. "Use up your arrows and then we'll take a break," he announced to the students. "Don't forget—no one collects their arrows until you hear my command. What's the command?"

"All clear," the group replied.

"That's right," Oscar said. "You wait for the 'all clear.' " He nodded to a man standing behind him and climbed down from his stand. "Gary is going to finish out today's lesson with you. And remember the first rule. "What's the first rule?" He pointed to a woman to his left.

"Always point your bows downrange, never at people," she said.

"Smart woman. You've got this." He approached Siobhán and Macdara, and they shook hands. "Would you like to find a quiet place to chat?"

"Do you mind if I watch for a minute?" Siobhán asked. She found it fascinating.

"Would you like to try?" Oscar asked.

"Can I?"

"Of course." He gestured to the group. "They'll be finished in the next ten minutes and you can have your choice of targets."

"This is your basic recurve bow," Oscar said, as he handed it over to Siobhán. "And we've sized the bows to your draw length. Are your arm guards and finger tabs secure?" He had taken her into the store located behind the manor house, outfitted her with all the equipment, and had run through the basics of holding it.

"They're secure," Siobhán said. Had the killer worn the same protective gear? She lifted the bow, feeling the weight of it in her arms, and tried to center her grip. Just holding it steady took a surprising amount of forearm strength.

"When you're ready you're going to place the arrow. Do you see the arrow rest?"

"This indentation here?" Siobhán asked, pointing to a groove at the end of the shaft.

"That's the one. It's called a nock. You'll hear a distinct click when it fits into the space."

Siobhán placed the arrow into the nock and heard the click. "Got it."

"Now. I'm taking you through the steps, but in the future you only nock an arrow when you're on the shooting line and it's your turn."

"Understood."

"This is your first time, correct?"

"Correct."

"Stand sideways, feet shoulder-length apart. When you pull the arrow back, your body is going to form the letter T. It might look easy to draw back, but it's deceptive. It's at least a stone of draw weight. You'll be using muscles in your upper back and shoulders you didn't know you had."

"I believe you."

"I'm going to talk you through pulling it back, and then you can practice. You use three fingers to pull the bow back. Index, middle, and ring. Index goes above the arrow. You're going to raise your bow arm—that's the one holding the bow—toward the target. The string is going to resist. You need to strike a balance between forcing it and coaxing it. When you draw it back, you want to keep going until your fingers reach a point near your mouth, jaw, or chin. That's called the anchor point."

"Anchor point." Siobhán felt a rush of excitement. When was the last time she'd learned something new?

"It's going to feel awkward at first. If it does—that means you're doing it right." Siobhán took a deep breath, held the bow in the lifted position and pulled. As promised, it took quite a bit of strength and her arm shook as she held it in position. "Well done," he said. "Try it a few more times."

Siobhán practiced pulling the arrow back. On the third time he stopped her. "Good. Now we're going to shoot. Focus on the target, not on the arrow tip. You can keep both eyes open or you can close your nondominant one. You're going to relax your fingers and let the string slip free—this isn't a fiddle or guitar lesson—don't pluck it."

"I don't play either, so no worries there."

Oscar laughed. "Sorry, I'm used to working with musicians. Let your hand drift back naturally and keep your bow arm steady. And you're going to want to follow through—meaning do not drop your bow arm immediately after the shot."

Siobhán managed to release the arrow then watched it fly wildly off course and miss the target. "Again," Oscar said. "Next arrow." She shot until all six of her arrows were depleted. It was fun but none of them hit the target. She sighed as she set the bow down.

"I'll have the lads fetch your arrows," Oscar said. "What did you think?"

"I think it must take a lot of practice." The killer had been doing this for quite some time.

He winked. "Believe it or not, you did pretty good for a beginner."

"Good work," Macdara called out. Siobhán gave him a look and he laughed.

"Now," Oscar said. "I take it you want to have a chat about something else?"

"We do," Macdara said, approaching. "Is there a quiet place we can talk?"

"The restaurant here is top-notch," Oscar said. "And quiet this time of day."

Macdara lit up at the thought of eating. "Lead the way."

* * *

"I did hear that the murder weapon was made from the bow of Jim's double bass, alright," Oscar said. "But I have no idea what to make of that." They were seated in the grand dining room, which was indeed quiet at this time of day. A wall of windows overlooked the lush grounds. This was a destination for the wealthy. "You should see the view in the evening," Oscar said. "It's hopping." He was seated on a makeshift booster chair; it was carved of wood and blended in seamlessly. A server appeared and made his way over. Oscar ordered a pot of tea, three cups and "a sandwich tree." He leaned forward. "What do ye make of the case?" he asked. "Any idea who did it?"

"We're only at the beginnings of our inquiries," Macdara said. "But we understand a bit of trouble broke out last Monday evening in Fitzgerald's. Between yourself and Niall O'Malley."

"The fiddle player? The conniving double bass thief?"

"That's the one," Siobhán said. Had there been so much trouble that evening that Oscar wasn't confident who they were speaking about? Or was he stalling? If it was the latter, this often indicated deception. Making up lies took time.

"It's no secret I have a bit of a temper," Oscar said. He glanced at Siobhán. "I hear you can relate."

Before Siobhán could respond—to either Oscar or the smirk from her husband, the waiter reappeared, rolling a cart. Atop it sat a teapot, three cups, and a makeshift stand shaped like a tree. Every layer was covered in finger sandwiches. Macdara began to hum as he took it all in. Siobhán placed her hand on her belly. *If you want to wrap your father around your little fingers, know that food is always a quick way to his heart . . .*

"I think it's just the stereotype that follows me around," Siobhán said. "About redheads having tempers." She'd purposefully waited until Macdara had taken a bite of a sandwich. He froze in place, no doubt making sure he didn't choke on it.

"Same with fiddle players," Oscar said. "We're known to be aggressive."

"My brother Ciarán is a fiddle player," Siobhán said. "Although as far as aggression he's a late bloomer."

Oscar leaned his head back and laughed. "We only bloom when the tunes are flowing."

"Can you take us through that Monday evening?" Siobhán said. "Including whether or not you happened to notice anyone lurking about the pile of coats and instrument cases in the back of the pub."

Oscar raised an eyebrow, then held up a finger, as Macdara poured them all tea. Oscar then pointed to the milk and sugar, and Siobhán waited as he poured them into his cup and began stirring slowly. He was definitely stalling.

"Due to my stature, when there's a large crowd as there was Monday night, my sightlines are greatly diminished."

"I never even thought of that," Siobhán said. "I'm sorry."

"No apologies necessary. I understand that unless you have a little person in your life, well, you don't know what you don't know."

"Well said," Macdara said, in between bites. Siobhán eyed the sandwiches. She was hungry, but she was also afraid to take any chances—she was starting to feel a bit queasy.

"You brought your fiddle with you that evening, is that correct?"

Oscar nodded. "Correct."

"By any chance did anyone slip—a note, or anything at all into your case?"

Oscar shook his head. "No. Why? Did someone else receive a note?" He sounded excited at the prospect.

Macdara set his tea down. "Unfortunately, we will be asking you questions today but not answering them."

Oscar held up his hands. "You caught me. I'm sorry. I

admit it—I'm a mad one for gossip. But of course, I understand."

"Why don't you tell us what led up to the incident between yourself and Niall," Macdara said.

Oscar raised an eyebrow. "His assistants didn't tell you?"

"Assistants?" Siobhán asked. "You mean Grace and Ron?"

"That's them," Oscar said. "The entire 'incident' was a setup." Siobhán and Macdara stared at Oscar. He stared back.

"A setup?" Siobhán repeated. Oscar aimed a finger gun at her, winked, and nodded.

"We're going to need a bit more detail," Macdara said.

Oscar gestured with his sandwich. "Here's what I think went down. Liam Noone wanted to cause a bit of drama. I suppose it was his way of getting everyone's attention. Niall was instructed to take Jim McVeigh's double bass and start their own trad session—competing with ours, mind you—and then I was to storm over and yank the bow out of Niall's hands. Which I did. I stirred the pot, and it seemed to work—everyone was focused now on them—thus knocking the first session out of commission while everyone focused on the 'argument.' "

This rendition was knocking Siobhán for a loop. "Liam staged the entire thing?" She was having trouble believing it.

"Why on earth would Liam want to cause that kind of disturbance?" Macdara asked.

Oscar shrugged. "I guess all publicity is good publicity."

"That's categorically untrue," Siobhán continued. "Why did you agree to do this?" She wasn't sure she believed him, but calling anyone a liar was rarely a good interviewing technique.

"I was paid," Oscar said. "In cash."

"How much?" Siobhán was genuinely curious. Liam seemed more the type to ask—or blackmail—for money, and if Oscar was to be believed, here he was giving it out.

"Five hundred euro," Oscar said. "Hard cash." He grinned.

The same amount Liam had offered to Jim McVeigh before he realized the true worth of the bow and was forced to give him a harp instead. But this offer made no sense at all to Siobhán. Had Liam been the one delivering the blackmail pages? Was he using this distraction to do it? Instead of dueling pianos he wanted dueling sessions? She had no doubt that during the argument, no one was paying attention to the pile of instruments in the back of the room. "Did you question Liam at all about his reasons for wanting this kind of disruption?" Siobhán pressed.

"I'm a musician," he said. "And no stranger to drama. All I can tell you is that it was a fun role. And that bow snapped easily which is not normally the case. They're built to be strong. When this one cracked like an egg it solidified that this was all staged. That bow had to be messed with beforehand."

"Messed with, how?" Macdara asked.

Oscar shrugged. "All I can tell you is it was weak and broke easily."

"Liam Noone personally told you to destroy property?" Siobhán wanted to make sure she was hearing this correctly.

"It was conveyed to me, but the message came from Liam."

"Conveyed to you how?" Macdara asked before she could.

"Through Barry. The publican."

"The bartender told you to do this?"

"No. The bartender was given a note from Liam to pass on to me."

Barry hadn't said a word about this. "Do you know for a certainty that Liam Noone was behind this?"

"I know for a certainty that the publican handed me a note and said it was from the matchmaker."

"We're going to need to see that note," Macdara said.

Oscar shook his head. "I tossed it. When your one seemed startled that I took the bow—well, I started to think there was something funny about the whole thing. I felt used."

"Where did you toss this note?" Siobhán asked.

A sheepish look came over his face. "The toilet." He grimaced. "If you don't mind, not a word to the publican. He'll give out to me—in front of everyone, he'll ask me if I can read." He put on a pinched face. "What's the matter with ya? Can you not read? Are you soft in the head?" His imitation of Barry wasn't bad.

"I'm missing something," Macdara said. "What does reading have to do with tossing the note in the toilet?"

Oscar sighed. "That's about another note. This one taped to wall in the jax. Big poster." Oscar stretched out his arms in either direction. "Threatens you with death if you throw anything other than toilet paper in the 'throne.' " He shook his head in disgust. "*Throne.*"

"Then why did you toss the note in?" Macdara asked.

The sheepish look intensified. "Because of the fecking note. Like we're all five years of age and need to be taught how to use the toilet." He shook his head. "I'm a bit of a rebel like that."

"Was this note typed or handwritten?" Siobhán asked.

"Handwritten but looked enough like type. Block letters in black ink."

"Why do you think Liam—or whoever was behind this so-called musical coup—choose you to get in the row with Niall?" Macdara asked.

"I suppose when you see a little person coming at you, it seems less threatening than if he sent some giant to snap the bow. Or maybe they knew I had enough muscles from archery to make it snap." He chewed on a sandwich. "Or maybe they took advantage of the fact that I was browned off with the group. Maybe they knew about me reputation for having a temper."

"How did you not know it was Jim's bow and double bass? He brought it specifically to show you."

"I can't tell one bass from another. I mean look at me. Does it look like I play the bass? I'd barely be visible behind the bloody thing."

Oscar O'Brien was turning out to be even cheekier than his reputation. "Then why on earth did you ask him to bring his bass?" Siobhán asked.

Oscar laughed. "You'll love this." He brought out his mobile phone, thumbed through it and showed a photo to Siobhán. It was a bespoke Christmas card. Oscar stood in Fitzgerald's pub behind a double bass with a Santa hat on. He was right, you could barely see him, apart from him sticking his head out and grinning. The card read: HAPPY CHRISTMAS. KISS MY BASS.

"What took place first? Did you get the note instructing you to do this first, or did you ask McVeigh to see the bass first?"

"Monday morning, I asked McVeigh about the bass. I know Christmas isn't for a few months but I want a good card this year, so I'm making several. This way I can see which one is the best." He put his phone away. "I think that's the one, alright."

"Monday morning you asked to see the bass, so when did you get the note from Liam?" Siobhán pressed.

"Ah, right. You're a real stickler for the details, aren't ya?" He tapped his chin with his index finger and stared at the ceiling. "McVeigh brought the bass Monday evening, and Barry handed me the note about a half an hour later."

Had the killer thought of this on the spot? That seemed like a stretch. This entire case was maddening.

"I take it Jim didn't know about Niall's plans to nick it or your plans to snap the bow?" Macdara asked.

"I was told another yoke brought a double bass, and I didn't dream one of the newcomers would be so bold as to steal McVeigh's bass. I wouldn't have snapped it if I knew it was worth ten thousand euro. I might be a rebel, but I'm no fool."

"Ten thousand euro?" Macdara said. "For a bow?"

"That's what *I* said," Siobhán exclaimed. "But apparently if you have Brazilian wood and it's crafted in France a hundred years before you're born, it's a big deal."

"Learn something every day," Macdara said. He turned to Oscar. "So you snapped a bow worth ten thousand euro."

Oscar bared his bottom teeth. "I felt bad about that, sure I did. But I heard Liam made it right."

Macdara looked to Siobhán. "He gave McVeigh a thirteen thousand euro harp," she explained. "Although to be fair, in return he gave Grace a chord zither."

"A chord zither," Macdara repeated.

"It's an autoharp. And before you ask—no, it doesn't play all by itself like a player piano. It simply has a button that makes it easier to play chords."

Oscar seemed intent on their conversation, happily ping-ponging his gaze from one to the other, a finger sandwich in each hand.

"What happened to you?" Macdara asked Siobhán. "It's like those children who hit their head and end up speaking a foreign language."

Oscar pointed a sandwich at Macdara and nodded.

"I may not have an ear for music," Siobhán said, "but I guess I've got one for the lingo."

"One last question," Macdara said. "Didn't it strike you as odd that Liam would spend all this money just in order to create a scene in the pub, and stir up bad publicity?"

"You know what they say. No publicity is bad publicity."

"You know how Liam Noone was murdered—is it your expert opinion that the killer is most likely an experienced archer?" Siobhán was eager to hear the question.

"That one just said 'last question,' " Oscar said.

"Well, it's a good thing I'm asking ya then, isn't it?"

Oscar tipped his index finger to her with a bow of his head. "I don't know how close this killer was standing in relation to the matchmaker, but if it was a precise shot? In the dark? You can bet it was an experienced archer."

Siobhán turned to Macdara. "You really shouldn't have said 'last question,' because I have one more."

"Fire away," Oscar said. "Pun intended."

"Do you know if any of the musicians are archers?"

Oscar shook his head. "Apart from that one stunt with Niall O'Malley, I've had no interaction with them."

Siobhán sighed. "I guess I'm done."

Macdara nodded. "Thank you for your time." Himself and Siobhán stood at the same time. Macdara set down fifty euro. "For the tea and sandwiches."

"I'll need another fifty," Oscar said. "For the archery lesson."

Siobhán frowned. "I thought you were giving away free lessons?"

"Free lessons? What do I look like? A charity shop?"

"Someone said they saw fliers around town advertising free lessons."

"Huh," Oscar said. "That explains the look on their faces when I collected the fee."

Chapter 22

Today's sessions were being played at multiple venues in Kilbane and the singles were encouraged to dance and mingle. Grace, it seemed, had talked Ron out of making official matches, as this was more of a tribute to Liam, and she pointed out it would be up to his next of kin to choose another matchmaker to take over the business, if that's what they wished to do. Ron looked none too happy about it, but he acquiesced and instead encouraged all the participants to write down their preferred match and hand it to him. He promised to notify the couples who chose each other. Siobhán took a moment to peek in on Ciarán who was dancing to jigs and reels in Fitzgerald's. Her jaw nearly touched the floor when she saw he was dancing with Sara O'Grady. The very redhead he had denied being interested in. She exited straight away so that she wouldn't ruin the vibe, a smirk clearly planted on her face.

Edward Kavanaugh had miraculously recovered from his stomach bug and had agreed to be interviewed at the garda station. They set him up in Interview Room 1 and made him wait, albeit they offered him tea and biscuits which he accepted. Siobhán was more convinced than ever that the stomach bug was a lie. By the time Siobhán and Macdara walked in, he was sweating and the tin of biscuits was empty.

"I'm the only one you brought into the station for questioning," Edward said. "Why is that?" He was trying to sound confident, but his voice wobbled.

"Sometimes there's a good place to talk, and sometimes there isn't," Siobhán said. "Today is the last day of the activities, and afterward, we'll all have dinner at The Six, but for now we have to stay downtown, and all the pubs have sessions going on."

"The Six?"

"It's a local restaurant," Siobhán said. "Best in town." It was true. She also loved the commute.

"It's a relief that today is the last day," Edward said. He may not have had a stomach bug, but he certainly looked haggard. Bags and dark circles underneath his eyes, hair unkempt, and a look of unease painted a picture of someone who was not doing well.

Macdara leaned back in his chair. "Why are you relieved that the week is ending?"

"Why?" Edward sounded astonished. Macdara knew the reasons one would wish this week to be over, but often a question was designed to poke the bear. "I think it's morbid that we continued with a love fest after a man was murdered."

"His employees thought Liam would have wanted the festival to continue," Siobhán said. "And they weren't officially matching people—only letting them mingle."

Edward shrugged.

"We're going to give you a chance to confess," Macdara said.

Edward suddenly shot up straight. "Confess?"

"We know you received pages from Liam's Lucky Book on Monday evening," Siobhán said. "What we want to know is, why did you lie about it when we questioned you in the gazebo?"

"How do you know?" he asked. "Róisín?"

"Why did you lie?" Macdara repeated.

Edward shrugged. "First, Liam was dead, so there was no use mentioning it. Second, it was meaningless. There was no real threat."

"You weren't worried about Róisín finding out that you had paid to be her match—when originally it was supposed to be Niall?" Siobhán wanted to make sure he was aware that they knew everything. Everything except why he was so evasive.

"I was not worried about it. She already knew."

"Is that why you weren't worried about it?" Macdara asked. "Or was it because by this time you were making moves on her sister Helen?"

A look of disgust came over Edward's face. "Róisín told you everything, did she?" He stared at them defiantly.

"I don't know," Siobhán said. "Did she?"

Silence. "You're not even going to try and defend yourself?" Macdara asked.

"Is it against the law to fall in love with your girlfriend's sister?" Edward asked.

"Maybe it's not against the law, but it could be a motive for murder," Siobhán said.

Edward frowned. "And how do you figure that?"

"Love triangles are always messy," Siobhán said.

"Yeah? And what does that have to do with Liam?"

"I heard that pipers are quiet," Siobhán said. "But you're rather cheeky."

"I guess you heard wrong then."

"If I were you, I'd start showing a little more respect," Macdara said.

"Sorry." He didn't sound it.

"I actually wasn't talking about a love triangle between yourself and two sisters," Siobhán said. "I was talking about a love triangle between yourself, Helen, and Liam Noone."

"What?" He sounded genuinely shocked. "What are you on about?"

"Let's go back to Monday evening after the row at Fitzgerald's," Macdara said. "Did anything happen later that evening? When you got to the inn?"

"I still don't understand why you think Helen, myself, and Liam were in a love triangle. That simply isn't true."

"We don't need to supply you with answers," Siobhán said. "What happened after you returned to the inn on Monday evening?"

He shook his head. "Nothing. Walked around the grounds for a bit. Went to bed."

"That's interesting," Macdara said. "We heard you got in your car and drove somewhere."

Edward looked stricken. "Right," he said. "That." His gaze flicked between Siobhán and Macdara.

"I drove to see if there was a market open. We needed some snacks."

"And did you find one open?" Siobhán asked. Every place in Kilbane bar a petrol station would have been closed.

"Nah," he said. "Just drove around."

"It was awfully late to just drive around," Macdara said. "Especially after such a long day."

"I don't know what to tell you," Edward said. "Sometimes I get a notion to do something and I just do it."

That was a lie. He knew to tell them everything but the truth.

"Let's jump to the night of the murder," Macdara said, opening a folder in front of him. Siobhán knew the page he was looking at had nothing to do with the investigation, but it might help keep Edward on edge if he thought they had a file on him.

"What about it?" Edward said. "The lights suddenly went out, and next thing I knew I heard someone screaming over that lousy harp."

"You're not a fan of the harp?" Siobhán asked.

"She couldn't have picked more generic songs."

"Where were you standing when the lights went out?" Siobhán asked. "Be as precise as possible."

"I was having a pint at Fitzgerald's," Edward said. "I was thirsty."

That should be easy enough to check.

"Give us a minute," Macdara said, gathering his folder and nodding to Siobhán. She stood and they headed for the door.

"You're not going to be long, are you?" Edward said. "I'd like to join some of the last sessions."

"Only a minute," Macdara said. Out in the hall they leaned against the wall.

"He's lying and omitting," Siobhán said.

Macdara nodded. "I know—which is why I say we let him go, and one of us follows him to see what he does."

"Brilliant," Siobhán said. "I'll do it." She was feeling antsy, and she wasn't nauseous for a change.

"Be careful," Macdara said.

"Seriously?" Siobhán said. "You don't think I could take on a piper?"

Macdara laughed. "You're right," he said. "He's the one that should be careful."

Most police officers know that stakeouts are usually a whole lot of nothing. Siobhán was planted on Sarsfield Street across from Fitzgerald's Pub. She was partially hidden under an awning, away from any streetlights. If anyone looked over, they might be able to see someone in the shadows but it would be hard to identify her. Edward had been inside for the past half hour. Siobhán was debating whether or not to go inside when the door opened and he appeared. He stood in front of the pub staring at his phone. Was he waiting for someone? She waited and watched him waiting and watching. Nobody ever said detective work was always thrilling. She had a sudden craving for curried chips, but Murphy's Law said that if she dared leave her post that's when something would happen. Sure enough, five minutes later a woman exited the pub and stood next to Edward. It was either Róisín or Helen. Edward opened his arms to hug her, but she put her hand out to stop him. The two began to argue. From inside the pub, Siobhán could hear trad music starting up, and their voices began to rise over it.

"Liar," the woman said. "I have proof."

Róisín. It had to be her. Was the "proof" that Edward had made moves on her sister? Because if it was Helen—then what was Edward lying about and what proof did she have? As if sensing her presence, they suddenly lowered their voices and began to look around. Siobhán was contemplating crossing to the other side of the street when they parted ways. Róisín—if indeed it was her—headed back inside the pub, and Edward continued down the street. Siobhán crossed over and began following from a distance. Edward was getting into a car a few meters away. Siobhán hadn't considered that he would take off in a vehicle. But she should have. She wasn't on her game. Her squad car was all the way back at the garda station. It was too late: Edward had already sped off. Someone was in a hurry. Siobhán took out her mobile and dialed a number.

"Kilbane Inn, Emma speaking."

"Hi, Emma, it's Siobhán. I believe one of your guests might be on his way back to the inn, and I was wondering if you could keep a look out and call if a car pulls in—say in the next ten minutes."

There was a moment of silence. "Did this guest do something wrong?"

The twins were sticklers for following the rules. He had done something wrong—he had just lied to Siobhán and Macdara. He said he wanted to go and join one of the last sessions. Instead, he'd argued with either his match or his unrequited love, and screeched away. "Nothing wrong, I just need to know whether to come to the inn or figure out where else he might have gone."

"Isn't he entitled to privacy?"

This had been a mistake. "No one is invading his privacy. He took off before I could call out to him."

"If that's the case, I will have to mention it to him before I call you."

Siobhán sighed. "That's fine. You can tell him I had a few follow-up questions, and I'd appreciate if he remained there until I arrive."

"Not a bother." The phone clicked off. Siobhán turned to head back to the garda station for her squad car. If he arrived at the inn and Emma indeed told him she was looking to speak with him, her stakeout would be over. But if he wasn't there . . . perhaps he was going to the Charlesville Hotel. He had left the inn the first night for several hours. Maybe Siobhán wasn't the only one tailing someone, maybe Edward had been following Helen. And if he was, it was quite possible that he saw Liam Noone go to that hotel one night and not emerge until the next morning. Jealousy was a prime motive for murder.

By the time she reached the station, her phone still had not rung. Should she go to the hotel? Maybe this was all a waste of time. For all she knew, he could be taking a drive. If he and Róisín were fighting that would be something a person might do. Drive around, cool off. She could go back to the pub and ask Róisín if she knew where he was going, but from the way they parted, she probably didn't know. Siobhán was mulling this all over when Macdara came out of the garda station.

"What's the story?"

"Edward took off in a car, so I'm getting the squad car."

"Change of plans." He motioned for her to follow. She did. "I received a call from Jim McVeigh—he's playing over in Fitzgerald's."

"Why did he call?"

"He got an alert on his phone from his security camera. He said someone is nosing around his shop—so he reached into his jacket to get his keys, thinking he'd head over—but his keys were gone."

Interesting. "Edward was in Fitzgerald's for about thirty minutes before he came out. He argued with either Róisín or Helen and then took off in his car."

"You're thinking it was him?"

"I think it's highly likely."

"Why would he want to break into the music shop?"

"That's exactly what I'd like to know."

"This job," Macdara said. "There's never a dull day."

"It's just as well," Siobhán said. "It should prepare us for the twins."

Chapter 23

When they arrived at the shop a familiar car was parked in front of it. "That's Edward's," Siobhán said. She instinctively felt in her pocket for her mobile phone. An image of it lying on the table in the interview room flashed through her mind as she found her pockets empty. "I left my phone at the station."

"We can swing by after this." Macdara pointed to the shop. There wasn't a single light on. "What do you think he's doing in the dark?"

"This killer seems to like the dark," Siobhán said.

Macdara put his finger to his lips and then tried the door. It swung open. They looked at each other. "Do you hear that?" Siobhán listened. From inside came the sound of something methodically ticking, but it was different than a clock. Louder, heavier, methodical.

"It's a metronome," Siobhán said.

Macdara nodded. "That's why it sounds so familiar." When he first started playing the fiddle, Ciarán used a metronome. Siobhán understood that it was an important tool for musicians, but for the casual listener it was torture. The door squeaked as Macdara edged in further. "It's Detective Sergeant Flannery and Detective Sergeant O'Sullivan," he announced. "If someone is in here, identify yourself now."

The only answer was the metronome continuing to tick. "If there was someone here, surely they would shut it off," Siobhán said.

Macdara found a light switch and soon the small shop was illuminated. "Hello? Anyone here?"

"Edward?" Siobhán said. "We know you're in here. Your car is parked right outside."

They scanned the shop. There was no one up front. Siobhán pointed to the back. The ticking was coming from the far corner. They began to quietly make their way toward it. In front of them, a sea of guitars were propped up on stands. Macdara, who was in the lead, came to a sudden stop. He put his arm out. Siobhán peered around it. A man was lying facedown on the floor. Blood pooled from a gash on the back of his head. Propped in the middle of the growing red puddle, was the metronome, also covered in blood. "It's Edward," Siobhán said. She recognized the outfit. They stared at the metronome as it continued to swing back and forth, back and forth, as if marking each second of life that Edward Kavanaugh was never going to live.

Jeanie Brady knelt next to the body while Siobhán and Macdara suited up, and Aretta cordoned off the outside of the shop. Either Róisín or Helen was the last person to speak to Edward, and it was vital not only to find out which one of them it was but also to know what had been said. Why had he come to the shop? Had he planned on stealing something?

It was odd, the coppery smell of blood mixing with the sweet, woody smell of the harp. There was only Edward's car parked in front of the shop. Either the killer had left just before Siobhán and Macdara arrived, or they had parked away from the shop and come on foot.

Jeanie stood. "Looks like one blow to the back of the head with the metronome. The killer used the sharp corner, and the poor man never saw it coming." Siobhán returned to the front of the shop and walked the distance to where Edward had been standing. The stone floors muffled any sound. She then returned to the door and opened it. Just as she thought—it squeaked.

"Could you hear that from where you're standing?" Siobhán asked Jeanie.

"Clear as a bell." *Bell.* Siobhán returned to the door. It was missing its bell.

"What's the story?" Macdara asked.

"Two things. The squeak in the door is obvious. If Edward didn't hear it, either he had a hearing loss or, when he entered, he left the door open behind him."

"That tracks," Jeanie said.

Macdara jotted down a note. "And the second thing?"

"When I visited this shop previously, there was a bell that jangled when the door opened. And now?" She opened and closed the door once more. *Silence.* "What happened to the bell?"

"The killer removed it," Macdara said.

"If that's the case, the killer knew in advance that Edward was going to break into the shop. How is that possible?"

"I never knew musicians could be this devious," Jeanie said. "They seem so happy."

"Until they hit a sour note," Macdara quipped. "And start playing out of tune."

"We need to speak immediately with Róisín and Helen," Siobhán said.

"I'm going to get a few guards to take Edward's car to the impound and conduct a thorough search," Macdara said. "Just in case."

"He was headed toward the back corner of the shop," Jeanie said. They all turned to look at that specific corner. It was filled with sheet music, squeeze-boxes, ukeleles, the harp Liam Noone gave Jim, and smaller harps, which Siobhán knew now to be autoharps.

"There was a full session going on in Fitzgerald's," Macdara said. "When we find out who was playing, we can eliminate some of our suspects."

"Unless they worked in pairs," Siobhán said. "But if Róisín was in the session then we'll know it was Helen he was arguing with on the footpath."

"Edward seemed taken aback when we mentioned a love triangle between himself, Liam, and Helen," Macdara said. "Perhaps he was confronting her?"

"Perhaps," Siobhán said. "But she in turn called Edward a liar and said she had proof."

"Isn't it possible Róisín was playing in the session but took a break to speak with Edward outside?" Macdara asked.

Siobhán nodded. "We'll have to verify whether or not she was in the circle and whether they took a break. Hopefully, the other musicians will remember." Because of the loose nature of trad sessions, musicians could come and go from the circle.

The door opened and Aretta poked her head in. "The funeral director is here for the body."

"Brilliant," Jeanie said. "I'd better get to Cork Hospital, then, although I think we already know how he was killed."

"Jim McVeigh is on his way over," Macdara said. "Maybe he can tell us what Edward might have been after."

Siobhán nodded. "That would definitely help."

"Would you rather stay here and speak with McVeigh, or do you want to bring Róisín and Helen into the station for questioning?"

"Róisín and Helen would be my preference." This time she was going to question them together. That way she could check them on the spot if they gave conflicting answers.

"Niall O'Malley wasn't Edward Kavanaugh's biggest fan," Aretta pointed out.

"This is why we have to question every single one of them again," Siobhán said with a nod. "And when Jim gets here, ask him to carefully check the shop—see if there is anything odd or out of place."

"I'm on the same wavelength," Aretta said.

"We need to keep the murder weapon quiet," Macdara said. "Only the killer knows it was a metronome."

"Absolutely," Siobhán said. They hadn't been able to do that with the bow and arrow, but now they would at least have a slight advantage. She glanced at a clock on the wall shaped like a guitar. It was nearly one in the morning. "Is the session still going on in Fitzgerald's?" The pubs stayed open until 2 A.M.

"It was up until Jim called about the break-in. He said they all agreed to shut down after that."

"I'll head to the Kilbane Inn, then," Siobhán said, "and round up all the usual suspects."

Chapter 24

Siobhán debated whether she should go to the station and get her phone, or go straight to the Kilbane Inn. Since she was going to bring the twins in to the station, she decided on the latter. It took her no time to get there, and minutes later she was pounding on Róisín's door. Her lights were off, and Siobhán was greeted by silence. That's when she noticed something odd. Not a single room had its lights on. That wouldn't have been unusual on a normal day, but these musicians had just been playing a session and couldn't have been back long, so it gave her pause. What were the chances that every single one of them had come back and immediately fallen asleep?

Siobhán tried peeking through the window but the curtains were drawn. She moved over to the next room and knocked on its door. No answer. She repeated this until she had knocked on every single door. There were a few cars parked in the car park but the musicians had been carpooling into town. She debated walking over to Emma and Eileen's dwelling, which was located upstairs from the office next door, but their lights were off too, which meant they wouldn't have a clue as to where all their guests were.

It was possible they were still drinking at the pub, or maybe one of the musicians suggested they continue a trad session at their home. It wasn't unheard of, and given this was the last night of the matchmaking festival it made sense that they wanted to pull an all-nighter. But something was tugging at Siobhán—it all felt wrong. She headed back to her squad car and drove back to the station. She made a beeline for the interview room, where her phone was still sitting on the table. She picked it up and was astonished to see she had a ton of missed calls from Ciarán. She counted twelve. She then looked at her texts. There were six of them, all from Ciarán:

Call me

Sara is with me and she is scared

Where are you?

I think we're being set up

Siobhán!!!!

Her hand trembled as she pulled up Ciarán's number and called him. It went straight to voicemail. She hurriedly texted him:

Left my phone at station. Just came from the music shop. Where are you now?

She stared at the phone, hoping for an immediate reply. Seconds later, she called Macdara. His phone went to voicemail as well. He'd call back as soon as he saw the missed call. She headed to the reception desk and asked the clerk if anyone had called in about anything other than the man breaking into the music shop. The clerk said it was all quiet. If Ciarán had been in real trouble, wouldn't he have called the station? Or Macdara? But the biggest question swirling around her mind—how did Ciarán know about the dead man in the music shop? Was the killer already spreading gossip? Then again, Ciarán said he thought he was being set up. What in the world did that mean? She called his number again and again got voicemail. She would call Eoin. He and

James, and Gráinne, for that matter were night owls. Hopefully, Ciarán would be home with them. She felt familiar little kicks in her stomach. Were the twins picking up on her adrenaline rush?

"Yo," Eoin said, upon answering. "I thought you were asleep upstairs."

"Macdara and I were called out. Listen. Is Ciarán with you?"

"I think he and Sara are still out on the town."

"Will you check his room?"

"What's the story?"

Siobhán sighed. "I've had numerous missed calls from him."

"Walking to his room now . . . James, Gráinne—have you heard from Ciarán?" Siobhán could hear them in the background, but could not make out their answers. "He's not in his room. Want me to give him a call?"

"It's going straight to voicemail," Siobhán said. "I'll look out for him."

"Aretta was called out too—there's something going on, isn't there?"

"When is there not something going on?" Siobhán sighed. "You'll hear about it soon enough. Just . . . lock the doors and stay in. And let me know if you hear from Ciarán."

"Wait," Gráinne yelled in the background.

"Hold on," Eoin said.

Moments later Gráinne was on the phone. "I heard from him about an hour and a half ago. He and Sara were starting the Midnight Scavenger Hunt."

"Midnight Scavenger Hunt? What midnight scavenger hunt?"

"I dunno. If I had to guess I'd say it's a scavenger hunt everyone was doing at midnight."

Cheeky. "Did he say anything else about it? Like where exactly he was going?"

"No. You sound worried. Should we be worried?"

Siobhán sighed. "I don't yet, but I'll let you know when I do." She hung up and exited the station, lightly jogging until she reached Fitzgerald's Pub. She walked in to find only a few stragglers left, and none of them the musicians. She headed for Barry, who had just announced "last call."

"Detective," he said with a grin. "Surprised to see you here this late." He leaned forward. "Is it about the break-in at the music shop?"

He knew about the break-in but not the murder. Maybe the gossip was slightly contained. "I'm hoping you know where all or any of our matched musicians went after the session?"

"You mean the scavenger hunt?"

"Yes. What can you tell me about the scavenger hunt?"

"After the session, the singles and matched musicians, as you call them, all found little clues in their instrument cases. A surprise scavenger hunt."

This was not good. "Who organized it? Was it Ron Gallagher?"

Barry shrugged. "I didn't ask. I assume so—if he's the one organizing all the events."

"Did you see anyone's clue?"

"Let's see . . . I know someone had the churchyard—I didn't see who had it—I just heard them talking about how creepy it was to go to a graveyard at this hour of the night."

It was creepy, alright. And if Siobhán's suspicion was correct and the killer had put all this in motion, they had no idea just how creepy. Had Ciarán been given a clue to the music shop? It would explain his texts. "How long ago was this?"

"I'd say just under two hours now."

The killer wanted to keep everyone busy. The question was—why? "And no one has come back?"

"We close soon—I told them all to take their gear—they weren't planning on coming back."

That meant they had to stash their gear somewhere, which meant some more time eaten up. It looked like she had a date with the graveyard.

The wind howled as Siobhán shone her torch on the weathered headstones. "Hello?" she called. "Is anyone here?"

"Who is it?" she heard a woman's voice whisper. Up ahead, she saw two figures moving in the dark.

"It's Detective Sergeant O'Sullivan, and I need you to come toward me." Considering where they were, it didn't seem right to say her first thought: *Come to the light.*

Moments later Niall O'Malley and Tara McCarthy stood in front of her, their faces stressed. "We've looked everywhere for the next clue," Niall said. "I think someone else might have beat us to it."

"Let me see your first clue," Siobhán said. Niall frowned but dug in his pocket and handed her a slip of paper.

THERE THEY LIE AS IF THEY'RE SLEEPING
THOSE WHO VISIT ARE OFTEN WEEPING
BUT IF THERE'S A MESSAGE THEY WANT TO IMPART
TRY NOT TO LINGER, LEST THOSE ETERNALLY SLEEPING
WAKE IN THE DARK

Creepy but slightly poetic. Was it penned by a songwriter? "It has to mean this graveyard, right?" Niall asked.

"If there's no second clue, I'm afraid someone is messing about," Siobhán said. *A killer.* Possibly one of the two standing in front of her. After all, the killer would want to go along with the crowd.

"What do you mean?" Tara said. "It's not a scavenger hunt if there aren't any more clues."

"That's what I'm trying to tell you," Siobhán said. "There is no scavenger hunt."

Niall cursed. "I told you we should have just gone to bed."

"Before you came to the graveyard, where were you?"

"Fitzgerald's," Niall said. "With everyone else."

"Everyone? Are you sure?"

Niall frowned. "What do you mean?"

"Think carefully—was anyone in your group missing?"

"Edward," Tara said. "One minute he was on the footpath arguing with Róisín, the next he was gone."

"How do you know it was Róisín and not Helen?"

"I can tell them apart," Tara said. "Once you get to know their quirks, their gestures, it's easy. But to answer your question, I'm sure because Helen was standing next to me watching them argue."

"And what happened after Róisín came in from speaking with Edward?"

"Helen and Róisín spoke out on the patio for a few minutes. Then Róisín found her clue, and the two of them left," Tara said.

"What was their clue?"

Tara took her time answering. "I don't know exactly—something about an old mill that's sweetened with time . . ."

The bakery . . . Whoever had written those clues wanted to scatter their suspects in different directions. Cause chaos. Misdirection at its finest. And Siobhán had no choice but to follow the threads. "Do you know who my brother is?" Siobhán asked. "Ciarán O'Sullivan? Fiddle player?"

"I know who he is," Niall said. "He's got the quite the confidence for a young lad."

"Did you see him in Fitzgerald's this evening?"

Niall shook his head. "Doesn't mean he wasn't there. The place was jammers."

"Do you know what anyone else's clues were?"

"No," Tara said. "Once Helen and Róisín announced theirs, everyone flocked to their instrument cases to see if they too had a clue. After that people just started running out of the pub."

"Was there some kind of prize promised?"

Niall shook his head. "But there has to be, right? I mean what else is the point of a scavenger hunt?"

To draw attention away from a killer.

"No one asked Grace or Ron about it?"

"We would have," Tara said. "If we had seen either of them."

"Were they there earlier that evening?"

"Like Niall said—it was jammers. I'm not saying they weren't there, I just didn't see either of them."

"Why would they play a prank like this?" Niall asked. "It's not funny."

"I need the two of you to go straight to the garda station. And unfortunately, it might be a bit of a wait."

"Are we in trouble?" Tara said. "It's not like we disturbed any of the graves."

"You're fine, pet. I just need all of you to gather in one place. Once everyone has reported to the station, we'll take it to my brother's restaurant."

"Ciarán has a restaurant?" Niall asked, his voice thick with disbelief.

"No. My brother Eoin."

"Will you please tell us what this is about?" Tara pleaded.

"In good time. Do I need to see you to the garda station myself?"

Niall shook his head. "We'll go."

"Thank you. I need you to head straight there."

Niall took Tara's hand. She yanked it back. He shook his head and headed out. Tara followed at a distance. As soon as their car pulled out, Siobhán called the station and alerted them that participants would start showing up. Just then

Macdara called. Siobhán quickly filled him in on all of the developments.

"I'll send a squad car around to look for Ciarán, and if they see any of the other suspects they'll pick them up too," Macdara said. "Try not to worry."

"I'll do my best."

"Don't go to the bakery alone. I'll send Aretta."

"Where is she now?"

"Still here at the music shop."

"I'll pick her up," Siobhán said. "Tell her to be outside in five."

The bakery was just outside of town, located in an old flour mill. It was only as they were pulling into the car park that Siobhán remembered that Helen didn't have a car, and Edward and Róisín had arrived in the same vehicle, the one that Edward had driven to the music shop and had been towed to the lot owned by the garda station. "If they're here they must have had a ride, or they took a taxi," Siobhán said. She parked up close to the building, and they sat there for a moment.

"It's dark," Aretta said. "Wouldn't they need torches?" There was no sign of any lights in the field surrounding the old mill.

"It's possible they've left already," Siobhán said.

"Do you want me to call the taxi companies?" There were only two in Kilbane.

"Yes, please." Siobhán got out her torch. "I'll do a quick sweep."

"Yell if you need me."

Siobhán left the car and turned on her torch. She swept it over the building, the waterwheel to the right, and the expansive field surrounding it. A chill had settled into the air, and it was deadly quiet. She took a few steps toward the bakery entrance. "Róisín?" she called. "Helen?" If they weren't outside, and neither taxi company had been called out to the bakery for a pickup, it was possible that they snuck inside the back of the mill. The front was where the bakery was located, but it was contained in a relatively small space. But the back of the mill was abandoned, and there were portions boarded up—if one was determined, one could get inside. First the cemetery and now this old mill at night. Where were Ciarán and Sara now and why hadn't he called back? She tried his phone again. *Voicemail.* If he turned out to be alright, she was going to kill him.

Aretta emerged from the car with a torch of her own. "Neither taxi company was summoned out here."

Siobhán groaned. "I was afraid of that."

"You think they're inside?"

"Unless someone else gave them a ride. We should at least check out the back of the building—if they broke in, there should be some sign of disturbance."

"I can't believe they all decided this nighttime scavenger hunt was a good idea."

"They're musicians," Siobhán said. "Highly competitive musicians."

"It's too bad they're not playing their instruments now—we could at least follow the melody."

"Ready?" Siobhán illuminated the side of the mill closest to them.

"As I'll ever be."

Their boots sunk into the soggy field. Days of rain had turned spots into muck. "Careful," Siobhán said. Aretta was tiny and Siobhán could imagine her getting sucked in and stuck in the mud. "Wait." She shone her torch again. "No footprints."

"Good catch," Aretta said.

"If I had thought of it earlier I could have saved us some mud."

"But they could have traversed the other side of the building—should we keep going and see if there's a back way inside?"

"Good thinking." They continued until they came to a chain fence erected at the back of the building. It was padlocked. Siobhán shone her torch through to the other side. There she caught a glimpse of brush that had grown up, but no fence. She maneuvered herself until she could clearly see the back of the building. She saw a stone window open to the elements and low to the ground a board was lying in front of it as if it had just been knocked out. "It looks like someone is in there but they must have entered through the other side."

"Róisín?" Siobhán yelled. "Helen?" The only sounds were crickets and the gurgling of the river.

"The other side? The side with the river and the waterwheel?" Aretta sounded as if she already knew what Siobhán was thinking and understandably, it did not thrill her.

"That's the one. Let's check it out." They returned to the front of the building and crossed over to the side by the waterwheel. In order to reach the back from here, they would have to wade into the river. They stared at the dark waters before them. Neither had brought their wellies. Siobhán's torch caught several impressions in the mud. "Two set of shoeprints. I think they did take this route."

Aretta sighed. "Tell me you have a raft."

"I have a raft."

"Really?"

"No."

"Are we really about to do this?"

"We could call the owner of the bakery to let us in, but that would take time. We could wait in this car park for them to arrive, but they might slip out the back. The only way forward . . . is through."

Aretta shone her light on the waterwheel. "It's not going to be easy getting past that."

"At least the water is relatively low and the wheel isn't churning." Although the waterwheel had been repaired a few years ago, it was only turned on for visual effect—it was no longer a working flour mill.

"Here goes nothing." With one more sigh, Aretta stepped into the river.

Chapter 25

The water was frigid, but it never came higher than Aretta's knees and Siobhán's shins. But the prospect of chasing down all these suspects the rest of the night in wet work boots and trousers was not appealing. By the time they reached the back of the mill, their feet and the lower part of their legs were thoroughly soaked. Now they faced a wall of bramble. Siobhán was glad Nancy Flannery could not see her now—no doubt she'd think the twins were being tortured.

"Did you happen to bring anything to cut our way through?" Aretta asked.

"Unfortunately, I left my scythe with the raft." Siobhán knelt. "But if the other two came this way there has to be some kind of opening." And a few meters away she found it. The brush had been pushed to either side, creating a passage. "Here it is." Siobhán climbed through with only a few scrapes. Aretta followed, and soon they reached the open window.

Aretta eyed it warily. "I suppose I'm the only one who can fit."

"You are," Siobhán said. "But maybe the interlopers before us sent one through that tiny window and that one opened the door for the other, and in that case maybe it's still unlocked." She sidled over to the back door, reached for the handle, and pulled. It creaked open. "One spot of luck."

Inside, the old stone warehouse smelled moldy and from somewhere within its depths came the sound of water dripping. "Róisín," Siobhán called. "Helen?" They took a few steps into the room. "They better not have broken into the bakery," Siobhán said. That section was housed at the front of the mill and separated by its own wall, much of it glass. If they vandalized anything in that vicinity, there would be repercussions. Siobhán knew from previous visits that the only other place Helen and Róisín could be was in the opposite section, where the flour used to be ground. The actual grinding stones were still in place there, as if waiting for their chance to work again.

They had taken a few steps in that direction when a door on that side burst open and two people rushed out. From the sound of their voices, it was indeed the twins. "Róisín?" Siobhán called for a third time. "Helen?" A yelp sounded from one of them and a genuine scream from the other. "It's Detective Sergeant O'Sullivan and Garda Dabiri," Siobhán continued.

The twins rounded the corner and came to a stop several meters away as if they still didn't trust their arrival. A few security lights about the place provided enough to see, but everyone's face was half-covered in shadow. "We thought you were the killer," one said. "I nearly wet my pants."

"Are you Róisín or Helen?" Siobhán asked.

They glanced at each other. "Róisín," she said.

"You'd be in good company," Siobhán said. "The two of us have already wet ours."

"You peed your pants?" Helen asked.

"I'm only messing. Our pants are wet from wading through the river."

"The river?" Róisín said. "Did you know that if you walk further up, there's a crossing, and from there, you walk a path to the back of the building?"

"I knew that—of course. We preferred the shortcut." Next to her, Aretta groaned.

"What are you doing here?" Helen asked.

"I hope you're here to give us the next clue," Róisín said. "It's ridiculous to expect us to find it in a building this large." She sounded annoyed, but casual. Either she had no idea her boyfriend had just been murdered or she was an actress in addition to being a musician.

"Take us through finding your clue, and if you have it, I'd like to see it."

"I have it," Helen said. She reached into her pocket and pulled it out. "It was in Róisín's drum case."

Siobhán took the scrap piece of paper. It too had been written on the back of a bartender's pad. The same block letters greeted her:

A GIANT WHEEL
HOW IT DOES CHURN
IF YOU HAVE THIS KIND OF TOOTH
YOU'LL WANT TO TAKE THIS TURN

Underneath someone had drawn a little map, with a turn in to the flour mill. "Do you recognize this handwriting, or did you see anyone slip this into the drum case?"

"No," they said in stereo.

"Isn't the scavenger hunt part of the festivities?" Helen asked. "I assumed these were from Ron."

"The scavenger hunt was not part of the festivities. It's urgent that we figure out who wrote and delivered the clues."

"You mean someone is messing with us?" Helen sounded incensed.

"The killer," Róisín said. "The killer is messing with us."

"I have a guess," Helen said, curling a strand of hair around her finger. "But it's only a guess."

Siobhán would take anything at this point. "Yes?"

"Songwriters like to rhyme. Out of all of us—Tara McCarthy is the songwriter."

"Do you have any other reason to believe Tara is behind this?" Aretta asked.

"You mean besides the fact that Liam Noone stuck her with Niall O'Malley?" Róisín said. "Spend five minutes with your man and you'll want to murder someone too."

Just then a noise sounded from the back of the mill. Before Siobhán and Aretta could reach the door, it opened and people began to pour in. Musicians carrying instruments and folding chairs, Saoirse and Aisling, Niall and Tara, even Ciarán and Sara and Grace. She had told Niall and Tara to go to the garda station but apparently playing all that music had damaged their drums—ear drums that is.

Siobhán wanted to run up to Ciarán and baby him, but she'd have to settle for knowing he was alive and well. "What are you doing here?" Siobhán asked, as the musicians began setting their chairs up in a circle.

Grace approached, pulling her autoharp on a dolly. "Everyone's next clue led here."

"When and how did everyone get a next clue?"

"Ron sent me a text and I notified the others," Grace said.

"Where is Ron?"

Grace shrugged. "Maybe he's picking up refreshments."

Siobhán gestured to the harp. "How on earth did you get this back here?"

"It's on a little trolley with wheels," Grace said, pointing out the obvious.

Siobhán glanced at Grace's shoes. They were dry and so were her trousers. "You didn't wade through the river."

Grace raised an eyebrow. "Why would I do that?"

"Did you find where to cross over the river?" How did everyone know about this path but her?

"No," Grace said. "We came in the other side."

"How did you get past the padlocked fence?"

"The fence was wide open." Someone had been lurking about, knowing the others would arrive. Someone had opened that gate so that they could lock them in. Ironic. "Is there something wrong?" Grace asked.

"We'll speak later. I need to talk to my brother." Siobhán ran over to Ciarán. "What happened to you? I rang and texted you back several times."

He shrugged as if he hadn't sent her half a dozen panicked messages and another half a dozen voicemails. "Don't get your knickers in a twist. My phone died."

"You sounded like you were in trouble. What's the story?"

"We got locked in the old arcade," Sara O'Grady piped up. She had adorable freckles all over her face. But if Siobhán showed even an ounce of approval, Ciarán would probably rebel, so she forced herself to stay neutral. "Let me guess—you received a clue that said to go in there."

Ciarán nodded. "Someone even loosened a board for us to crawl in, but when we couldn't find another clue and tried to get out, the board was back in place."

This killer was certainly making the rounds this evening, which meant they had a vehicle. "How did you finally make it out?"

"I texted James when there was just enough power left on me phone to send one more message."

Siobhán glanced at Sara. "Are you alright, pet?"

Her cheeks flushed red and she nodded. "I just don't like

dark and abandoned places." She looked around the dark and abandoned place they were currently in.

Siobhán turned back to Ciarán. "Do you happen to have the clue with you?"

He shook his head. "Was I supposed to keep it?"

"Not a bother." She saw something flickering out of the corner of her eye. Grace was setting candles down in between the circle of chairs. Siobhán headed over.

"That's a hazard," she said, feeling like the bad guy. "And we aren't staying."

"They're LED," Grace said. "But I'm so chuffed that they look like real flames."

"You brought a harp and candles all the way back here?"

Grace looked perplexed as if Siobhán's question made no sense. "A lot can fit in me harp case," she said. "And it's our last night."

"Where's Edward?" Finally, someone asked. *The killer?* The question came from Róisín.

"Why did you say we aren't staying?" Grace asked. "I assumed Ron cleared this with you."

Before Siobhán could answer, the back door slammed shut. Next, the light from the window Aretta almost had to crawl through went dark. Aretta, who was closer to the exit, reached the door first. She began to pull on it. She gave Siobhán a look and Siobhán hurried over. "It's locked," she whispered.

"Check the window," Siobhán said. Aretta hurried over and kicked the board with her boot. It didn't budge. Someone had lured all of them there and locked them in.

Siobhán checked her phone. No signal. "Same with me," Aretta said. The musicians began to play their warm up tunes. "Are we going to stop them?"

"Not until I can figure out a plan," Siobhán said. "The last thing I need is for everyone to panic."

"Is there a back way into the bakery portion of the mill?"

"No. The entrance and exit is the front door." They were well and truly locked in. And the only person who was missing was Ron. Siobhán headed for Grace, who had finished setting up candles and was seated at her harp. She was huddled in a coat that was way too big for her. The musicians had completed their warm-ups and were seated, ready to go but just chatting. Siobhán had yet to figure out what to tell everyone.

"Does Ron know that you're here?" she asked Grace, keeping her voice low.

"Of course. He's the one who texted me and told me to get everyone here."

"I see."

Grace studied Siobhán. "You don't think—you don't think Ron *lured* us here, do you?'

"Why would you say that?" Siobhán asked, as Grace's eyes flicked about. She shrugged. "You thought it for some reason. Might as well say it."

"It could be nothing." Grace reached into the coat pocket and removed a business card. She cocooned it in her palm. "This is Ron's coat. He left it in the back of my van. When I got the message to come to the bakery in the old flour mill, I grabbed it. I would have asked permission, but he was nowhere to be seen." She uncurled her fist and held out the card. Siobhán took it.

Archery Lessons
Oscar O'Brien
First lesson free!

Siobhán didn't have time to dwell on the fact that he'd conned them into paying for a free lesson. There were bigger things at stake. But she would tuck it away for later. "Have you mentioned this to anyone?"

Grace shook her head. "Not a soul."

"Keep it mum."

Grace nodded. "I don't know why he had this card in his pocket—but for what it's worth, I don't think he killed Liam."

None of them seemed to know about Edward's murder. The scavenger hunt had succeeded in distracting them. "Leave the thinking to me," Siobhán said. She pocketed the card and headed back to Aretta.

"How long do you think until Macdara comes to check on us?" Aretta asked.

"Not long," Siobhán said. "But probably long enough for the person who locked us in to accomplish whatever they are trying to accomplish."

"Are you thinking it's Ron? He's the only one who isn't here." They were interrupted by Helen.

"Nobody knows where Edward is," she said. "And I can't get a signal on my phone. I need to go check on him." She headed for the door.

"Why you?" Siobhán said. "And not Róisín?" Now that Róisín's hair wasn't tucked under a cap it was easy to tell them apart.

Helen stopped in her tracks. "She's too upset to do anything."

"Wait," Siobhán said. She hurried over to Helen. "The door is locked."

"Locked?" Helen said. She continued to the door. She had to tug on it a few times before she was convinced. "Why are we locked in here?"

"I'm going to need you to stay calm and keep this to yourself," Siobhán said. "Detective Sergeant Flannery will be here soon."

Helen put her hands on her hips. "You came to get us out. And now we're locked in?" She scanned the room. "Who's doing this?"

"It's either Edward or Ron," Róisín said. She had been

standing a few feet away, but Siobhán hadn't realized she'd been listening.

"Why would it be Edward?" Helen asked.

"I didn't say for sure it was him, but he and Ron are the only ones missing."

Helen was sounding more like Edward's girlfriend than Róisín. Had his unrequited feelings been reciprocated?

The musicians began to play "Dirty Old Town." It was one of Siobhán's favorites, but now was not the time to enjoy it. On the other hand, Macdara should be able to hear the music when he arrived, and even if he didn't, he would see the squad car parked out front. To top it all off, nature was calling. Siobhán could only hope that Macdara would arrive before she was forced to answer. Until then, she needed to take advantage of all their suspects being here. If she waited too long to tell them about Edward, she risked alienating them. But since they were stuck here for the moment, it was best to take advantage of it. She could gauge everyone's reaction to the news. Who would be truly shocked and who would be forced to pretend? Unless, of course, Ron was their killer. If he wasn't—where was he?

Siobhán stepped into the middle of the trad session and brought it to a stop by waving her arms. "I'm sorry," she said. "But I need to share some news with all of you." The musicians eventually stopped, none of them looking too happy with the interruption. Siobhán asked the rest of the group to come forward.

"We're locked in, aren't we?" Grace asked, her gaze nervously flicking toward the door.

"Momentarily," Siobhán said. "But Detective Sergeant Flannery will be here soon."

Several heads snapped toward the door. "Don't worry," one of the older trad musicians said. "We'll play as long as we're in here."

"A few hours ago, myself and Detective Sergeant Flannery were alerted that there had been a break-in at a music shop not far from here." She scanned the group to see if anyone's expression had changed, but all she could see was curious faces. Under better circumstances Siobhán would have pulled Róisín aside and delivered the news to her privately, but that might have clued her in as to what type of news she was about to impart, and Siobhán needed all of their honest reactions. If Róisín was a killer, then she already knew Edward was dead, and tipping her off would have given her time to prepare a reaction. Even a matter of seconds could be to her benefit.

"What is it?" Helen called out.

Siobhán couldn't stall any longer. "When we arrived at the shop, we found Edward Kavanaugh."

"You're saying Edward broke into the shop?" Róisín said. "Why would he do that?"

"We're trying to figure that out," Siobhán said. "But I'm afraid that isn't the news. Unfortunately, by the time we arrived, Edward was deceased."

"Deceased?" This came from Helen. "You're messing with us."

"I'm not. Edward was attacked. I cannot say how, and at this point we cannot say who—but I'm sorry to tell you—he was murdered."

Chapter 26

Helen let out a scream that startled not only Siobhán but everyone in the vicinity. The music shut off at once. Róisín stared at Helen as she began to hyperventilate. Róisín crossed her arms and eyed her. She seemed to be taking the news on the chin. "Let's find a private corner where we can talk," Siobhán said. She nodded to Aretta to keep her eye on the rest of the group, and she had Róisín and Helen follow her in the small space near the door to the bakery. "I'm sorry for delivering such horrific news."

"What happened?" Helen asked. "Did he take an arrow to the heart?"

"I'm afraid I cannot divulge any specifics at the moment," Siobhán said.

"Was he struck by an arrow?" she persisted.

"Don't," Róisín said, holding her stomach.

"I'm aware that one of you spoke to Edward last night on the footpath in front of Fitzgerald's."

"It was me," Róisín said. "It seems so petty now."

Helen's lip began to quiver. "We need to tell her everything," she said.

Róisín seemed to collapse in on herself. "I suppose it's time." She straightened her spine. "As you know, Liam was devious. He was squeezing money out of Edward, he was hitting on Helen, and he would have made a mockery out of this entire festival."

"But we didn't kill him," Helen said. "And we definitely didn't kill Edward." She took a deep breath. "Edward and I are in love." She gasped. "We *were* in love." A sob tore from her. Róisín put her arm around her sister.

"It was fine by me," she said. "Helen and Edward have been a couple for the past six months."

"Wait," Siobhán said. She looked at Helen. "You were the one staying with him at the inn?" Helen nodded. "And you—" She turned to Róisín.

"I was at the Charlesville Hotel."

"So the woman I thought was Róisín was really Helen and vice versa?"

Róisín nodded. "We promised Liam we would put on the charade throughout this festival and that was it. This time we were all going to take his money for it."

"I didn't steal my sister's boyfriend," Helen said. "Róisín and himself realized early on they weren't a match."

"We didn't have that spark," Róisín said. "But himself and Helen did."

"Then why pretend?"

The twins exchanged a glance, and Siobhán saw the moment something was decided. They could speak to each other without words. "Because we saw this as an opportunity to stop Liam once and for all," Róisín said. "Not by killing him, mind you. But giving him a taste of his own medicine."

"Give me the entire story," Siobhán said. "Leave nothing out."

"Liam was constantly trying to contact Edward before coming to Kilbane. You see, once Helen and Edward got together, there was no reason for Edward to continue to pay Liam to keep quiet."

"When you say 'keep quiet' you mean about the fact that originally you were supposed to be matched with Niall," Siobhán guessed.

Róisín nodded. "Once Edward stopped paying, Liam was angry. He started showing up at Helen and Edward's place."

"Only he thought I was Róisín," Helen said.

"This time he tried blackmailing Edward by threatening to tell me that Edward was in love with Helen."

Helen nodded. "Which of course, she already knew."

"I set up a meeting with him to set him straight," Róisín said. "But the minute I walked in, he mistook me for Helen."

"And he was all over her, like," Helen said. "*Gross.*"

Róisín laughed. "He had a horrible personality, but you have to admit he was attractive."

Helen shrugged. "Until you realized what a devious person he was." She gave Siobhán a look. "Róisín has always had a thing for men she shouldn't or can't have."

Róisín nodded and then shrugged.

"Róisín," Siobhán said. "Are you saying that from that meeting on, you started seeing Liam while pretending you were Helen?" *What was the point of that?*

"Let me be clear that nothing ever happened between myself and Liam apart from a few harmless kisses. But yes. We decided—myself, Edward, and Helen—that if I was able to play along with Liam's advances, then maybe I could get close enough to get his Lucky Book."

"And once we had his Lucky Book, we could expose all of his blackmail schemes," Helen said. "We could ruin him."

"But not kill him," Róisín quickly added.

"But let us assure you—we never got our hands on the Lucky Book. And we certainly didn't shoot him with a bow and arrow."

Siobhán turned to Róisín. "You say nothing happened between the two of you other than a few—what did you say? 'Harmless kisses.' "

"I swear."

"I should tell you that we have Liam on CCTV camera entering the Charlesville Hotel shortly after you did, and not exiting until the next morning."

"That's correct," Róisín said. "But it's not what you think." She stared at the ground.

"Tell her," Helen said. "It's best she hears it from you."

"I helped him to sleep."

"Helped him to sleep? Are you saying you drugged Liam?"

Róisín held up her hands. "Not like anything illegal or awful—just over the counter cold medicine. Just enough to keep him asleep while Helen and Edward searched his room at the Kilbane Inn."

With this revelation, Siobhán's attention switched to Helen. "We convinced a cleaning lady that Liam wanted us to fetch something out of his room. But she watched us the entire time, so I had to pretend to look for his notebook but I couldn't really do a deep dive like I wanted."

"They didn't find his book," Róisín said.

That's because it was in Grace's possession at that time, but they didn't know that. "And that's everything," Helen said.

"Did either of you text Liam while he was meeting with you after the opening session?"

They shook their heads. "But he did get a text," Helen said. "And after reading it, he immediately told us all to take a break and he headed toward—well—his final resting place."

"None of you happened to see who texted him?'

They shook their heads.

"What did Edward say to you, Helen? What were his last words?"

Tears came into Helen's eyes. "He said he had an idea who the killer was—and he was going to get proof."

"Who did he think it was?"

Helen shook her head. "The music was really loud and I could barely hear him. He said something about . . . going in somewhere with a pair of shears?"

"A pair of shears?"

Helen nodded. "I asked him to repeat it, and he removed a photo from his pocket and said it was a clue."

The photo should have been sent to the garda station. Everyone in town had heard the request to turn them in. Was it still on his person? She would have to talk to Jeanie Brady straight away. "Did you see this photo?"

Helen nodded. "It was taken of the town square the night of the murder. But everyone's heads were cut off like it was taken by a child. And I think it was taken by a young one because Edward said something about a little girl and a ghost."

A little girl and a ghost? With every word out of Helen's mouth the picture became cloudier. "What did he mean?"

"All I know is, there was a little girl in the photo, and she was pointing at something—but I have no idea what it was. Somehow Edward thought he figured it out."

"I know how," Róisín said. "At least I'm guessing—I saw him talking to a young girl at the session. This was just before he pulled you out onto the footpath."

"Do you know who she was? Did you hear what they were saying?"

"I don't know her name—but she was with your brother's girlfriend. The redhead?"

Sara O'Grady and her younger sister, Margaret. "What did he say to her?"

"All I know is he showed her the photo. She must have been the one in it. I didn't hear anything else, but he wore this satisfied expression when he finished speaking with her. He said he had to go get the proof."

The proof he thought was in the music shop. What could it have possibly been? Siobhán's thoughts were interrupted by the sound of pounding in the next room. Macdara was here, breaking down the door. "Do not say a word to anyone about any of this," Siobhán said.

"We swear," Róisín said.

"Please," Helen said. "Just tell me. Did he suffer?"

Siobhán hesitated. "I think it was quick, and he never even saw it coming. I'm sorry that's all I can say for now."

Helen's face stilled. She finally nodded, as she tried to hold back tears.

"You mentioned that not many of us had a motive to kill both Liam and Edward," Róisín said. "Well, I can think of someone. Niall O'Malley."

First, they had tried to throw Tara under the bus, and now, Niall. Maybe the twins were still playing games. Maybe Siobhán shouldn't listen to a word they said. "You can be assured we'll be speaking to everyone," Siobhán said. They stared back toward the warehouse. "Wait." Siobhán stopped. "Liam had lipstick on his neck—neon-pink glow in the dark—was that from you, Róisín?"

Róisín's cheeks flushed. "After his little meeting with us, he grabbed me and pulled me into him. My lips smashed up against his neck. He was always doing that."

"Where did you get the lipstick?"

"From the welcome package," she said.

"You mean *my* welcome package," Helen said with a laugh. "It was in my room at the Kilbane Inn."

"What's mine is hers," Róisín said. "And what's hers is mine."

"Except," Helen added, "when it comes to men."

Chapter 27

Cheers rang out as everyone filed out of the old flour mill. Macdara threw a blanket around Siobhán, then waited in front of a patch of woods while she finally answered nature's call. No one could see her, but she wasn't bothered. Pregnancy had a way of making one less fussy. No doubt that would be reinforced when she was changing nappies on two babies all day long. Or should she say when *they* were changing nappies. For once, she let her husband fuss over her. He assigned guards to the mill and surrounding area, and insisted on driving Aretta and Siobhán home to get out of their wet clothes. "Any idea who locked you in?" he asked on the drive back to town.

"The only one not present was Ron," Siobhán said. "And Grace found a business card for the archery in his coat pocket."

"Any reason in particular she was rummaging through his coat pocket?"

"She said he left it in the back of her van, and she put it on when she knew she was making a trek to the mill." Siobhán proceeded to fill Macdara and Aretta in on her conversation with the twins.

"Switching places and switching men," Aretta said. "It's too cliché."

"People often are," Macdara said. "Let's ask if they'll voluntarily turn their phones over so we can verify that they did not text Liam and summon him to his death."

"Will do." It was morbid but necessary. "I'm also going to text and ask if Ciarán will come to the house with Sara in the morning," Siobhán said. "I'd like to see if they overheard what Edward spoke to Margaret about."

"Are you sure you're not just checking out his love interest?" Macdara teased.

"I can do both."

"A pair of shears and a ghost," Macdara said. "Who called that tune?"

Siobhán shook her head. "How long have you been holding onto that one?"

Macdara grinned. "Since this festival began."

"With the festival well and truly over—won't all of our suspects be leaving town?" Aretta asked.

"I don't see how we can stop them," Macdara said. "But in the morning, I intend to hold one last interview with each before we let them go."

"You should station a guard or two at the Kilbane Inn," Siobhán suggested. "In case any of them try to sneak out in the middle of the night."

"Remember that tip for when our twins are teenagers." They dropped Aretta off at her town house and then headed home. Once there, they stopped a moment to look at the skies and just breathe. Macdara pulled her in to him and kissed her. As she kissed him back, she allowed all the stress to melt away. When they parted Macdara touched her cheek. "How are you feeling?"

"I'm grand. I'm starting to get over the morning sickness."

"Perfect," Macdara said. "All the better to catch a killer."

* * *

Early the next morning, Ciarán was playing his fiddle on the hill behind their house, as if serenading the rising sun. Siobhán, groggy but determined, made her way up to him clutching a decaf coffee, and looking forward to a day when she could go back to her cappuccinos. She listened to Ciarán's lovely but slightly mournful tune and took a moment to take in the colors of the sunrise, striations of pink and orange painting the horizon. At the moment there was no wind or rain, only a slight breeze and the smell of earth and rain. Siobhán pulled her cardigan tight and waited for Ciarán to finish.

"Is it time for the inquisition?" he said.

"It was bound to happen, no?"

"To be honest, I thought it would come sooner."

"I just want to hear how you and Sara ended up together," Siobhán said. "She's a redhead and not a musician."

"She's loves trad music though. Said she could listen to me play all day and all night." *There it is.* Siobhán smiled. "And you're totally right. Your hair isn't red, no one has ever called you ginger, you're auburn. You might as well be a brunette."

"Let's not go over a cliff here," Siobhán said. "Auburn is not brunette."

"Do you think the twins will be redheads?"

"I think it tends to skip a generation."

"I can't believe I'm going to be an uncle."

"I can't either." She paused, wishing she could bottle this moment. Maybe she could imagine him as an uncle. "Do you remember Edward Kavanaugh speaking with Margaret O'Grady at Fitzgerald's yesterday evening?"

Ciarán shook his head. "I was in the middle of a session."

"Did Sara mention it?"

"She said he had a photo of Margaret pointing at something in the town square. He wanted to know what she was pointing at."

"Did you see the photo?"

Ciarán shook his head. "But Sara thinks it was taken by another child—every adult's head was cut off."

Taken by a child . . . or Oscar?

"And what was she pointing at?"

"She said she saw a ghost. Obviously, she was making it up."

"I'd like to speak with her."

"Bad timing."

"What do you mean?"

"They left last night for Dublin. I won't see Sara for a fortnight."

She was going to have to find the photographer. "Next time you speak with Sara, tell her I'd like to arrange a video call with Margaret."

"Do you think the ghost is the killer?"

"I think it relates to the case somehow. I just don't know all the pieces."

"I'm glad I don't have your job," Ciarán said. "I'd much rather play the fiddle." He looked thoughtful. "That said, it would be kind of cool if the killer was a ghost."

"Maybe," Siobhán said. "But impossible to catch."

"What's the plan?" Siobhán sat at one of the communal tables in The Six with Eoin, Gráinne, and James. Eoin had made them all a full Irish breakfast.

"We had a video call with Ann last night," Gráinne said. "I think somehow she tuned into the vibe of the matchmaking festival, for she actually told us about a girl she was seeing."

Siobhán perked up. "Details."

"Her name is Katie," James said. "That's honestly all we could get out of her."

"But she was beaming," Eoin added.

"Ciarán and Ann, both in love . . ." Siobhán said. "Eoin and Aretta are finally admitting their love to the world . . ."

"Easy now," Eoin said.

Siobhán laughed and eyed Gráinne and James. "Now it's time for ye to find someone."

"Are you joking me?" Gráinne said. "Do you know how many tourists come in and out of Inch? There's never a lack of dates." She gave James the side-eye.

"What was that?" Siobhán asked.

James shook his head. "I told you not to mention it."

Gráinne put on her most innocent expression. "Did I say a word?"

"Spill," Siobhán said.

"I've been seeing someone," James said.

"She owns a bakery," Gráinne said. "And she's divorced with two kids."

"Gráinne!" James had just gone red.

"What is the matter with you?" Siobhán said to James. "That's not shocking. What's her name? What are the kids' names? How old are they?"

James sighed and pulled out his mobile phone. He scrolled through it until he found a photo and turned the screen to Siobhán. She noticed Eoin and Gráinne did not lean in—they had already seen it. A touch of jealousy reared up—but who could blame him for convening without her, she'd been so engrossed in this case. "Her name is Erin. The boy is Rory, he's eight. The girl is Brigid, she's ten."

An adorable threesome, all with white-blond hair and big smiles. Erin was beautiful, and even more to Siobhán's liking, she looked kind.

"The kids are a hoot," Gráinne said. "Sometimes James brings them to the inn, and they tear around the place like little racehorses. Bakeries and children," she said, shaking her head. "What was she thinking?"

James laughed. "She monitors their sugar level."

"Would you listen to all of us?" Siobhán said. "It's like we're all grown-up."

The door opened, and Jeanie Brady walked in. "Something smells incredible."

"Have a seat," Eoin said. "Full Irish breakfast?"

"Why not," Jeanie said. "And after that, I'm going to sleep like the dead."

"All-nighter?" Siobhán asked.

Jeanie nodded, as she sunk onto the communal bench. Gráinne and James got up and cleared their plates.

"Good to see you, Jeanie," James said. "We're going to let you two talk murder."

Jeanie laughed. "How's Lahinch?" she asked them.

"We love it," Gráinne said. "There's always a place for you at the inn."

"Would you look at that," Jeanie said. "Room at the inn. And here I thought I'd have to look for a stable." Gráinne and James disappeared, and after delivering her plate, so did Eoin. Siobhán let Jeanie enjoy her breakfast, and then she answered all of Jeanie's questions about her pregnancy and the joy and terror of expecting twins, and finally, they switched to the topic of Edward Kavanaugh.

"Did you find a photo on him?" Siobhán asked.

"A photo?" Jeanie shook her head. "Wallet, car keys, a key to the inn, and a key to the music shop."

"Did you search his wallet?"

"Yes. Cards, motor license, some cash."

"Someone took the photo and left the cash." That was telling.

"What was this photo?" Siobhán filled her in on the photo, ghosts, and shears. "Something in that photo triggered Edward to go to the music shop."

"Ghost and shears," Jeanie repeated. "Does that mean anything to you?"

"Not a thing." She sighed. "Tell me you have something for me."

"It was pretty straightforward. No surprise, the blow to the back of the head with the metronome was the cause of death." She shook her head. "It's hard when it's someone that young." She paused. "However, I did find something a bit odd."

"I'll take odd."

"He had a few cuts on his fingertips and a splinter."

"Like someone who fashioned an arrow out of the bow of a fiddle?"

"I would say that's possible, but—"

"But?"

"These looked like fresh injuries, so they wouldn't be from the arrow made for Liam's murder. But maybe he was planning on making a second one?"

"Maybe," Siobhán said. "And whereas it is possible that Edward killed Liam—after all, Liam was trying to sleep with the woman Edward paid to be matched up with—I feel like we're looking for one killer. And Edward certainly didn't hit himself on the back of the head with a metronome."

"He did not. And it couldn't have fallen off a shelf or some such—it was a deliberate blow."

Chapter 28

Siobhán headed for the garda station, where she found Macdara in his office with Aretta. She filled them in on her conversation with Jeanie Brady. "We've located Ron Gallagher," Macdara said. "Apparently, he was locked in the bookshop."

"Now," Siobhán said, "if you're going to be locked in anywhere, it might as well be a bookshop." Siobhán hadn't been a huge reader until the bookshop came to town. She started with a romance here and there—and little by little, Oran and Padraig began suggesting titles for her—and not only had she branched out to sampling different genres, now she could officially call herself a reader. Time often caused an obstacle, especially with her promotion—and of course the upcoming arrival of the Dynamic Duo—but the thought of cracking open a new book still brought her a shot of excitement.

"And you're not going to believe what Ron found there," Macdara said.

"Knowledge?" Siobhán guessed. "Entertainment."

"Funny gal," Macdara said.

Siobhán grinned. "Tell me."

"Liam's Lucky Book," Aretta said. "He said he found it on one of the carts that Oran and Padraig had rolled outside for the festival."

"Appropriately nestled between romance novels," Macdara added.

"I don't understand. What was he doing in the bookshop after hours?"

"He said he'd been in there since late that afternoon. Apparently, he was looking for the rest room and ended up in their storage room instead. The carts had been stored there. Once he spotted Liam's Lucky Book, I guess he started reading it on the spot. Padraig, not realizing anyone was in there, padlocked the door. He's only just found him this morning."

"And he admitted to finding the Lucky Book," Siobhán said. "I find that interesting."

"In what way?" Macdara asked.

"Someone stole the Lucky Book out of Grace's harp cover. Only someone familiar with her harp cover would have even thought to look there. If Ron is the thief, and the killer, he might have pulled this entire stunt just so he could produce the Lucky Book, and have us thinking he's an upstanding citizen." She stared across the square at the bookshop. Padraig was rolling out the carts, and Oran was watering their flower containers. The sun was out, and nothing but blue skies were above them. "And what about this scavenger hunt?"

"He said he knew nothing about that—he insisted he did not leave the clues," Aretta said.

"And CCTV confirms that he was locked in the storage room," Macdara said.

"Have either of you had a peek at the Lucky Book?"

Macdara nodded. "Liam Noone had detailed notes on every person he'd ever matched."

"And he made more money on his blackmail schemes than he did matchmaking," Aretta added.

"Let's hope Ron isn't eager to follow in those corrupt footsteps. Does he have a section on Grace or Ron?"

Macdara shook his head. "No. And before you ask—there aren't any pages ripped out."

Aretta picked up a chain of paper clips made no doubt by Macdara, and held them up as if marveling at the design before setting them back down. "Do you think this eliminates them as suspects?"

Siobhán had been thinking about that very thing. "As far as Grace is concerned, she seemed to worship Liam. And if he wasn't blackmailing her . . ." Although she did have his Lucky Book for a spell. Maybe she read it and it was too much to see the man she'd put on a pedestal for what he really was—a con man who took advantage of people's deep need for love. And all the things they did for it. "But there wasn't enough time between reading it and his murder to make an arrow, let alone learn how to hit her target in the dark."

"And Ron?" Macdara asked.

"Ron coveted Liam's job. And that Lucky Book. Liam seemed like one of those people who was never going to retire. Maybe this was Ron's way of taking the throne."

"Except there was nothing stopping him from setting up a matchmaking business of his own," Aretta pointed out.

"I'm still shocked he admitted to finding Liam's Lucky Book. None of us would have been the wiser had he simply absconded with it."

"True," Aretta said. "Oran and Padraig hadn't even noticed that it had been slipped into the cart."

"Then again, Ron could have been the one to slip it in there."

"Ron did say that once he realized the extent of Liam's schemes, he wanted nothing more to do with them," Macdara said.

Siobhán knew, if they discussed this any more, they were going to keep going in circles. "Where is Ron now?"

"We let him go back to the inn," Macdara said. "He's wrung out. Let him have a shower and a meal and a rest. We'll bring him in to the station in the afternoon."

"I'm actually on my way to the inn," Siobhán said. "I need to speak with them about the 'welcome package' that Helen claimed to have received."

"I'll leave you at it," Macdara said. "And do let me know if anyone seems to be making a run for it—and that goes double for Ron Gallagher."

"Welcome package?" Emma said. For once she was on her own. Eileen was at the market. It was always odd to see them on their own: it was like looking at a person who had just lost a limb. Siobhán didn't want her twins to feel like half of a whole. She was going to do everything she could to encourage individuality. Then again, she hoped they had the kind of tight bond that only twins share. "We don't have a welcome package."

"That's what I thought." They stood outside the rooms at the Kilbane Inn. According to Emma, the musicians, as well as Ron and Grace, were still there, but they were all sleeping in.

"Is there any way I can speak with the cleaning attendants who would have been here during their arrival?"

Emma tilted her head. "Do you think my cleaning attendant left the musicians a welcome package?"

"*Someone* did. I need to know if anyone went into Edward and Helen's room—"

"Helen?"

"Sorry, that's her twin. Edward and Róisín—"

"Róisín has twin?" Apparently Róisín had not been hanging around the inn.

Siobhán nodded. "Identical."

Emma's eyes twinkled. "Why haven't they been together?" She placed her index finger on her chin. "I suppose I wouldn't have known unless they were standing next to each other."

"You would have known." They were getting off track. "They are identical, but they wear their hair different."

Emma touched her hair. Herself and Eileen had identical bobs. "What was in this welcome package?" Emma asked.

"I just really need to speak with the attendant and see if anyone went into that room for any reason."

Emma's disappointment was obvious. "I'd have to check the schedule, or I can call her."

"A call would be fine."

"I will say that before guests check in, she does tend to leave the doors open to run around and fetch towels and the like."

"I see. I'm sure that explains it. But do let me know if she saw anyone in particular go into a room that wasn't his or her own."

"She wouldn't know who was assigned to each room."

Siobhán nodded. Emma was right. And if all the doors were open, it could have been any of them.

"But if she has anything to report, I'll let you know straight away."

"I appreciate it."

"Maybe we *should* put together a welcome package," Emma mused out loud, as she sauntered away.

Before leaving, Siobhán taped notes she had written at the station to each door:

Before leaving town, please meet for a final dinner at The Six. 7 PM.

If you wish to stay one more night, we will pay for the room.

Dinner is on us and we may have a few closing questions.

Leaving town is not advisable.

Detective Sergeant O'Sullivan

By the time Siobhán returned to the station, Aretta was waiting to drive them to the music shop. Jim McVeigh was waiting for them there. "I hear he's distraught," Aretta said.

Siobhán nodded. "Who wouldn't be." She didn't know if he owned or rented the building, but it would be hard to work in such a small shop without thinking of the horror that had occurred. Then again, if McVeigh was a killer, murdering Edward in his own shop might have been part of the plan. Who would suspect him of doing that? Siobhán knew of no motive, but the nature of this job was to be suspicious of everyone, no matter how charming they seemed.

By the time they pulled up, Jim was smoking in front of the shop, looking as if he hadn't slept all night. His hair was sticking up, his shirt barely covered his paunch and his eyes were red. The minute Siobhán stepped out of the squad car, he approached. "He must have taken my keys while I was playing a session. I had no idea."

Siobhán took a moment to retrieve her notepad and biro from her handbag. She was still in these ridiculous maternity clothes, and they did not have pockets. At least, this time, she wasn't sprouting strawberries: instead she wore a white maternity dress dotted in light-blue flowers and a jumper. The more professional outfits she'd ordered were too dressy. She needed to find a happy medium. A trip to Dublin would be in order. "Didn't you notice your keys were gone when the session was over?"

"I keep my house and car keys in me pockets, and my

shop key in me coat pocket," he said. "I had no intention of going to the shop until this afternoon." He gulped. "The blood," he said. He shook his head.

"I can give you the name of a cleaning service," Siobhán said gently.

"It's ruined. Me shop is ruined."

"I'm sorry. And I do not mean to dismiss your feelings—anyone would be upset to find someone has been murdered in their place of business—but I'm afraid I must focus on Edward."

"Of course, of course. I didn't mean to sound callous."

"I don't suppose you have security cameras?"

"Out here?" He shook his head. "I never needed them." He sighed. "I suppose I should say, I never needed them *till now*."

"Let's step into the shop." The guards had finished processing the scene. Siobhán headed for the spot where Edward's body was found. "Do you have any idea what he might have been looking for?"

Jim looked around. "He was a piper, is that right?" Siobhán nodded. "I suppose he could have been headed for the uillean pipes." He pointed to a back corner where a set of pipes hung behind the harps. "He didn't take any money from the register, and I cannot think of any reason he'd break in."

"Edward told a few witnesses that he had figured out who Liam Noone's killer was, but before he spoke to the guards, he needed proof. I believe he was convinced that the proof lay somewhere in your shop."

Jim opened his arms and gestured around. "I sell instrument and sheet music. I don't know what any of them has to do with the matchmaker's murder."

She believed him. "Was the metronome from this shop?"

He nodded and pointed to a shelf just behind the spot where Edward's body had been found. Two other metronomes sat there, but there was a space at the very end that was empty, and only a faint outline framed in dust showed one had indeed been sitting there. "Do you think only a musician would realize these were heavy enough to kill a man?"

"I suppose anyone in a panic would have grabbed anything," Jim said. "But if it wasn't premeditated—why did someone follow him into the shop?"

"Is it possible a friend of yours—or a neighbor—was driving by and saw Edward break in? Maybe this person thought they were interrupting a robbery."

"He let himself in with a key, and there's barely any traffic by here at night, I'd say that is a very slim possibility."

Siobhán thought so too, but it was good to eliminate all possibilities. "Do you remember seeing Edward at the session last night?"

Jim shook his head. "When I'm fully engaged in a session, the outside world falls away." Siobhán found herself staring at the harp Liam had given him. Jim followed her gaze. "You think he came in here to nick a harp?" McVeigh asked. "It wouldn't fit in his car."

Siobhán thought of Grace hiding the Lucky Book in the cover for the harp. It triggered a thought. "Is there any way someone could hide something inside a harp?"

Jim nodded. "Yes. The interiors are hollow." He squinted at the harp. "You think something is hidden inside?"

"To be honest I don't know what to think. But could you have look?" Maybe Edward had heard of Liam or Grace hiding something in the harp before giving it away. Jim walked over to the harp, knelt down, then gently grasped each side and gave it a shake.

"I don't hear anything," he said. "And if you want me to reach me hand in there, I risk breaking a string. But if you think it's really necessary . . ."

"That's alright. If you don't hear anything inside that's good enough for me."

He shook it again. "Nothing." He stood. "Anything else?" He glanced at the blood still on the floor. "I don't want to be in here right now."

"I understand." There were no footprints in the blood. Someone had banged him in the back of the head and quickly stepped out of the way. "One more question, but I can ask it outside." Once outside, Jim put a padlock on the door. The keys to the shop were currently in evidence. "Did you know that Edward was showing people a photo that night?"

Jim shook his head. "What photo?"

"Do you know Margaret O'Grady?"

Jim smiled. "She's a wee dote."

"It was a photo of her the night of the murder. She was pointing at something out of the frame. Apparently, she said something about a ghost—and Edward said something about shears."

"Shears? As in sheep shears?"

"I suppose."

"Sorry. I don't know a thing about that either."

"He also said that all the heads of adults were not visible in the photo—as if it was taken by a child."

"I know nothing about this."

"I was just thinking of Oscar O'Brien."

"Now that sounds plausible. He does fancy himself an amateur photographer. He said he wanted to make a book out of photos taken from his perspective. Give people a glimpse into his day-to-day view."

"That sounds creative. I hope he does that." Ron Gallagher had the calling card to Oscar's archery in the pocket of his coat. She definitely needed to speak with Oscar again. "Any idea what his hours at the archery are?"

Jim glanced at his watch. "He'll be there right about now."

* * *

As promised, she found Oscar at the archery. "I knew you'd be back," he said. "You're a natural."

"Unfortunately, I'm here on business."

"Right, so. Fire away." Arrows flew from the line of people toward the targets. Oscar yelped and whirled around, shaking his finger at the group. "I was speaking to *her.*" He sighed, then started to chuckle. "But well played." He gestured to his assistant. "Shall we take a stroll?"

They walked the field. "We're going to have a snowy winter," Oscar said. "I can feel it in me bones."

"If I said the name Ron Gallagher, would you know who that is?"

"Aye. The matchmaking protégé."

"Did he come to the range?"

"He did . . ." He hesitated.

"Yes?"

"He was given a gift certificate for a series of lessons. Said it was from Liam. Only thing is—those gift certificates were last year's design. It was purchased by someone else but he never used it."

"Someone regifted it?"

Oscar shook his head. "I haven't had a chance to talk to him—but it doesn't ring true to me."

"And who is this person?"

"The publican from Fitzgerald's. Barry."

Interesting. "Please do not mention it. I'll speak with him."

Oscar sighed. "Is there any chance you can leave me name out of it?"

"I can't promise anything." She removed the business card from her pocket and handed it to him. "Did Ron pick this up on his visit?"

"I couldn't say for sure. But there are a pile of them on the counter in the shop."

"Did he come with anyone?"

"He came with the harp player. Grace, is it?"

"It is."

Oscar shook his head. "She gave up after *two* tries."

"This was before the murder?" If it was after, Siobhán didn't see how they would want to be anywhere near bows and arrows.

"Yes. Two days before. On the Wednesday."

"Did Ron have the knack for it?"

"I'd say he was like any other beginner."

"You said Barry never used the certificate. Has he ever taken a lesson?"

"Barry wouldn't need a lesson. He practically grew up with an arrow in his hand."

None of this was looking good for Barry. Had Liam done something that Monday evening to threaten Barry? Had he tried one of his blackmail schemes on him? Barry was also mentioned as someone who was ferrying notes to patrons from other patrons. What if the notes came from Barry himself? "Did you see any kind of interaction between Barry and Liam Noone on the Monday night they arrived?"

"He was browned off with how the group conducted themselves. And I suppose he was also browned off with me for snatching the bow out of that fiddler's hand, breaking it in two and almost starting a row." He shrugged and gave a look like it was unreasonable to be upset with him over *that*.

Siobhán gave it a beat before switching directions. "I heard you were taking photos that Friday evening before the murder."

"I'm always taking photos. From my perspective."

"Meaning?"

"I don't try to adjust my size—I'm putting together a book of the world as I see it. That's the title too." He gestured in the air as if the title were written in the clouds. "*The World As I See It*."

"I think that's a brilliant idea." He grinned and took a little bow. "One particular photo you took was of Margaret O'Grady pointing at something."

"Margaret O'Grady?"

"A young girl. Night of the opening. She stood pointing at something. Apparently, a ghost."

"Ah, right, so. Yes. I just happened to catch the moment."

"Do you have any idea what she was pointing at?"

"Funny you ask. I too was curious, so I went over and asked her."

Siobhán felt a tingle up her spine. "And?"

"You know kids and their imaginations."

"Go on, so."

"She said she saw a ghost—"

Siobhán sighed. "We already knew that."

"A ghost playing a broken guitar."

Chapter 29

"Broken guitar?" Macdara asked. Herself, Aretta, and Macdara stood in the town square, watching as volunteers dismantled the festival. Vendors were packing up their food carts, volunteers were removing the string lights, and Ciarán and Sara were folding up chairs. Eoin insisted his Cupid and heart needed to be put to rest, especially since they had helped a murderer with their deadly scheme. Siobhán agreed, in fact, they should burn them.

"I feel like we were bested," Siobhán said. "Played by a ghost." If only an autoharp did play by itself. She could see how that would look something like a broken guitar.

"We know we had a broken bass bow," Aretta said. "Maybe there's a theme at play."

Siobhán thought about this. Was Oscar going around breaking other instruments as well? She felt her phone buzz in her pocket and pulled it out. "I have a missed voicemail from Jim McVeigh."

"Can you put it on speaker?" Macdara edged in.

Siohban pushed play: "Heya, Detective O'Sullivan, Jim here. I'm at the shop. You asked me if anything was missing, and I said there wasn't, but I just noticed this morning that I am missing a small recorder. Not sure if that's helpful at all but thought I'd let you know."

"A recorder?" Siobhán said. "Like a small audio recorder?"

Ciarán walked over carrying a folded chair. "A recorder is a musical instrument. It's in the flute family."

"Ah, right, so. I misunderstood."

Ciarán studied her. "Perhaps they made you a detective too soon." With that, her cheeky brother ambled away.

"Does he really think the killer decided to grab a flute on his or her way out?" Aretta mused.

"Musicians are a mysterious breed," Macdara said. "Which one of our suspects plays the flute?"

"Tara McCarthy," Siobhán said. "Who is matched with Niall—Niall hated Edward." Did he murder his rival and then nick a flute for Tara on his way out? None of this was adding up. Shears. Broken guitar. Ghost musician. Stolen recorder. Avid archer. And this entire matchmaking and music festival had been Siobhán's idea.

"There's Ron Gallagher," Aretta said, pointing toward King John's Castle. Sure enough, Ron was standing by Grace, who was directing the musicians to load their instruments into her van.

"Let's bring him into the station and have a chat," Macdara said.

"Actually," Siobhán said. "Can we bring him into Fitzgerald's? We need to have a chat with Barry as well."

The pubs had opened early, in case the volunteers got thirsty. Siobhán had filled them in on everything she'd learned from Oscar that morning.

"Fitzgerald's it is," Macdara said. "But don't tell Mam."

"Let me guess," Siobhán said. "She thinks the twins are too young to be hanging out in pubs."

Aretta's laughter filled the air, and she kept laughing until she saw the stoic expression on Siobhán's face. She then glanced at Macdara, who nodded and shrugged. She grimaced at Siobhán and mouthed her response: *Wow.*

They spoke with Barry first. "Gift certificate?" He glanced at a pint glass by the register filled with calling cards, pens, and coins. "It's been in there for ages." He began taking items out, one by one. "Well, I'll be. Gone."

"Is it possible someone could have taken it?"

"We've been jammers this entire week. It's more than possible." They glanced back at Ron, who was seated in the corner booth, staring at a full glass of orange juice.

"Have you had any discussion with any of the musicians on the subject of archery?" Siobhán asked.

"Not that I can recall."

"You're not aware if any of them are into the sport?"

"Subject never came up."

"Thanks." They headed over to the table where Ron sat. He looked up at the three of them.

"I feel like I'm in trouble," he said. "I hope you believe that I was locked in the bookshop during the scavenger hunt. I swear on me life."

"I just paid a visit to the archery," Siobhán said. "I heard you showed up there Wednesday with a gift certificate."

Ron did not look surprised or guilty. "I did. Liam gave it to me on Monday."

"Liam?" Siobhán asked. "Did he say why?"

Ron's expression changed instantly, and this time he did look guilty. "I know I should have said something. But I don't know how it relates to his murder." He gulped, then stared at his orange juice. "I was trying to go over the weekend schedule with him. I thought it was high time he let me participate. I wanted to run at least one of the events. Just one! But that was too much to ask. And yes—voices were raised. Grace broke it up—although for once it would have been nice if she had stood up for me. I swear she was so smitten with Liam, she didn't know where he ended and she began. Anyhow . . . on me way out, Liam blocked my path and shoved the gift certificate in me face. Said if I wanted to 'go to war,' I should at least learn how to shoot."

"All of that, because you asked to run an event?" Macdara asked.

Ron sighed. "I also said it was only fair that he let me read his Lucky Book."

"What did he say?"

Sweat trickled down Ron's face. "Over me dead body."

"Last night, did you interact with Edward Kavanaugh at all?" Macdara asked.

"Not a word," Ron said. "But I know Grace did." Ron frowned. "Come to think of it, he did say something odd."

The three of them leaned in simultaneously. "Go on, so," Macdara said.

"He said something about finding a recorder."

"A recorder?" Siobhán said. "The instrument? The one in the flute family?" She could feel Macdara giving her the side-eye, but she ignored it.

"That's what I gathered."

"What exactly did he say?"

"I only heard a bit as I was passing by—they were standing at the bar and he was showing her a photo. And then I heard 'find a recorder'—and that was it."

"Did you ask Grace about it?"

Ron nodded. "She said there was something really off about him, and that he was going on about a girl, a ghost, and finding a recorder."

This felt like one of those group games where each person would add on to a story, only with this one they weren't even trying to make sense. "And then?"

Ron moved his glass of orange juice around in a circle on the table, as if it was skating. "That's it. It was about a half an hour later that I was ready to go home—I guess I left right before everyone started getting the scavenger hunt clues."

"Hold on," Siobhán said. She headed back to Barry and pointed to the pint glass filled with cards, pens, and coins. "Did this pint glass ever hold anything else?"

Barry stared at it and tilted his head. "A small notepad."

"Yellow sticky notes?"

"Yeppers."

"The kind the scavenger clues were written on?"

"Never got a look at them," he said. "All I can tell you is there once was an entire pad in there and now there's not."

The killer had written the scavenger hunt notes on the fly. Which meant he or she was creative—but more to the point: the minute Edward left, someone figured out where he was going. *How?* Was Edward so foolish he threatened the killer? Or was it some innocuous comment that triggered their alarm bell? The faux scavenger hunt would have given the killer time—not only to disappear without being noticed, but to kill Edward and then clean up. No doubt blood splatters would have gotten on the killer's clothes. Siobhán was halfway out the door when a familiar trad song began to play over the speaker. Wistful. Mournful. Filled with a mixture of hope and longing. She stopped. Why was that song familiar? "That sounds live," she said.

Barry cupped his hand around his ear, then held up a finger and turned down the music. "Sorry, it's hard to hear with the music going."

It certainly was. "No worries. I just said that it sounds like a live recording."

Barry nodded. "A squeeze-box and a fiddle. Niall O'Malley played it last night with Aisling Byrne." He grinned. "It was a crowd favorite."

She didn't have to ask Barry the name of the waltz. The answer had come to her. And it was going to require some thought. "Can I use your patio?" she asked.

"Knock yourself out."

Siobhán went out back and began to pace. *Missing Lucky Book . . . a very tight timeline for a killer . . . bow and arrow. Liam's blackmail schemes . . . Liam's womanizing. Not just shears, wasn't it something like—'in for a pair of shears'? . . . ghost musician, find a recorder, broken guitar . . . guests at the inn switching rooms, a peep hole in the closet wall . . .*

What did she know for sure? The killer must have hidden the bow and arrow somewhere nearby, and yet—despite all the people outside day after day—it still hadn't been found.

Killers stuck to habits, didn't they? And this killer had done something habitual. Or at least, this killer *said* they did something. It was a lie, but it was probably something they would have done under different circumstances. The explanation didn't seem odd at the time. But now—it was all right there in front of her. She had missed a step at the very start. It was time to rectify that. The twins chose that very moment to kick, as if letting her know she was on the right track. Amateur sleuths in the womb. She placed her hand on her stomach and allowed the rush of love she already felt for these beings to fill her soul. Next, she picked up the phone and called Jim McVeigh. She needed a favor.

Jim agreed to gather some musicians to play one last session. This one would take place at The Six. No community invited, just the musicians, and their out-of-town matchmakers and musicians. Eoin would provide appetizers and drinks. And at some point in the evening, Detective Sergeant Siobhán O'Sullivan would accuse one of them of murder.

Chapter 30

Grace volunteered to transport all of the instruments to The Six in her van. Jim McVeigh and Oscar would join them to lead the session. When she was ready, Siobhán would cue Jim to play the song she needed the killer to hear. The same mournful favorite she not only heard playing in Fitzgerald's, but at the very beginning of the festival as well. And, as it turned out, the swan song—for the victim.

Aisling and Saoirse walked in hand-in-hand, laughing. Maybe the stressful events of this week were a reminder that life was short, and loving each other was worth it. Tara and Niall, however, walked in separately. Finally, Róisín and Helen entered followed by Jim and Oscar, and before they knew it, the session had begun, with Jim leading the way. Ciarán—who had already been present in The Six, along with James, Gráinne, and Nancy—was in the circle, whereas the rest of the family took a nearby farm table.

As requested, Jim had opened the session with waltzes. Since they usually played in threes, the song Siobhán requested would be the third. She had learned this week that reels were the bulk of the songs played in trad sessions, with jigs coming in second and waltzes a bit more rare—up to the discretion of the session leader and the players. But this was a special occasion, and Jim obliged without argument. The first two songs were zippy and foot-tapping, and as Macdara, Aretta, and Siobhán prepared themselves for the third song, her heart rate began to tick up.

Jim made eye contact with Siobhán, and she gave him a nod. Soon, Liam's favorite song began to play. "Inisheer" by Tom Walsh. It was normally played instrumentally, but lyrics were later added. It was a lovely song about the island in Galway Bay, with a line about fisherman whose stories you'd love to hear. . . . Today, the group would play it instrumentally, as it was played the first night of the festival. The song even continued to play through the blackout, through the confusion and screams.

Grace, who had decided not to join the circle with her harp (much to Ciarán's relief), began to sniffle. "Liam's song," she said when it began to play. It was a beautiful rendition, and when it was over, Grace clasped her hands under her chin as tears rolled down her cheeks. Ron Gallagher looked at her with disdain and was frequently caught rolling his eyes or shaking his head. The minute the song ended, Grace whirled around and pointed at Ron.

"What is your problem?"

"Nothing."

"Then why were you staring daggers at me?"

"Because you act like the man was a saint."

"Have some respect for the dead."

"Please," Tara said. "Could you not argue? We've had enough stress this week."

"Want to tell them why?" Niall piped up.

"Don't do it," Tara said.

"I don't have to pretend anymore," Niall replied. "Ladies and gentlemen, Tara and I are not together. We haven't been together in months."

Mouths dropped open. "We were supposed to be matched

from the beginning," Niall said, turning to one of the twins. "We can do it now. We can finally be together."

"Not on your life," she said.

"Why?" He stepped forward. "Is it too soon? I mean no disrespect to Edward. But life is short."

"How can you be so daft? I'm Helen."

Niall stared at her. "But I just saw you playing the bodhrán."

"We both play," Róisín said, approaching the group.

"You're Róisín?" Niall asked, still unsure.

"Last time I checked."

"Be with me." Niall clutched his hands in prayer. "Nothing is holding us back."

"You can't even tell me from my sister, Edward has been murdered, Tara is a perfectly lovely girl, and you think I'm just going to jump into your arms?" She shook her head.

"It's not like I murdered him," Niall said. The room fell quiet. He looked around. "What?"

"How do we know that?" Tara asked. "You were angry with both him and Liam."

Maybe Siobhán wasn't going to have to do much talking after all. Maybe they would be the ones to let their secrets fly.

"That's preposterous. Just because I think Róisín would have been a better match for me doesn't mean I'd kill for her." He turned to Róisín. "No offense."

"But wasn't Liam also blackmailing you?" Aisling said.

"He threatened to tell Tara that I preferred Róisín. But I refused to pay to keep that quiet." He glanced at Tara. "But that was right after we matched. And as I've already told you, we haven't been together in months."

Tara stepped forward. "We just pretended to because we both wanted to attend this festival."

"That is strictly against Liam's protocols," Grace said.

"Are you joking me?" Niall said. "It was *his* idea."

"See?" Ron said. "Grace, you are still totally under his evil spell."

"Evil?" Grace eyed Ron. "Maybe you're the one who's evil."

Ron looked stricken. "What do you mean by that?"

"Why don't you tell all of us why you had a calling card to the local archery in your coat pocket."

"You snoop!" Now everyone was staring at him. "What? Liam gave me a gift certificate."

"You were a natural," Oscar piped up. "A natural beginner, that is."

"A natural beginner," Grace scoffed. "Or maybe he was already a seasoned archer pretending to be a beginner."

"Why is everyone looking at me?" Ron said.

"Well," Aisling said, "you did happen to bring a double bass. And I never even saw you take it out of the case."

Ron shrugged. "I was told it wasn't a good idea to play one in a session."

"He listens!" Ciarán piped in. "I'll give him that."

The crowed stared at Ron. "Why is everyone looking at me? Niall and Tara are the ones who pretended to be a successful match. And Grace is right—Liam wouldn't have liked it."

"Liam knew we weren't together," Tara said. "He actually paid us to pretend we were this happy couple."

"My word," Ron said. "Is there no bottom to what that man was doing?"

"Ron!" Grace said. "Do not speak ill of the dead. Liam may have been a flawed man, but there was so much good in him too."

Ron didn't even try to hide the look of disgust on his face. "I'm so tired of your endless devotion to that man. Admit it—*you* wanted to be with Liam."

Grace's face flushed red. "He was my boss," she said quietly.

"I know better," Ron said.

"Is that right?" Grace replied. "What exactly do you think you know?"

"I read his Lucky Book," Ron said. "And I have my suspicions you did too."

"What do you mean? Of course I didn't read it. He entrusted it to me."

"Well, if you're telling the truth, let me give you some more cold, hard facts. He documented every time you tried to flirt with him. He thought you were like a lovesick puppy."

Siobhán missed that section. She should have read it more carefully.

"Stop it." Grace turned away.

"And then he waxed on about whatever single woman he was targeting at every matchmaking event. At every single event, he hooked up with someone new." At this, Ron glanced at Helen, who had been in the middle of shoving a sausage roll into her mouth. She and Róisín exchanged a panicked glance.

"Do not lie, Helen Doyle. I saw you kissing on Liam. You're the one who left that glow-in-the-dark lipstick on Liam's neck."

Heads snapped to Grace, then to Helen. "Someone left that lipstick in my room at the inn," she said. "Someone set me up."

Ron frowned. "But you didn't even stay at the inn."

Róisín stepped forward. "No more lies. I was the one who pretended to be interested in Liam. Helen and Edward were a couple. So yes—she did stay at the inn."

"Did you sleep with Liam?" Grace asked, taking a few steps toward Róisín.

"Not that it's any of your business, but no, I did not. Can you imagine?" From the look on Grace's face she had imagined it more than once. "The point is, Edward and my sister Helen are a couple. As in Tara and Niall's case—Edward and I haven't been together in over eight months. He and my sister were very much in love."

Helen began to cry. Róisín rushed to her side to comfort her.

Slowly, all the suspects began to nudge in closer to each other, forming an accusatory circle. It was time for Siobhán to step in. "Please, everyone. Back away from each other." Reluctantly everyone took a few steps back. "I invited you all to this last session under false pretenses. You see . . . we *know* who Liam's killer is."

Around her, faces stilled and mouths dropped open. Like a session, they were all in a circle. But this time, it was a circle of accusations.

"This murder was carefully planned. I think the killer was waiting to see whether Liam would be on the straight and narrow this weekend, or back to his old tricks. So, this killer was prepared for either eventuality. Unfortunately, Liam was like an old dog—performing the same tired, old tricks. And then, the plan was set in motion. The cut-out Cupid helped out—as an identifier. As soon as the opening session ended and Liam called for a break, the killer texted him and asked to meet him at the Cupid. He did. The lipstick on his neck also helped guide the arrow—but the person who kissed his neck was not in on the plot."

"Me?" Helen said. "Thank goodness you believe me."

Siobhán nodded. "Earlier, I believe the killer had seen you kissing Liam on the neck and rightly assumed you'd do it again. Which is why you received the lipstick. She thought you were Róisín, mind you, but the rest played out according to plan."

"She?" Róisín said. The women in the circle eyed each other.

Siobhán turned to Aisling. "You wrote *Traitor* on the mirror in the bookshop café."

Aisling bit her lip. "It was for Saoirse," she said. "Before we worked things out."

"I did betray her," Saoirse said. "But I also fell in love with her. And she's forgiven me."

"Well?" Grace said. "Which one of them is it?"

Macdara stepped in, right on time. "Grace?" he said. "Can you open the back of your van for me?"

A trickle of sweat formed on her brow. "Why?"

"We're going to start packing up the instruments."

"Of course."

"Are you just going to leave us hanging?" Aisling asked.

"For the moment," Siobhán said.

Siobhán and Aretta followed Macdara and Grace out to the van. Sensing something was up, the others began to filter out after them. Grace's hand shook as she unlocked the van. They stared at the empty space within. Macdara pointed to the mat used as a cushion for the instruments. "Lift that, please," Macdara said.

"I don't see why—"

"We can impound it and go through the courts. But this is always going to end the same way."

"Grace," Ron said, pushing his way to the front. "What have you done?"

Before anyone could react, Ron pulled out the mat. There, in plain view, a small trap door could be seen. "It's nothing," Grace said. "It's simply storage for a spare tire."

"A spare tire," Siobhán said with a groan. "You removed it from that compartment after you checked in to the inn. I had to swerve out of its way." If only she'd known it had belonged to Grace.

"That could be anyone's tire."

"Then show us your spare."

"I want my solicitor."

Ron shoved his way in again and opened the trap door. He stared inside, then whirled around. "Grace!"

"Back away," Siobhán said, donning gloves. She stepped forward and reached into the compartment. The first thing she pulled out was a recorder. Not an instrument in the flute family, but an audio recorder. She pushed PLAY and "Inisheer" rang out.

"It's Liam's favorite song," Grace said. "I like to listen to it . . ."

Siobhán handed Aretta the recorder and reached into the compartment again. This time she pulled out a bow. "The recorder was hidden in your autoharp. This way you could play the song, sneak away to kill Liam, and no one would ever know. But that didn't work out as planned—a little girl noticed that no one was at the harp. She thought a ghost was playing it." She also thought it was a broken guitar, which to be fair it did kind of look like one.

Grace gulped. "Someone must have . . ."

"Enough with the lies," Ron said. "Did you kill Liam?" Her lips began to tremble. "This is unbelievable," Ron said. "You—of all people—why?"

"Because he wouldn't stop! I loved him. I wanted to be with him. I worked for him nearly my entire life. And he couldn't even see what was right in front of him. He had to prey on some young woman at every single matchmaking event. I couldn't take it anymore. You were right, Detective. I was going to give him one last chance. If he had just stayed away from Helen—Róisín—he would still be alive. But he didn't change his spots. He was never going to change his spots."

"You tried to blame me!" Ron said.

"And me," Helen said. "With the lipstick."

"Wait," Aretta interrupted. "It was actually Helen staying at the inn. So how did Róisín end up with the lipstick?"

"I can answer that," Helen said. "I only wear lip gloss. Before I received my welcome package, Grace commented on it." Everyone looked to Grace. She refused to meet their eyes. "She must have known I'd give it to my twin—who she thought was me . . . Anyhow, she was right. I did give it to Róisín."

Róisín nodded. "We share everything."

"She saw Róisín kissing on Liam's neck earlier. She wanted to implicate her in the murder," Siobhán said. "And it just happened to help her aim her deadly arrow."

"Why did you kill Edward?" Tara asked.

"He figured it out," Helen said. "I'm not sure how—but he figured it out."

"The photo," Siobhán said. "Margaret O'Grady was standing near the harp. She heard music, but no one was sitting at the harp. A ghost musician. Edward guessed correctly that this little recorder was hidden inside the harp. And it's an autoharp. Which to a child resembled a broken guitar."

"You heard snippets of the conversation Edward was having with people that night and must have heard that he was going to get proof. You followed him," Macdara said. "Once we get your fingerprints, we'll be comparing them to the prints we found on the metronome."

"Don't be ridiculous," Grace said. "I wore gloves."

"And thank you for that confession," Siobhán said. Grace was the only one who could have done it. She was the one who was there anytime something happened. Always in the background. "Liam thought someone had been sneaking a look at his Lucky Book, and he was right." *He just didn't know it would lead to his murder*. "And several times I was told Liam was the one to do something—make a request that you, Róisín, and Edward switch rooms, offer up your harp to Jim McVeigh, or take a yellow sticky pad out of Barry's cup at the pub. That's because if you said it was Liam requesting it—everyone believed you. You were his right-hand woman. That's why it never occurred to me until now—*you* drilled the hole in the wall between your room and Liam's. He wasn't spying on you—you were spying on him."

Grace shrugged. "Someone had to do something about him."

"Was that what pushed you over the edge?" Ron asked. "All his notes about you, and all the other women over the years?"

Grace lifted her chin in defiance. Siobhán could tell they had reached the denial part of the confession. "He had to be stopped. I did it for him—his reputation."

"That's insane," Ron said. "I didn't even know you were an archer."

"Your arm and hand muscles have been developed from years of playing the harp," Siobhán said. "I can see why you would be good at it." Grace pursed her lips and remained silent.

Now that they had all the evidence Siobhán could see how Grace had pulled off Liam's murder. She started the recorder. As it played "Inisheer," his favorite song, she hid it inside the harp. Next, she snuck through the backstage curtains and killed the lights. Then she texted Liam on a burner phone and asked him to meet her at the Cupid. Ron had mentioned Liam saying something about Liam constantly checking his texts and looking quite upset. As if somebody had been harassing him. Siobhán now assumed that Grace had turned the tables, and she'd been pretending to blackmail the blackmailer. But it wasn't money she wanted—it was blood. She grabbed the bow and arrow from the van, which was parked near the passageway underneath King John's Castle. She waited until she saw those glowing pink lips on Liam's neck. She took her shot—then ran back to the van and rehid the bow and arrow. She slipped the Lucky Book into the outdoor shelves set up by Oran and Padraig at the bookshop. And then all she had to do was turn on the tears.

"There's one thing we haven't sussed out," Macdara said. "What did you do with his phone?"

Grace crossed her arms. "I am not going to incriminate myself any more."

They would get it out of her eventually. For now, they had everything they needed to make an arrest. "Garda Dabiri will read you your rights," Siobhán said. She turned to the crowd. "You won't be able to load your instruments into the van, but we have informed the taxi company that you'll all be needing rides back to the inn."

"Can it wait a few minutes?" Tara asked as they filed away from Aretta and Grace.

"Why?" Siobhán asked.

Tara gestured to the hill behind Siobhán and Macdara's farmhouse. "I think we should play 'Inisheer' from the hilltop. Under the moon. A tribute to Liam."

"That would be lovely," Siobhán said. The moment Grace was driven away, the rest of them gathered on the hill. The moon was fat and bright, casting a yellow glow over the musicians, standing in a circle. As they began to play, the smooth notes filtering through the evening air, the babies began to kick. Macdara camc up, and shc took his hand and placed it on her stomach.

"They're going to be night owls," Macdara said. "We'll have our hands full."

"And our hearts," Siobhán said. "And our hearts."

"Just keep that in mind all day tomorrow," Macdara said. "Emma and Eileen have asked me to drop you off at the inn."

Siobhán groaned. "An attack baby shower," she said. "If I'm going to have to suffer through it, so are you."

"What's this about a baby shower?" Gráinne was standing behind them, hands on hips.

"I'm being ambushed," Siobhán said, "but it won't be nearly as nice as yours."

"Think of it this way," Macdara said. "Emma and Eileen are throwing a baby shower for one of them, and you're throwing a shower for the other."

Siobhán laughed, and soon the rest followed suit. It was a sound that brought a smile to everyone that listened, making them feel joyous and lighter. It was music to their ears.